TEENAGE MUTANT NINJA TURTLES

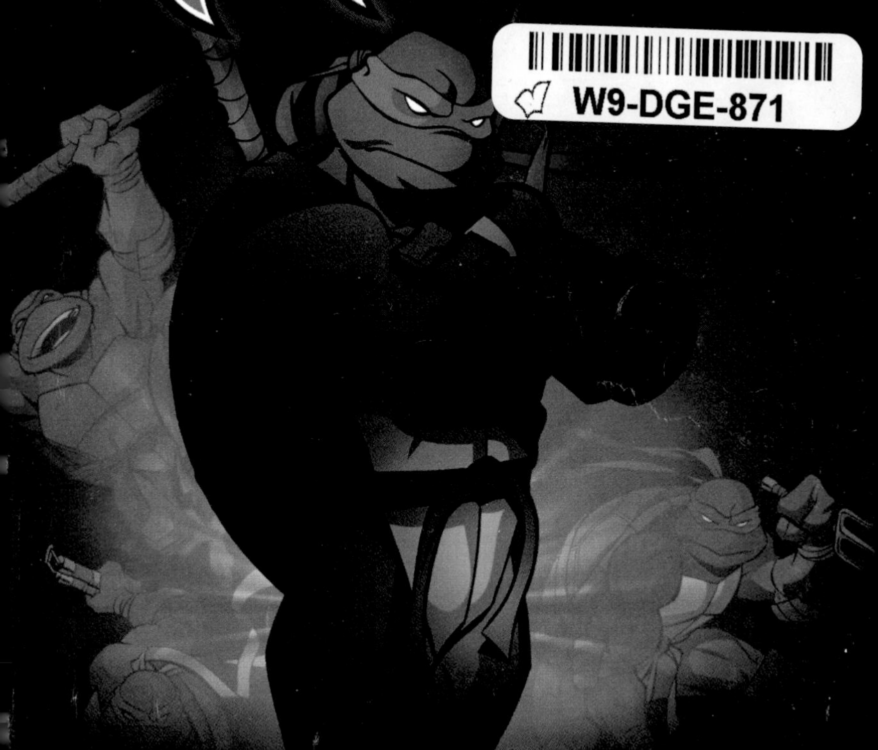

IT'S A SHELL OF A TOWN

TOKYOPOP®

HAMBURG • LONDON • LOS ANGELES • TOKYO

Contributing Editor - David Schreiber
Graphic Design & Lettering - Tomás Montalvo-Lagos & Anh Trinh
Cover Layout - Tomás Montalvo-Lagos

Editor - Erin Stein
Digital Imaging Manager - Chris Buford
Pre-Press Manager - Antonio DePietro
Production Manager - Jennifer Miller & Mutsumi Miyazaki
Art Director - Matt Alford
Managing Editor - Jill Freshney
VP of Production - Ron Klamert
President & C.O.O. - John Parker
Publisher & C.E.O. - Stuart Levy

E-mail: info@tokyopop.com
Come visit us online at www.TOKYOPOP.com

A **TOKYOPOP**® Cine-Manga™
TOKYOPOP Inc.
5900 Wilshire Blvd., Suite 2000, Los Angeles, CA 90036

Teenage Mutant Ninja Turtles: It's a Shell of a Town

ISBN: 1-59532-473-9
First TOKYOPOP printing: November 2004

10 9 8 7 6 5 4 3 2 1

Printed in Canada

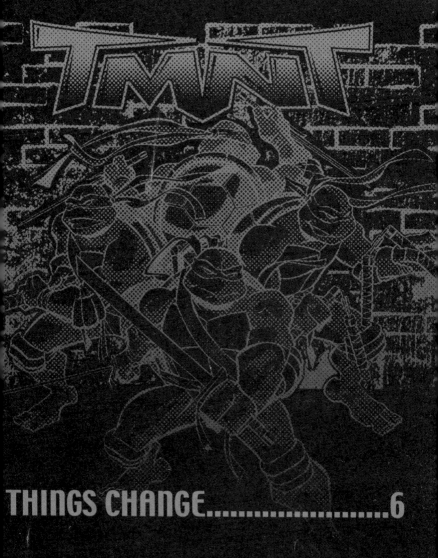

TMNT

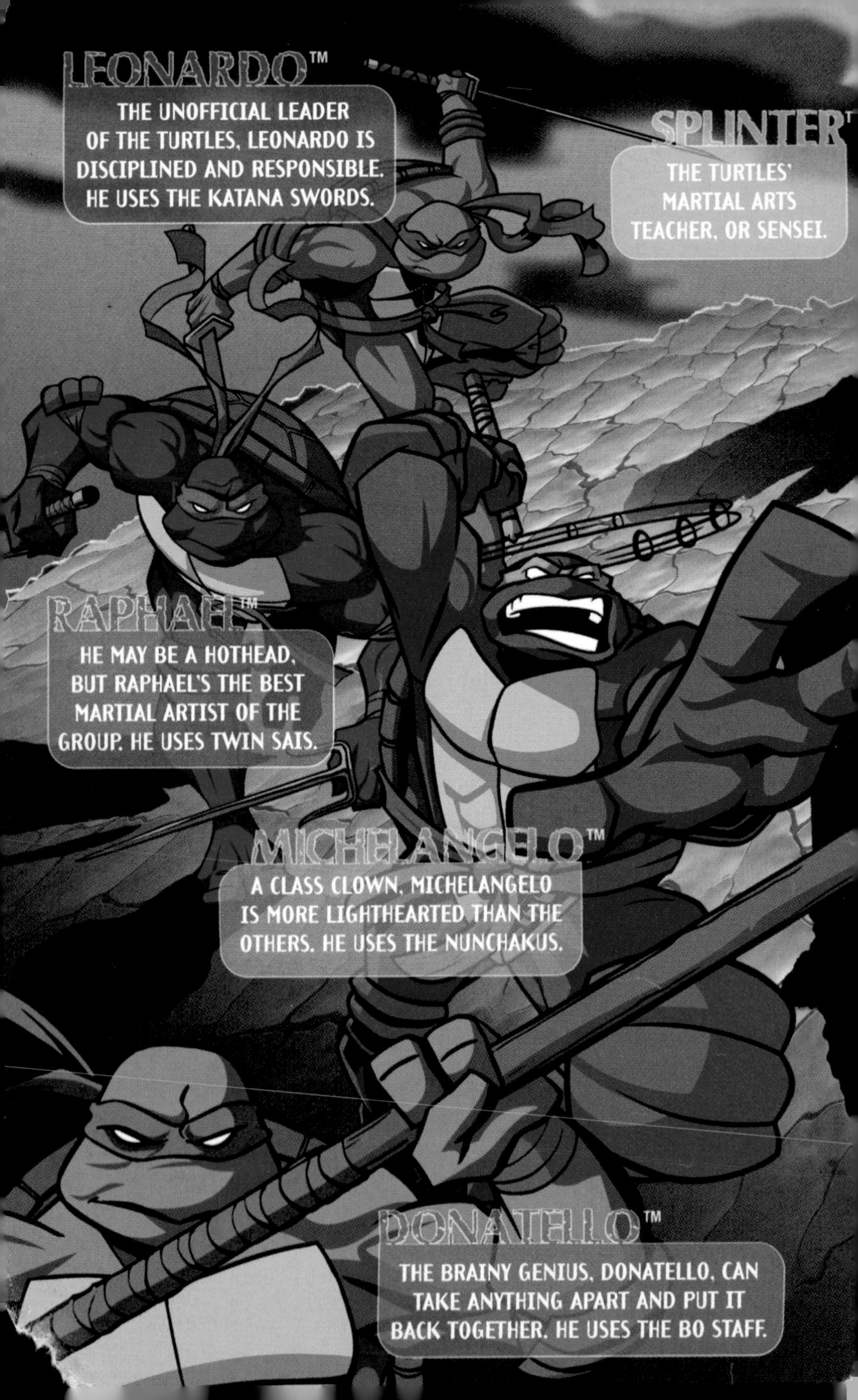
LEONARDO™
THE UNOFFICIAL LEADER OF THE TURTLES, LEONARDO IS DISCIPLINED AND RESPONSIBLE. HE USES THE KATANA SWORDS.
SPLINTER™
THE TURTLES' MARTIAL ARTS TEACHER, OR SENSEI.
RAPHAEL™
HE MAY BE A HOTHEAD, BUT RAPHAEL'S THE BEST MARTIAL ARTIST OF THE GROUP. HE USES TWIN SAIS.
MICHELANGELO™
A CLASS CLOWN, MICHELANGELO IS MORE LIGHTHEARTED THAN THE OTHERS. HE USES THE NUNCHAKUS.
DONATELLO™
THE BRAINY GENIUS, DONATELLO, CAN TAKE ANYTHING APART AND PUT IT BACK TOGETHER. HE USES THE BO STAFF.

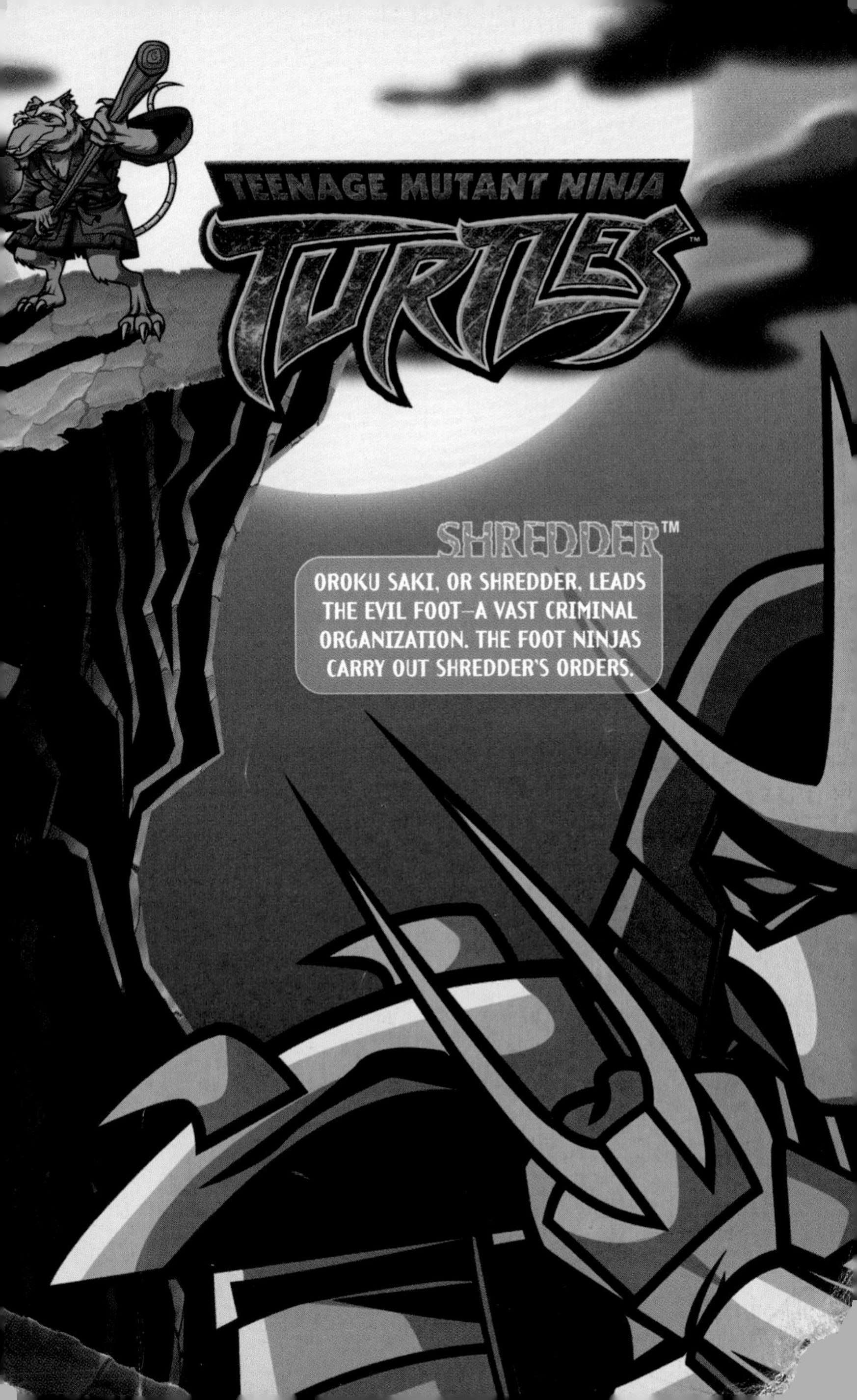
TEENAGE MUTANT NINJA
TURTLES™
SHREDDER™
OROKU SAKI, OR SHREDDER, LEADS THE EVIL FOOT—A VAST CRIMINAL ORGANIZATION. THE FOOT NINJAS CARRY OUT SHREDDER'S ORDERS.

THINGS

CHANGE

WRITTEN BY

MICHAEL RYAN

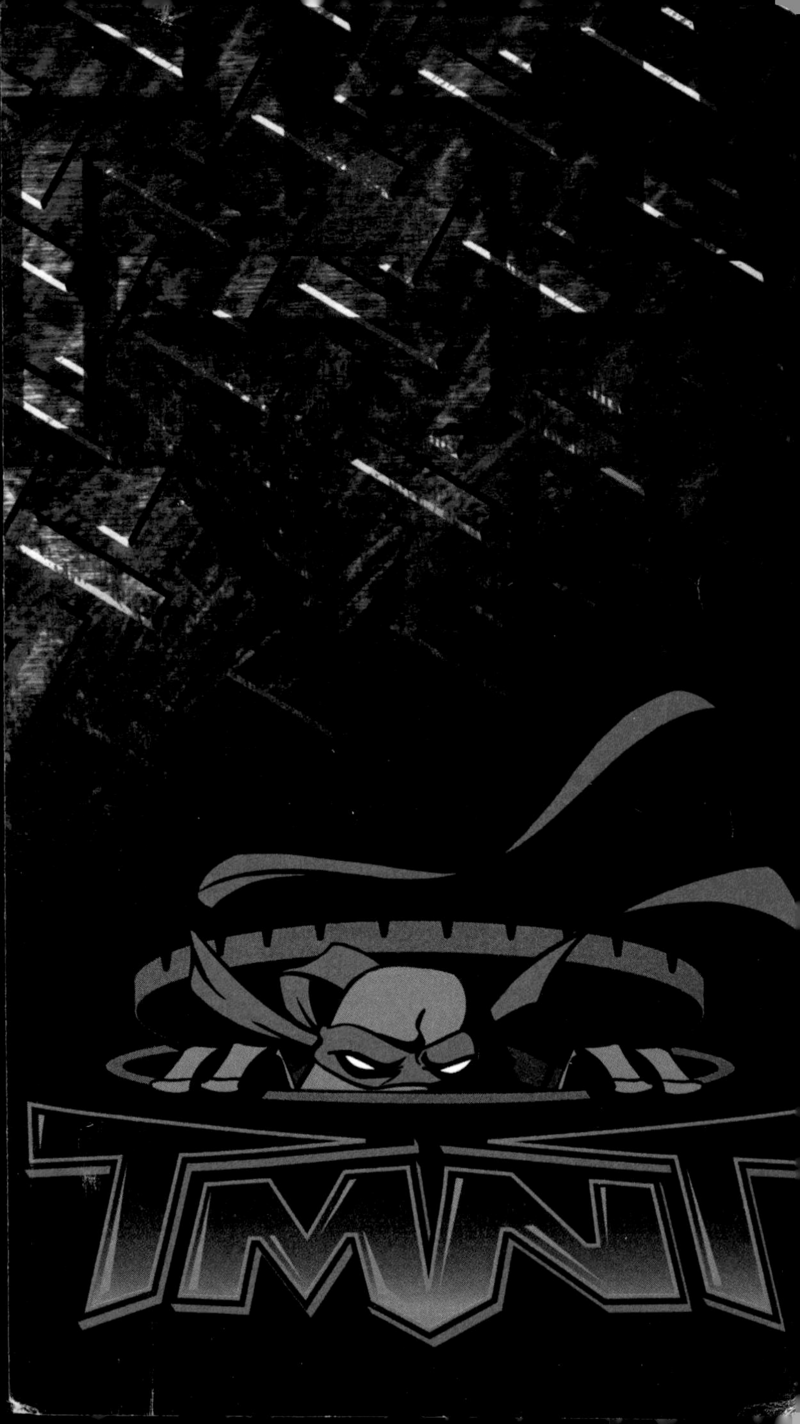
TMNT

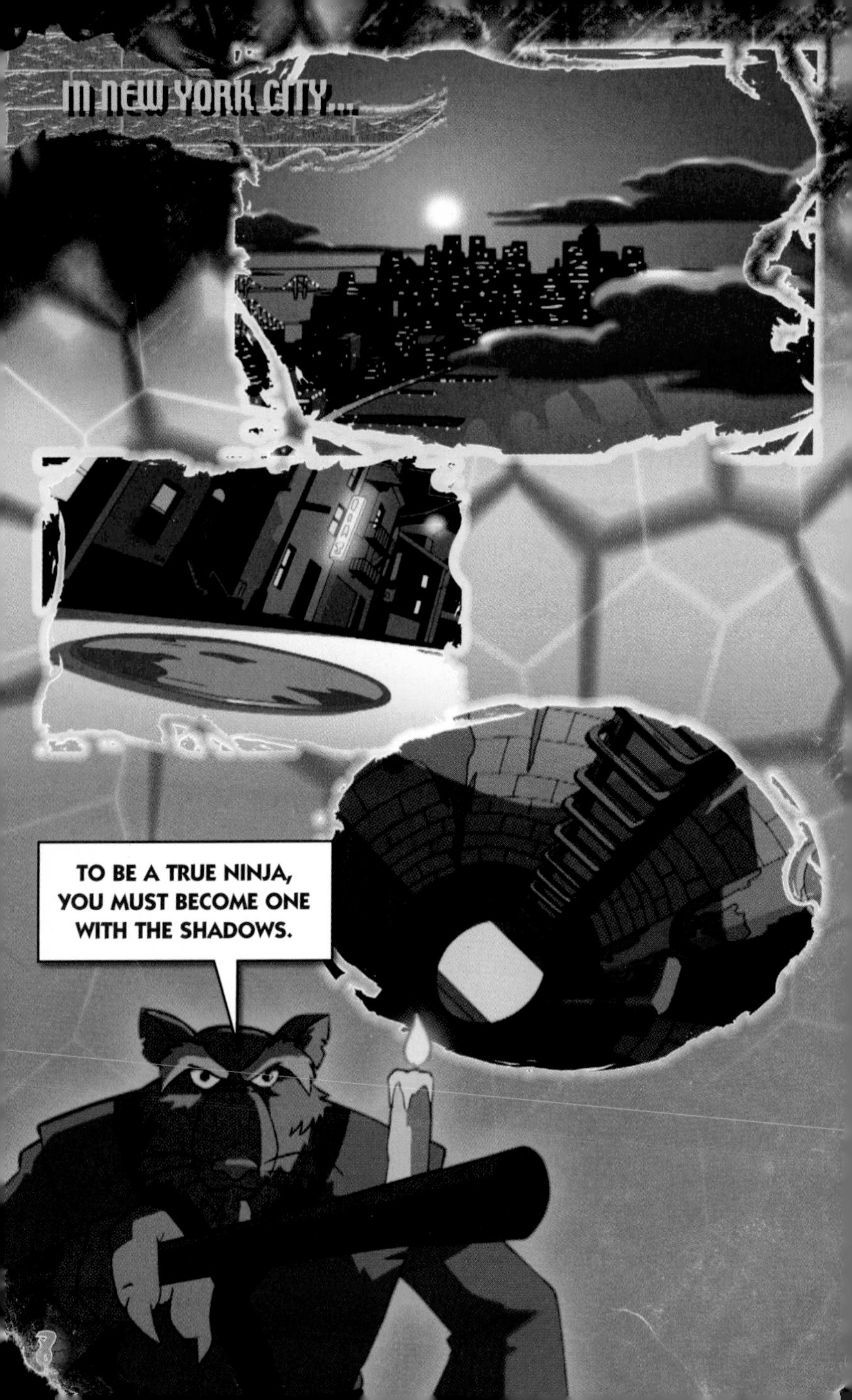

IN NEW YORK CITY...
TO BE A TRUE NINJA, YOU MUST BECOME ONE WITH THE SHADOWS.

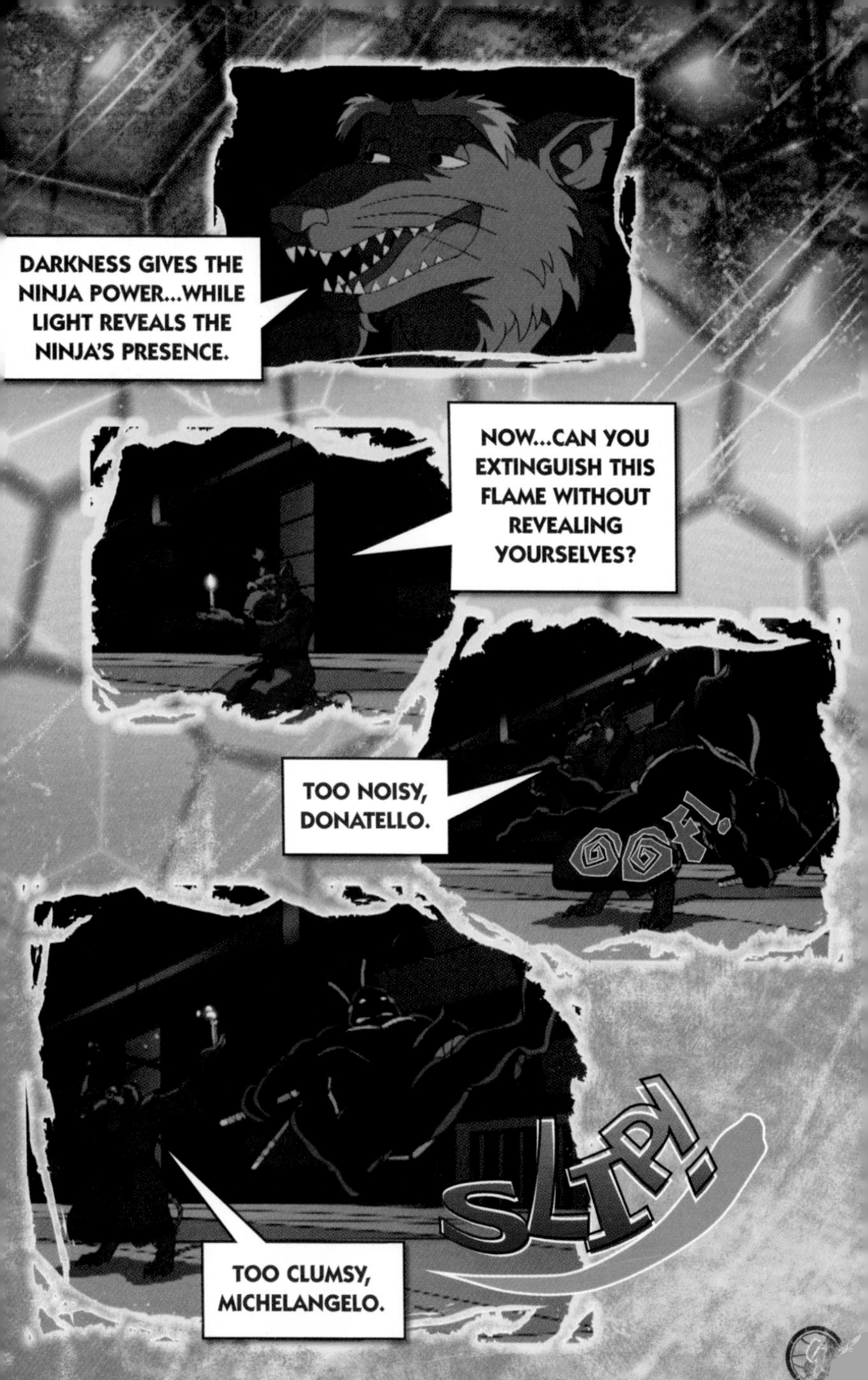
DARKNESS GIVES THE NINJA POWER...WHILE LIGHT REVEALS THE NINJA'S PRESENCE.
NOW...CAN YOU EXTINGUISH THIS FLAME WITHOUT REVEALING YOURSELVES?
TOO NOISY, DONATELLO.
OOF!
TOO CLUMSY, MICHELANGELO.
SLIP!

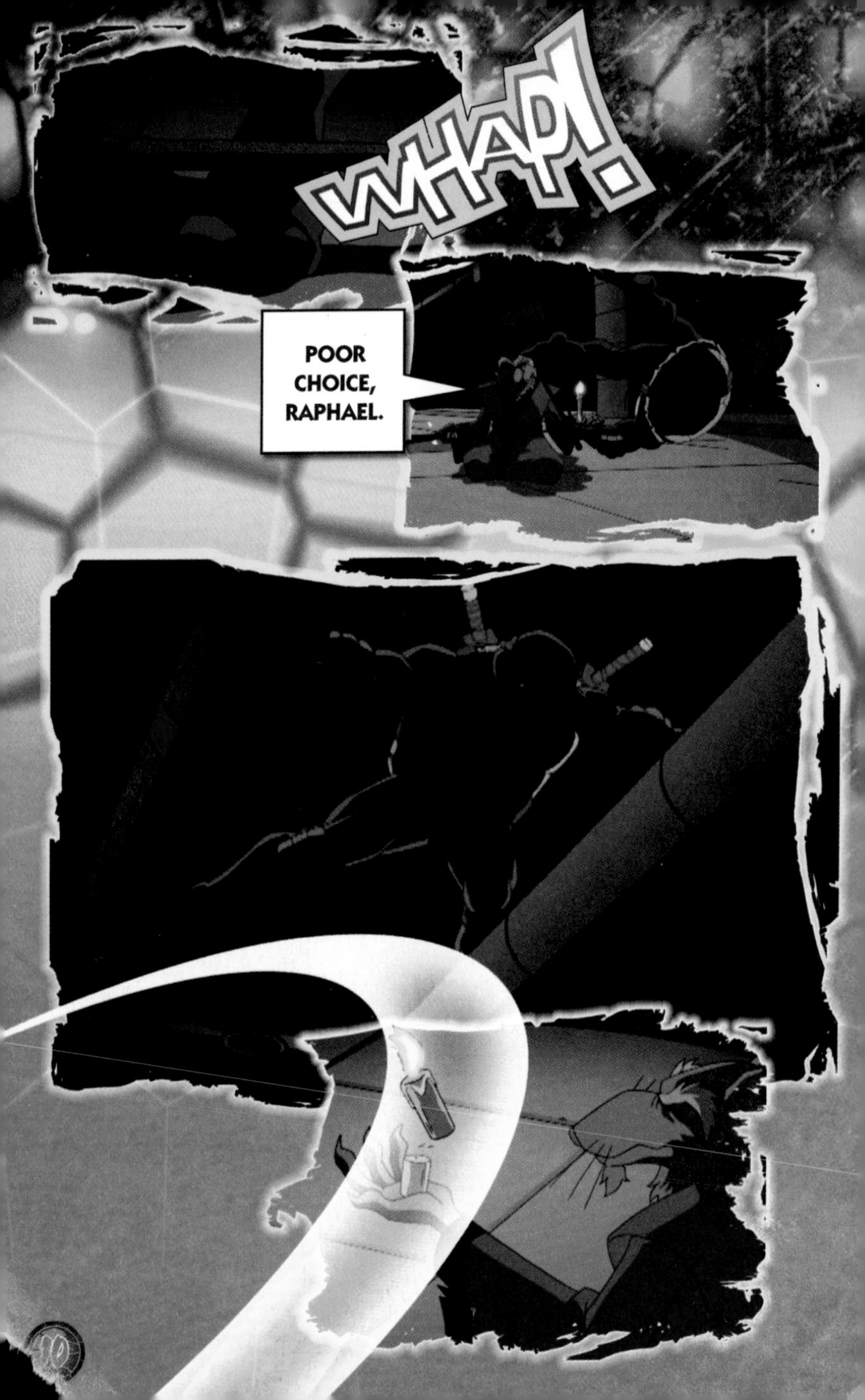
WHAP!
POOR CHOICE, RAPHAEL.

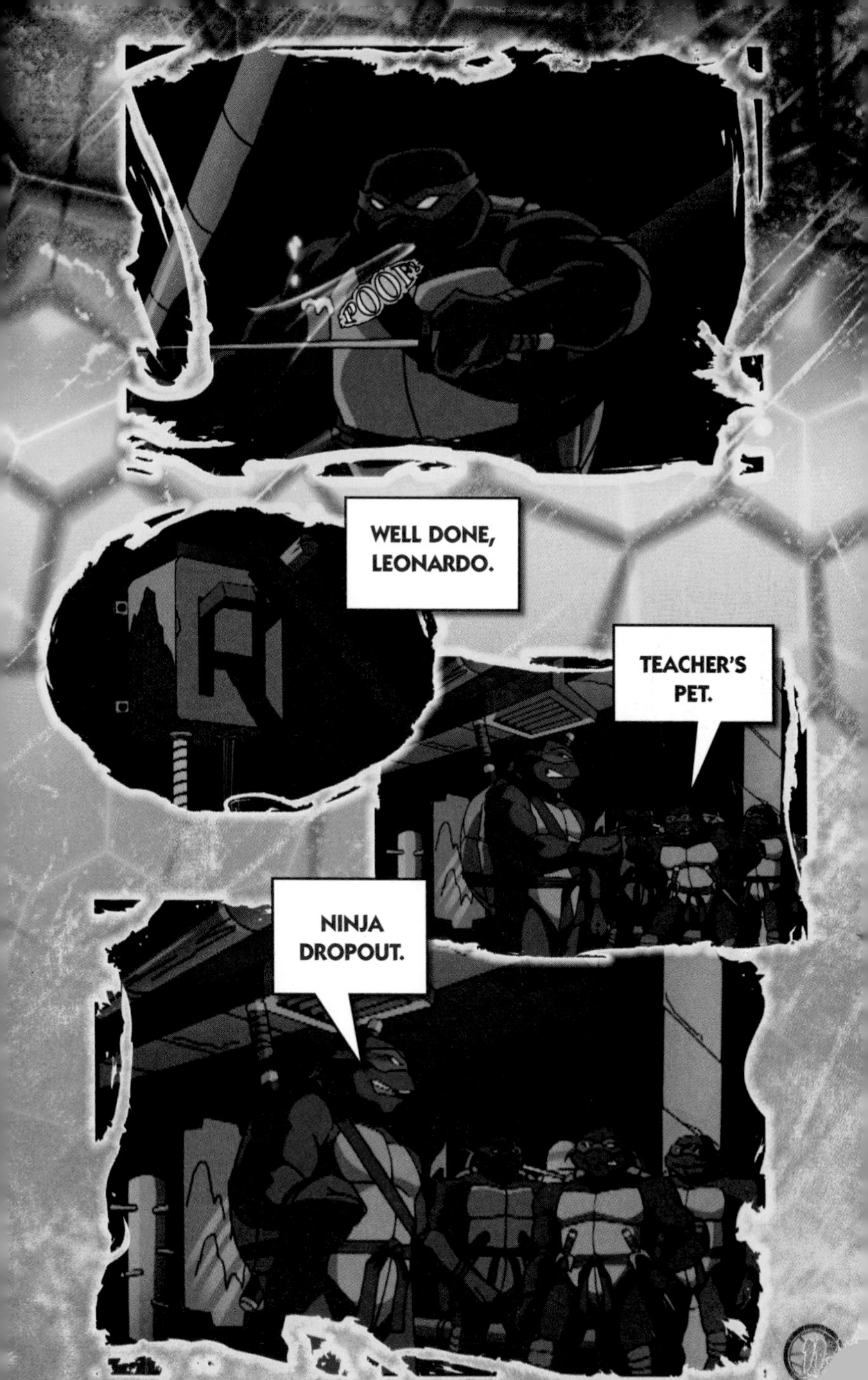
POOF
WELL DONE, LEONARDO.
TEACHER'S PET.
NINJA DROPOUT.

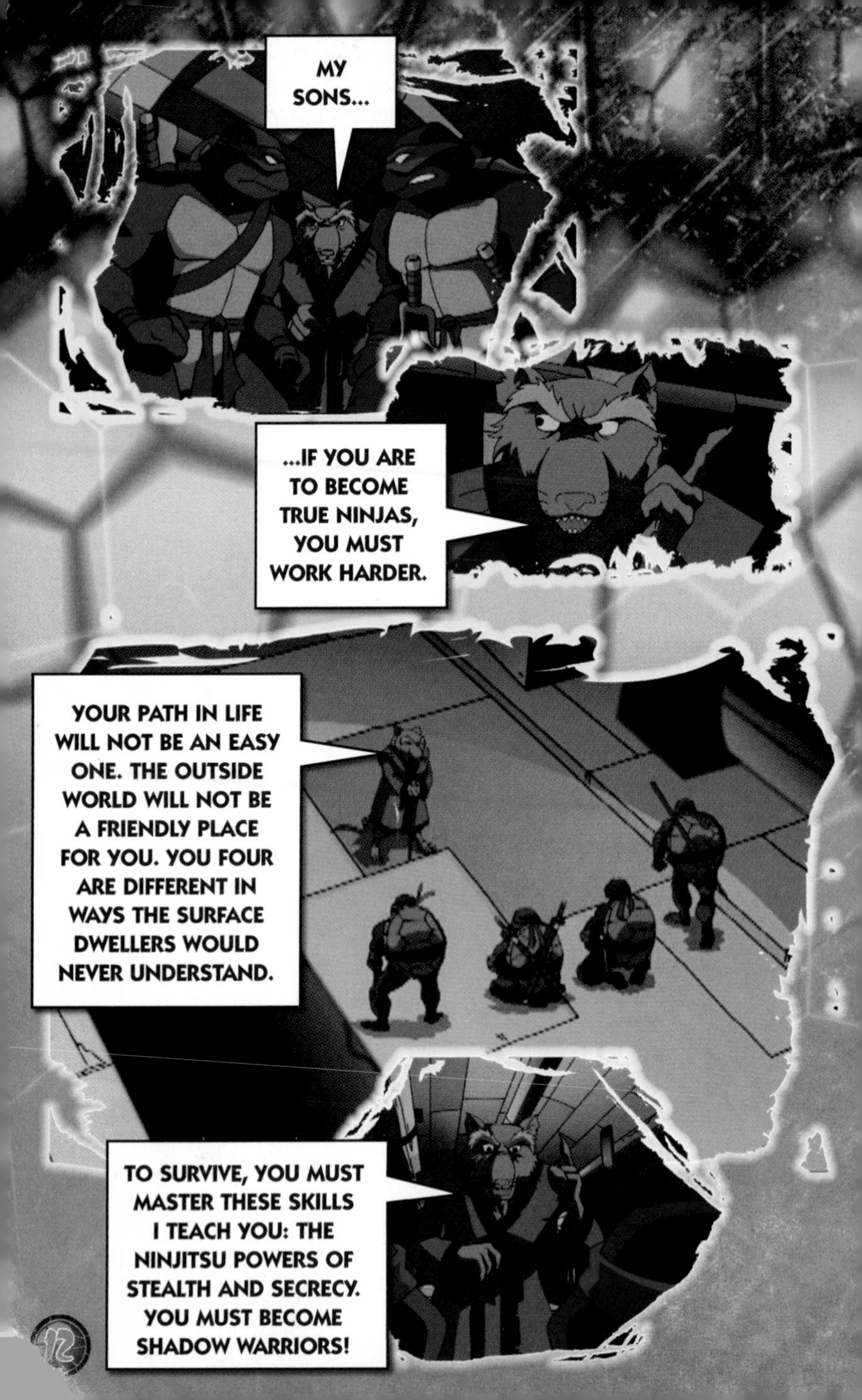

MY SONS...
...IF YOU ARE TO BECOME TRUE NINJAS, YOU MUST WORK HARDER.
YOUR PATH IN LIFE WILL NOT BE AN EASY ONE. THE OUTSIDE WORLD WILL NOT BE A FRIENDLY PLACE FOR YOU. YOU FOUR ARE DIFFERENT IN WAYS THE SURFACE DWELLERS WOULD NEVER UNDERSTAND.
TO SURVIVE, YOU MUST MASTER THESE SKILLS I TEACH YOU: THE NINJITSU POWERS OF STEALTH AND SECRECY. YOU MUST BECOME SHADOW WARRIORS!

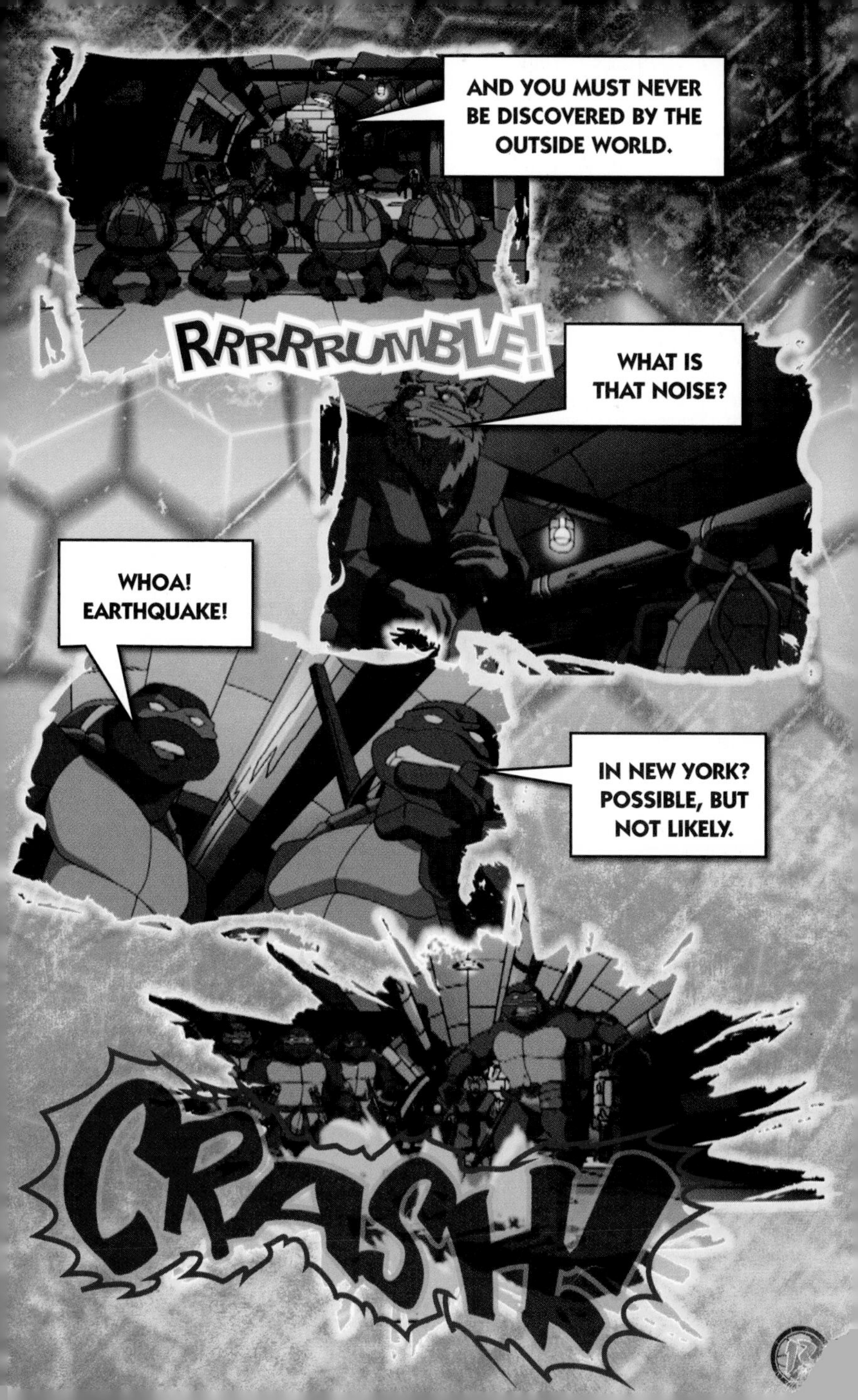
AND YOU MUST NEVER BE DISCOVERED BY THE OUTSIDE WORLD.
RRRRRUMBLE!
WHAT IS THAT NOISE?
WHOA! EARTHQUAKE!
IN NEW YORK? POSSIBLE, BUT NOT LIKELY.
CRASH!

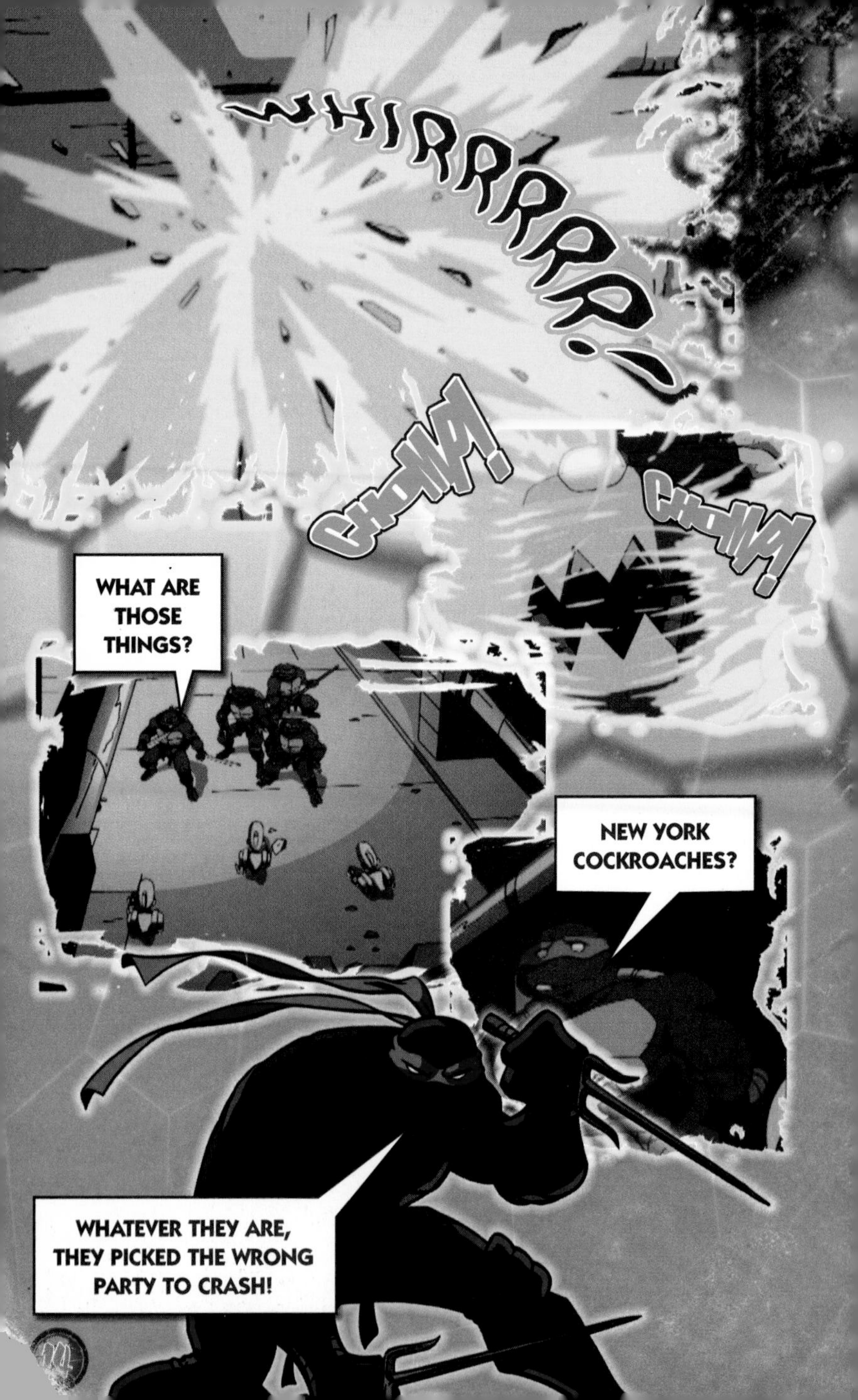
WHIRRRRR!
CHOMP!
CHOMP!
WHAT ARE THOSE THINGS?
NEW YORK COCKROACHES?
WHATEVER THEY ARE, THEY PICKED THE WRONG PARTY TO CRASH!

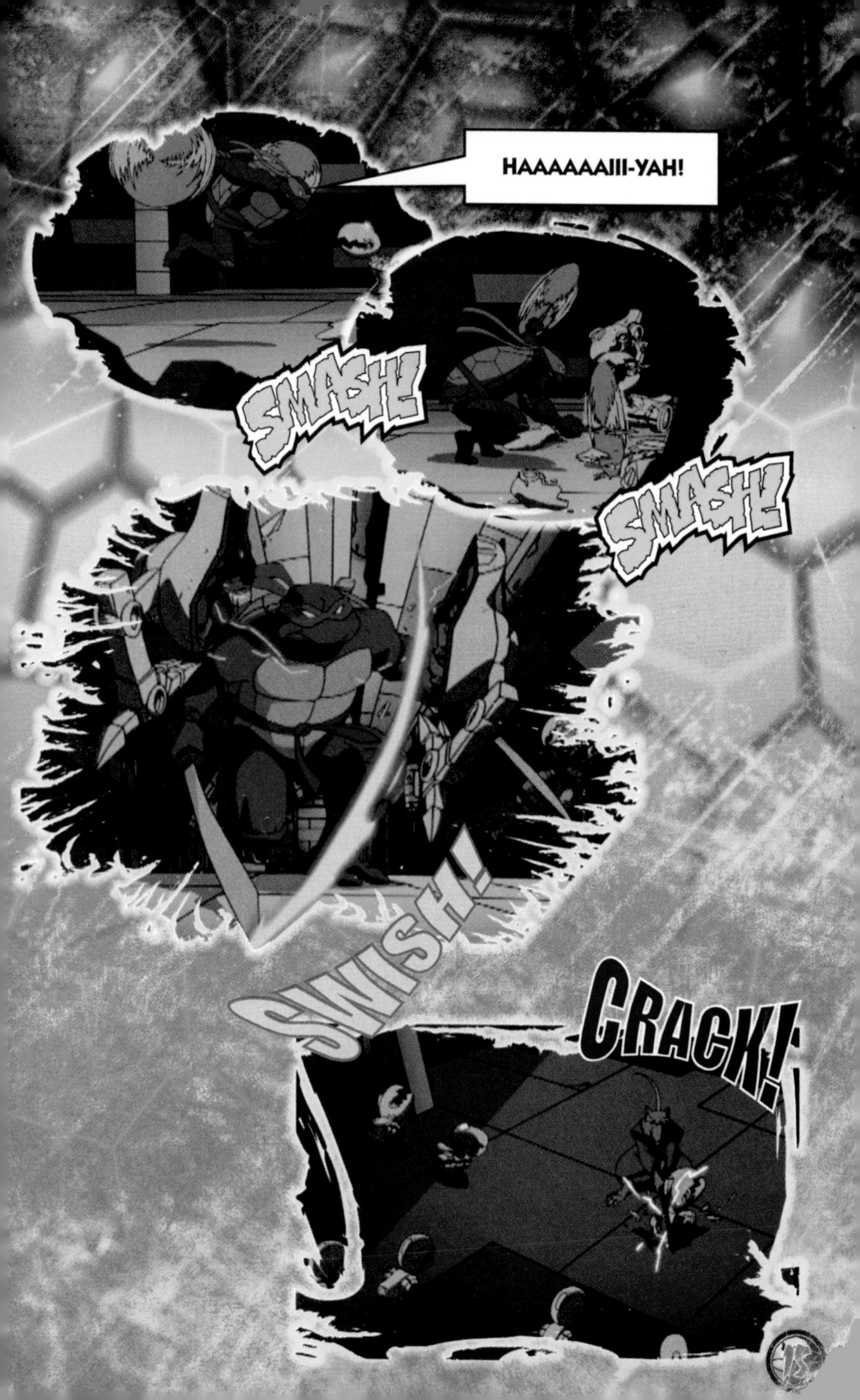
HAAAAAAIII-YAH!
SMASH!
SMASH!
SWISH!
CRACK!

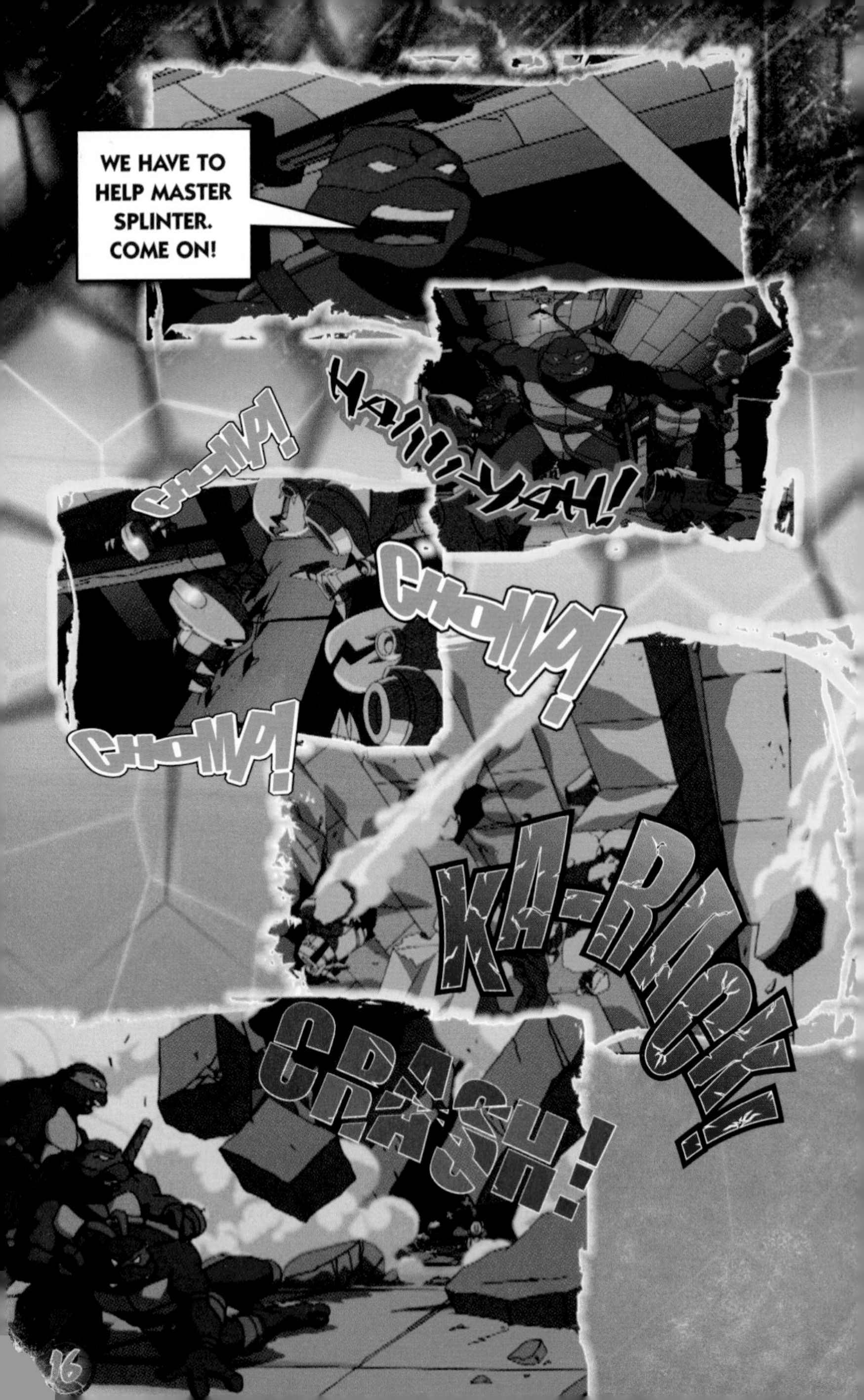
WE HAVE TO HELP MASTER SPLINTER. COME ON!
HAIIIIYAH!
CHOMP!
CHOMP!
CHOMP!
KA-RUNCH!
CRASH!
CRASH!

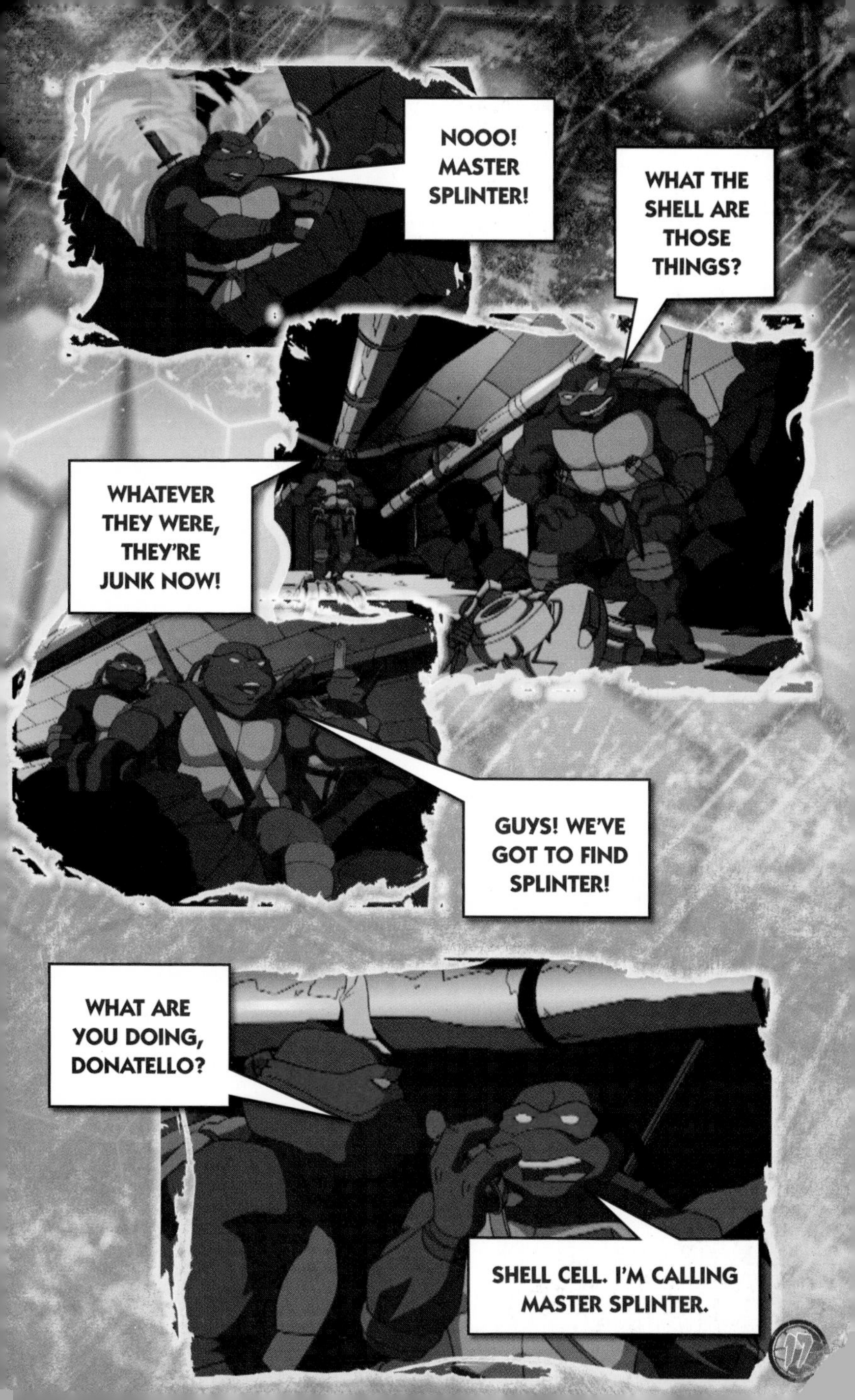
NOOO! MASTER SPLINTER!
WHAT THE SHELL ARE THOSE THINGS?
WHATEVER THEY WERE, THEY'RE JUNK NOW!
GUYS! WE'VE GOT TO FIND SPLINTER!
WHAT ARE YOU DOING, DONATELLO?
SHELL CELL. I'M CALLING MASTER SPLINTER.
17

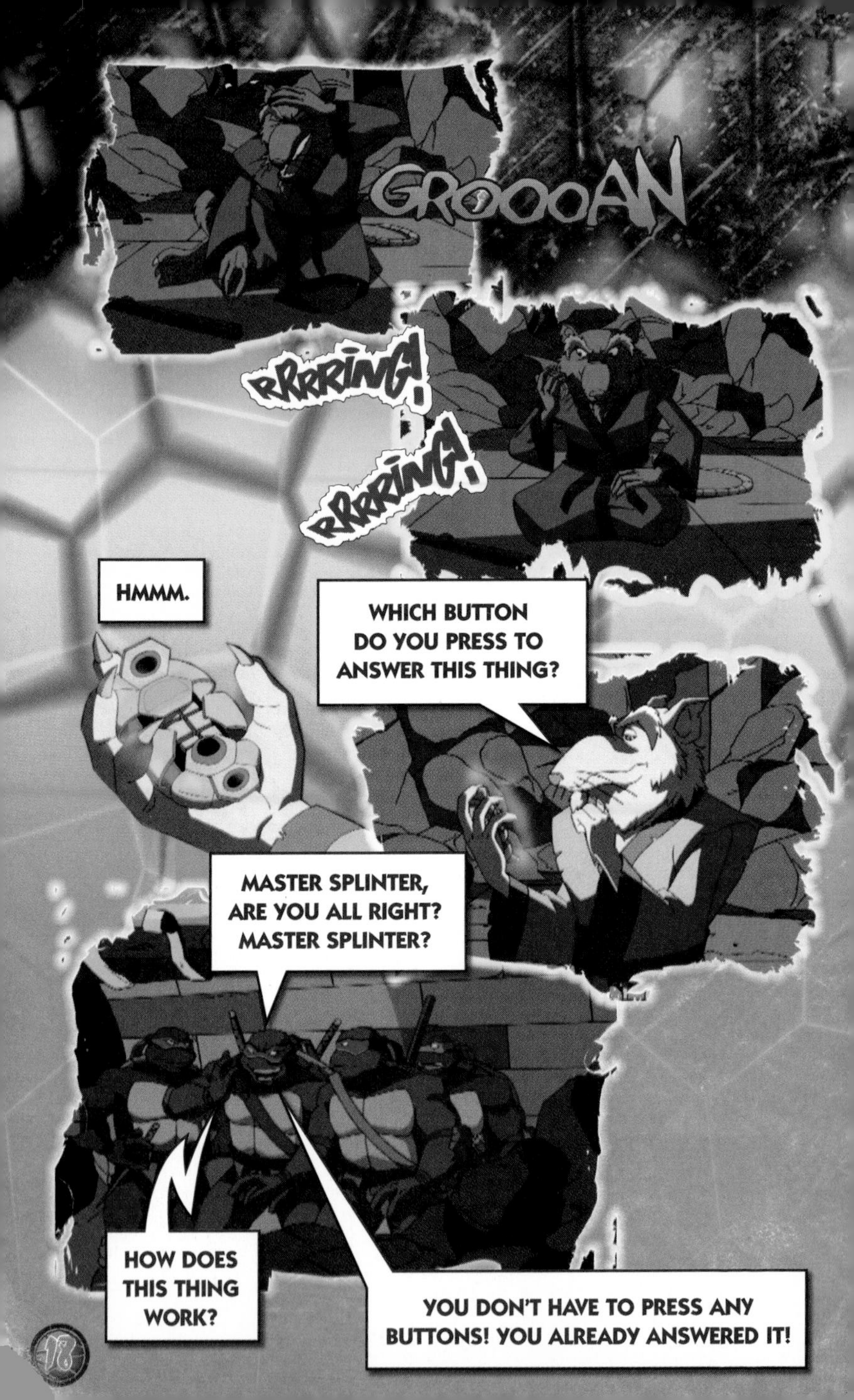
GROOOAN
RRRRING!
RRRRING!
HMMM.
WHICH BUTTON DO YOU PRESS TO ANSWER THIS THING?
MASTER SPLINTER, ARE YOU ALL RIGHT? MASTER SPLINTER?
HOW DOES THIS THING WORK?
YOU DON'T HAVE TO PRESS ANY BUTTONS! YOU ALREADY ANSWERED IT!

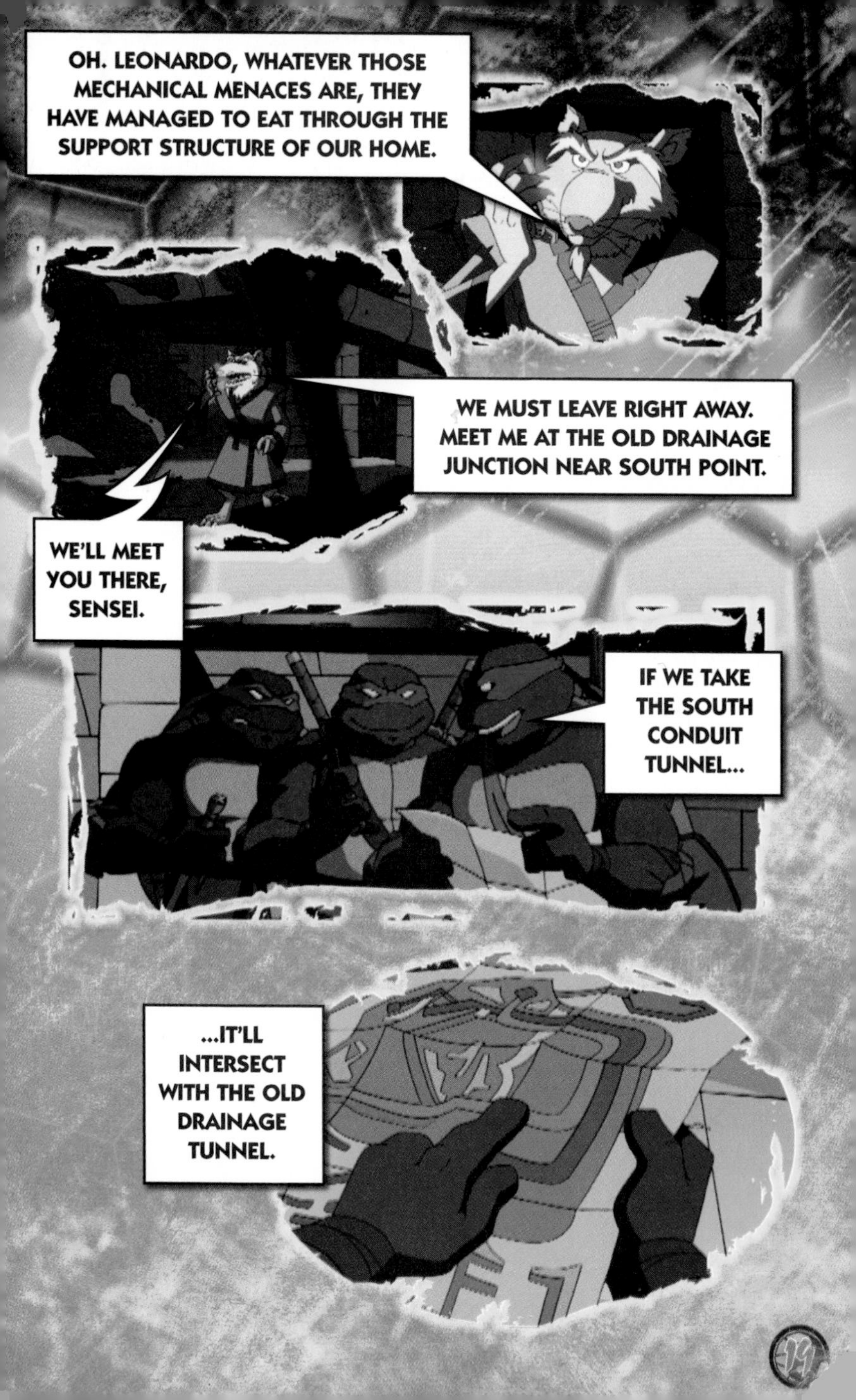
OH. LEONARDO, WHATEVER THOSE MECHANICAL MENACES ARE, THEY HAVE MANAGED TO EAT THROUGH THE SUPPORT STRUCTURE OF OUR HOME.
WE MUST LEAVE RIGHT AWAY. MEET ME AT THE OLD DRAINAGE JUNCTION NEAR SOUTH POINT.
WE'LL MEET YOU THERE, SENSEI.
IF WE TAKE THE SOUTH CONDUIT TUNNEL...
...IT'LL INTERSECT WITH THE OLD DRAINAGE TUNNEL.

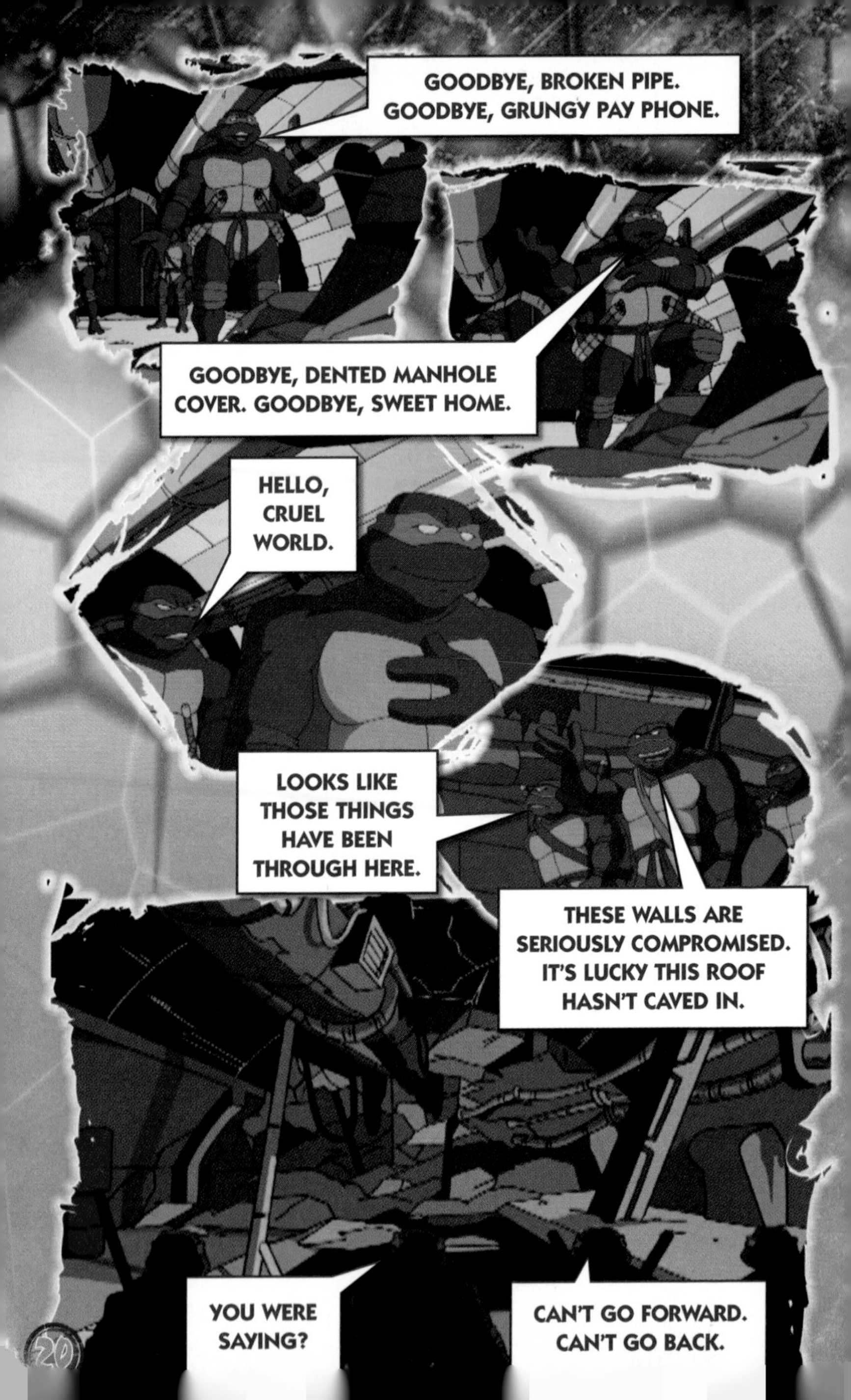
GOODBYE, BROKEN PIPE. GOODBYE, GRUNGY PAY PHONE.
GOODBYE, DENTED MANHOLE COVER. GOODBYE, SWEET HOME.
HELLO, CRUEL WORLD.
LOOKS LIKE THOSE THINGS HAVE BEEN THROUGH HERE.
THESE WALLS ARE SERIOUSLY COMPROMISED. IT'S LUCKY THIS ROOF HASN'T CAVED IN.
YOU WERE SAYING?
CAN'T GO FORWARD. CAN'T GO BACK.

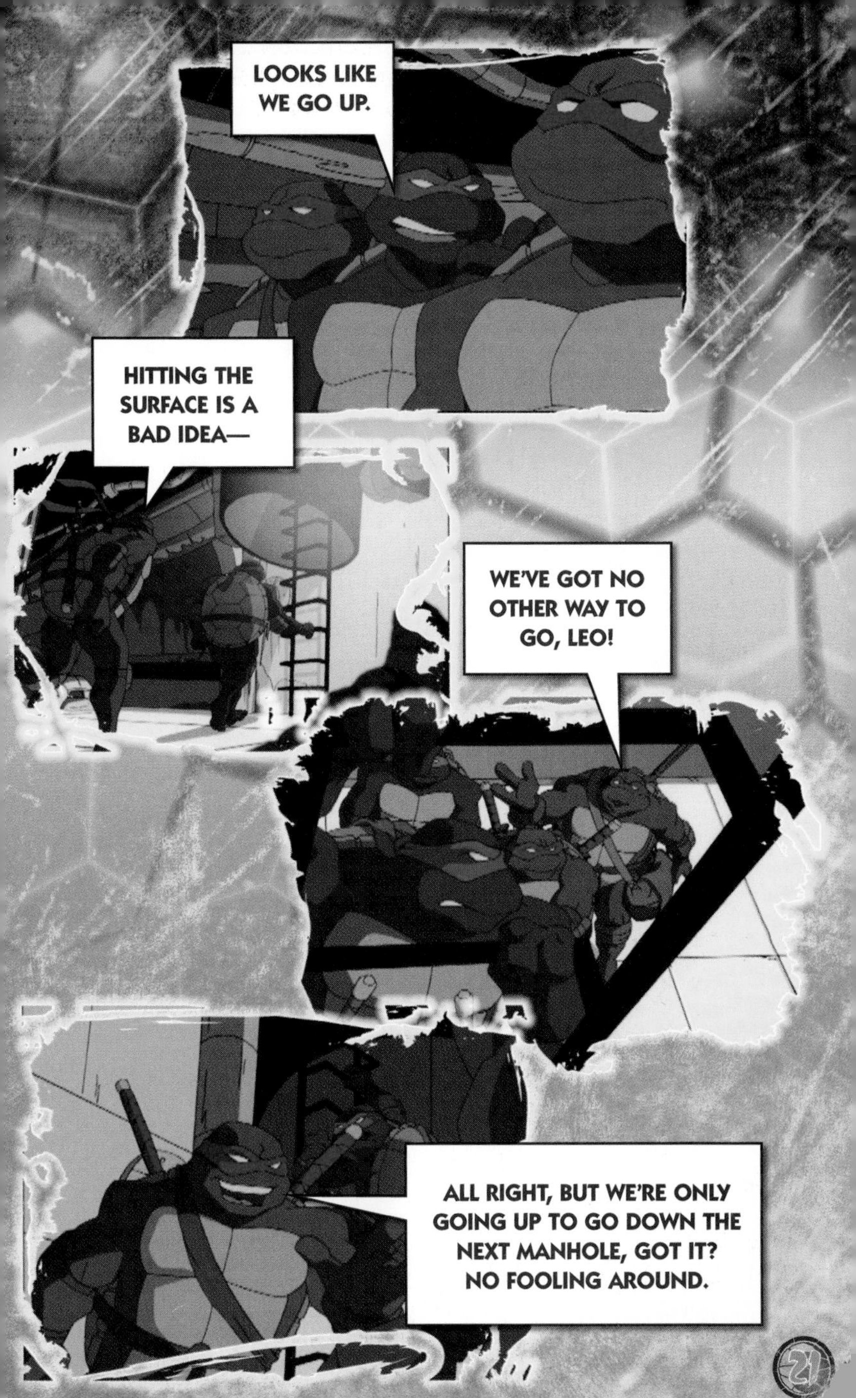
LOOKS LIKE WE GO UP.
HITTING THE SURFACE IS A BAD IDEA—
WE'VE GOT NO OTHER WAY TO GO, LEO!
ALL RIGHT, BUT WE'RE ONLY GOING UP TO GO DOWN THE NEXT MANHOLE, GOT IT? NO FOOLING AROUND.

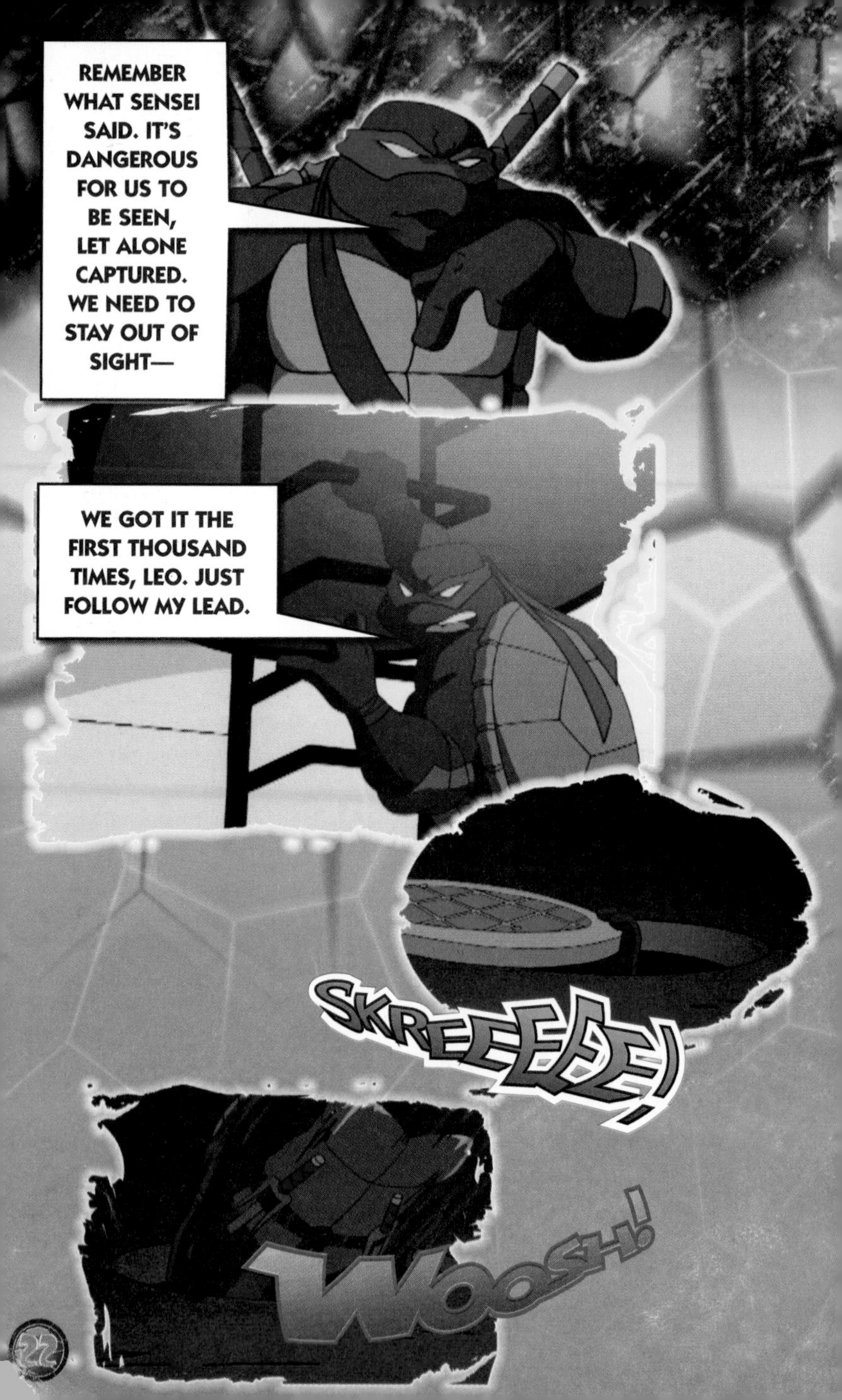
REMEMBER WHAT SENSEI SAID. IT'S DANGEROUS FOR US TO BE SEEN, LET ALONE CAPTURED. WE NEED TO STAY OUT OF SIGHT—
WE GOT IT THE FIRST THOUSAND TIMES, LEO. JUST FOLLOW MY LEAD.
SKREEEEEE!
WOOSH!

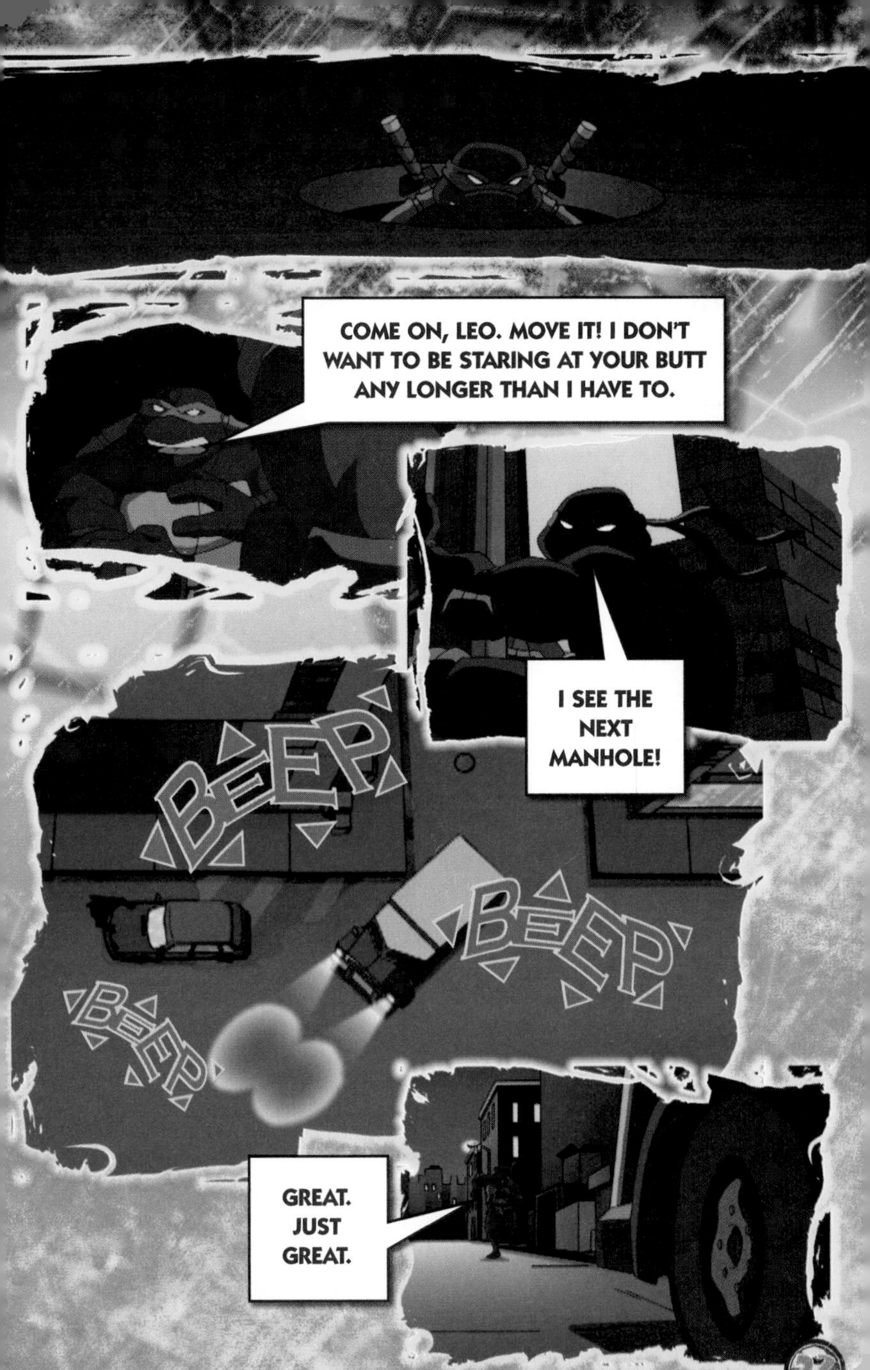
COME ON, LEO. MOVE IT! I DON'T WANT TO BE STARING AT YOUR BUTT ANY LONGER THAN I HAVE TO.
I SEE THE NEXT MANHOLE!
BEEP
BEEP
BEEP
GREAT. JUST GREAT.

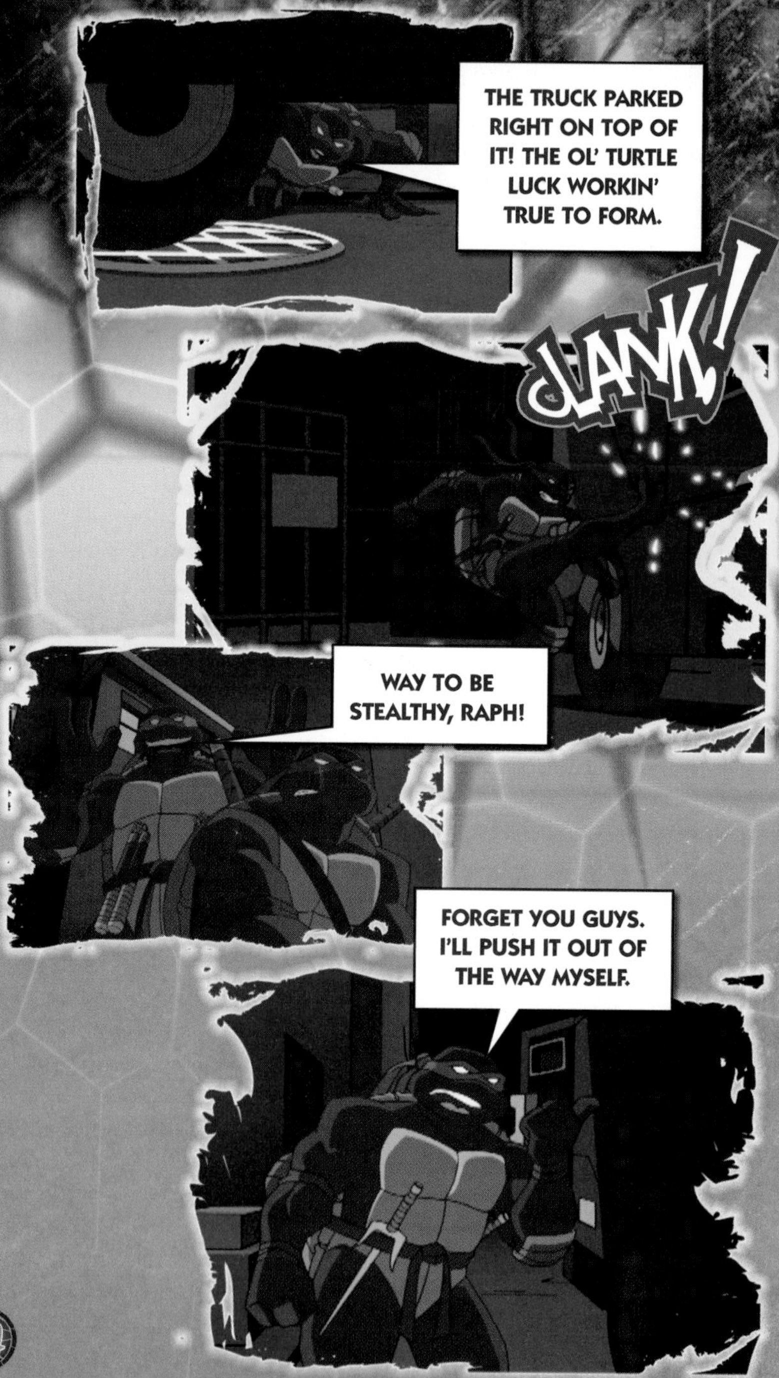
THE TRUCK PARKED RIGHT ON TOP OF IT! THE OL' TURTLE LUCK WORKIN' TRUE TO FORM.
CLANK!
WAY TO BE STEALTHY, RAPH!
FORGET YOU GUYS. I'LL PUSH IT OUT OF THE WAY MYSELF.

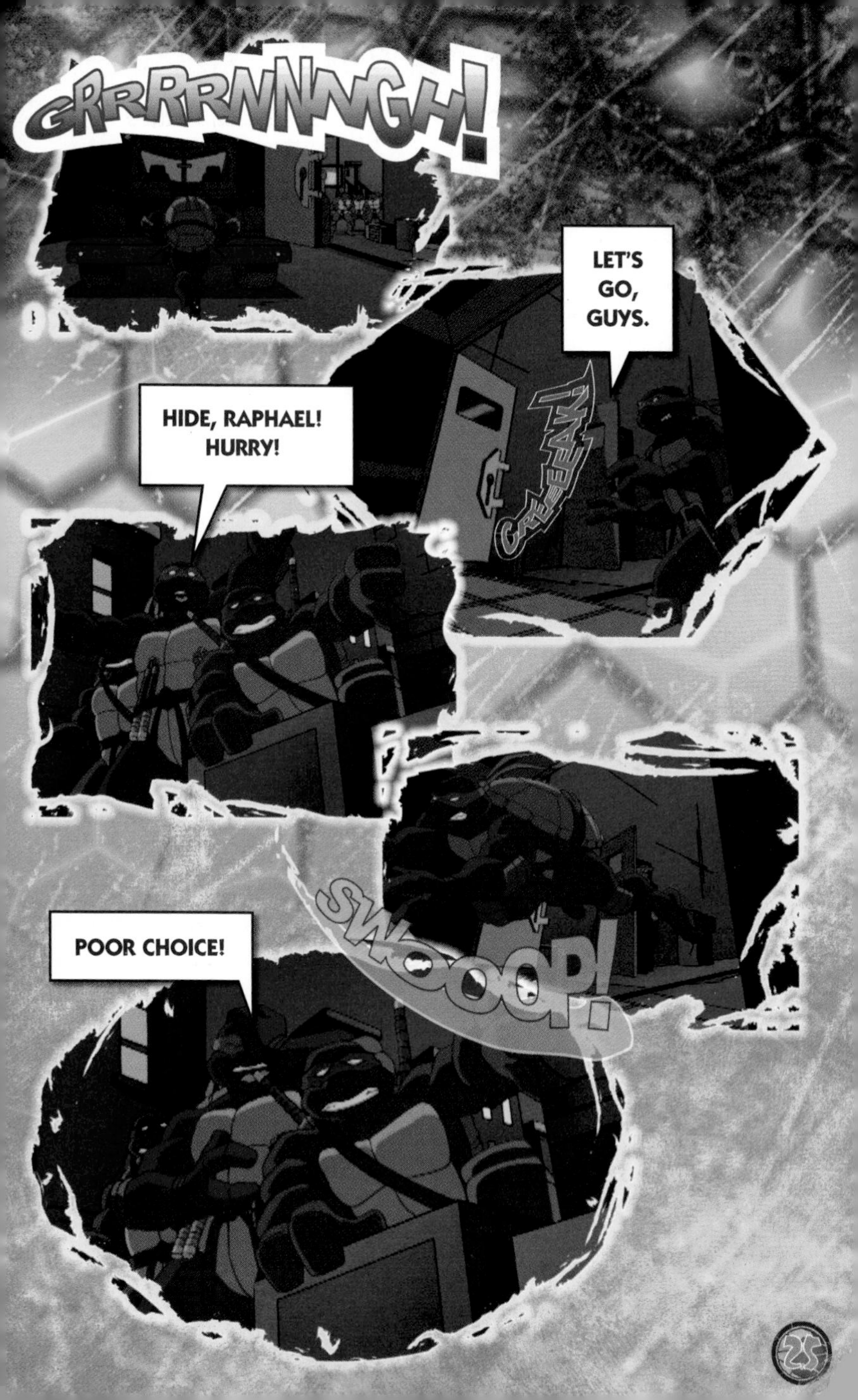
GRRRRNNNGH!
LET'S GO, GUYS.
CREEEAK!
HIDE, RAPHAEL! HURRY!
SWOOOP!
POOR CHOICE!

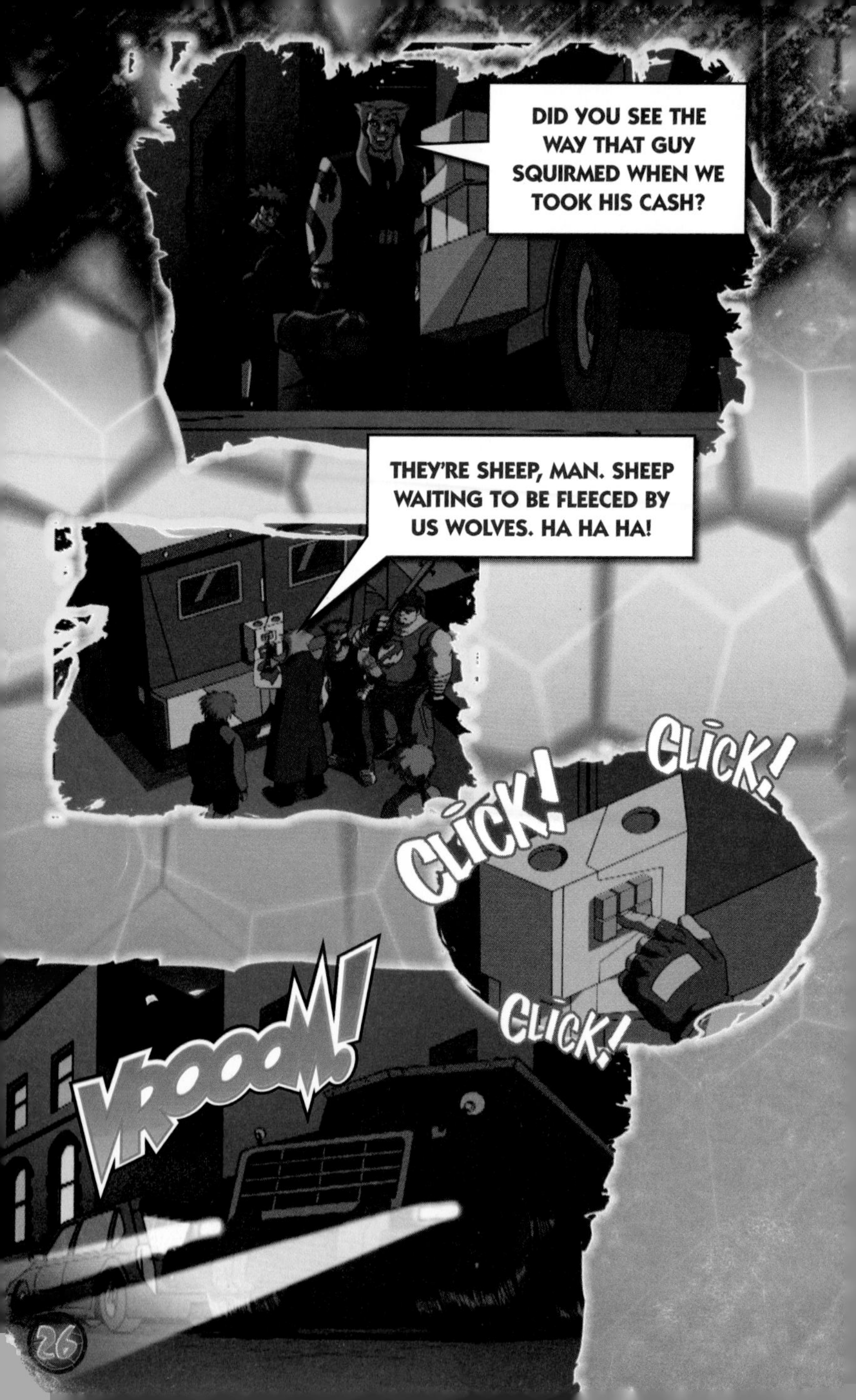
DID YOU SEE THE WAY THAT GUY SQUIRMED WHEN WE TOOK HIS CASH?
THEY'RE SHEEP, MAN. SHEEP WAITING TO BE FLEECED BY US WOLVES. HA HA HA!
CLICK!
CLICK!
CLICK!
CLICK!
VROOOM!

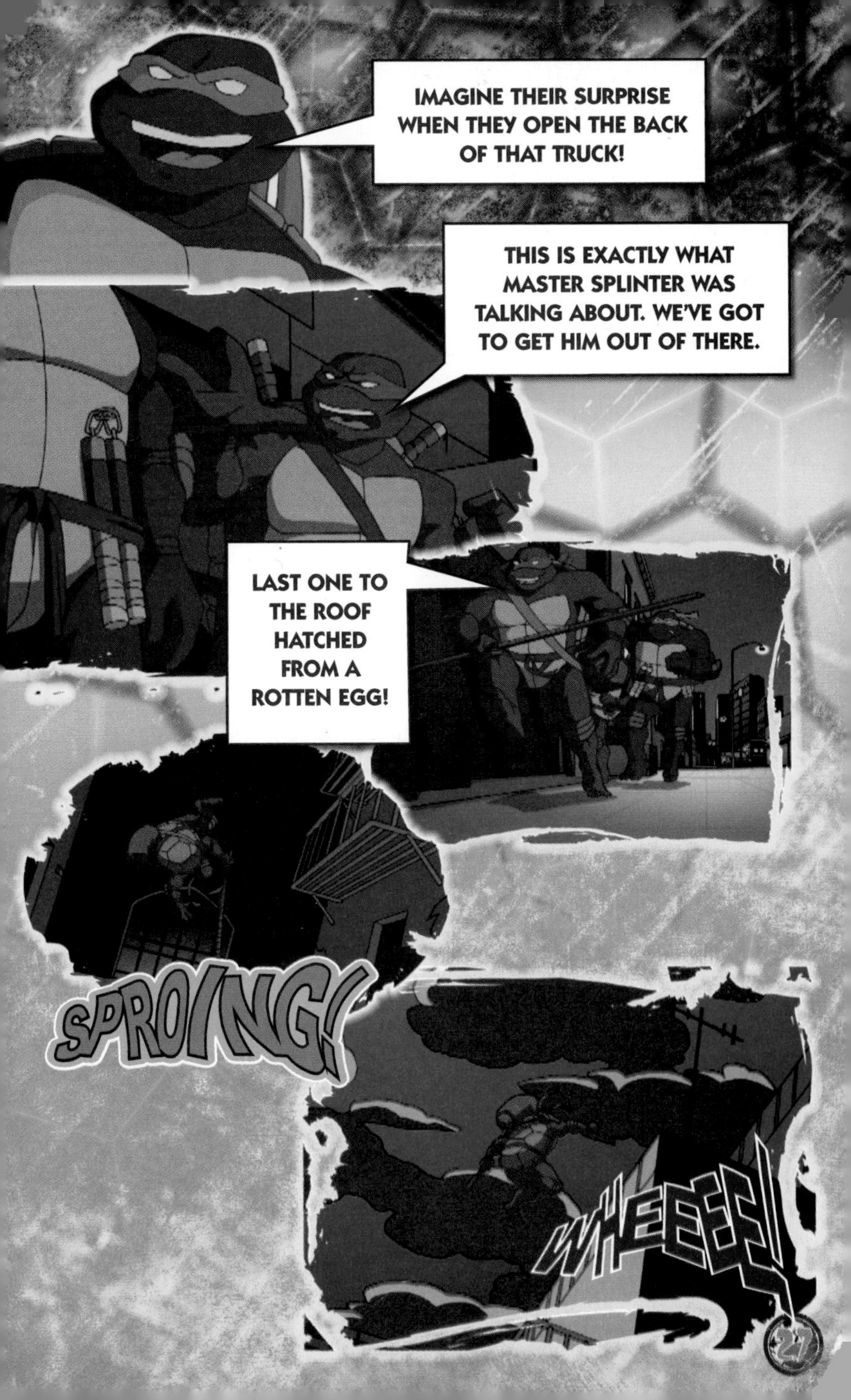
IMAGINE THEIR SURPRISE WHEN THEY OPEN THE BACK OF THAT TRUCK!
THIS IS EXACTLY WHAT MASTER SPLINTER WAS TALKING ABOUT. WE'VE GOT TO GET HIM OUT OF THERE.
LAST ONE TO THE ROOF HATCHED FROM A ROTTEN EGG!
SPROING!
WHEEEE!

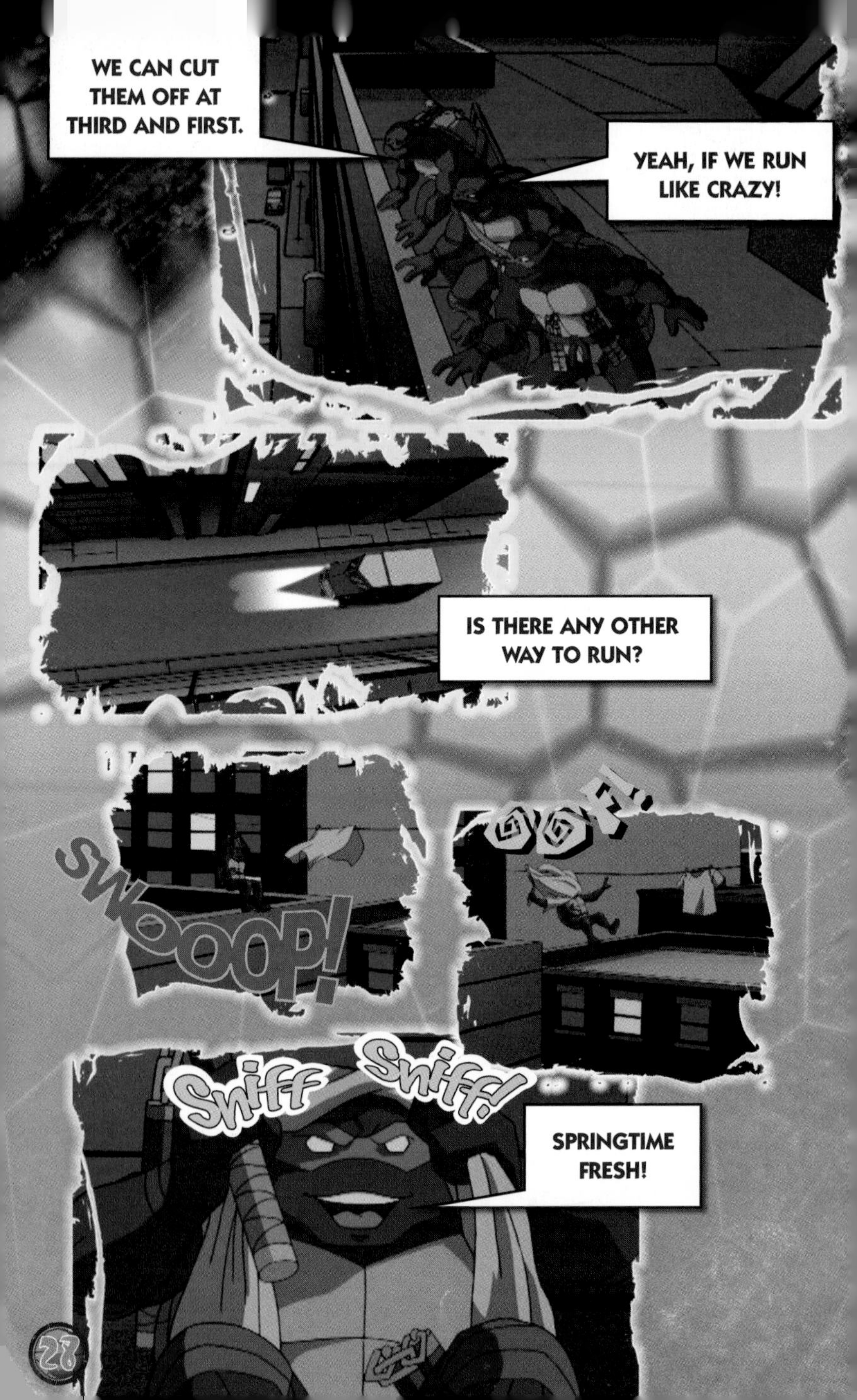
WE CAN CUT THEM OFF AT THIRD AND FIRST.
YEAH, IF WE RUN LIKE CRAZY!
IS THERE ANY OTHER WAY TO RUN?
SWOOOP!
OOF!
Sniff Sniff!
SPRINGTIME FRESH!

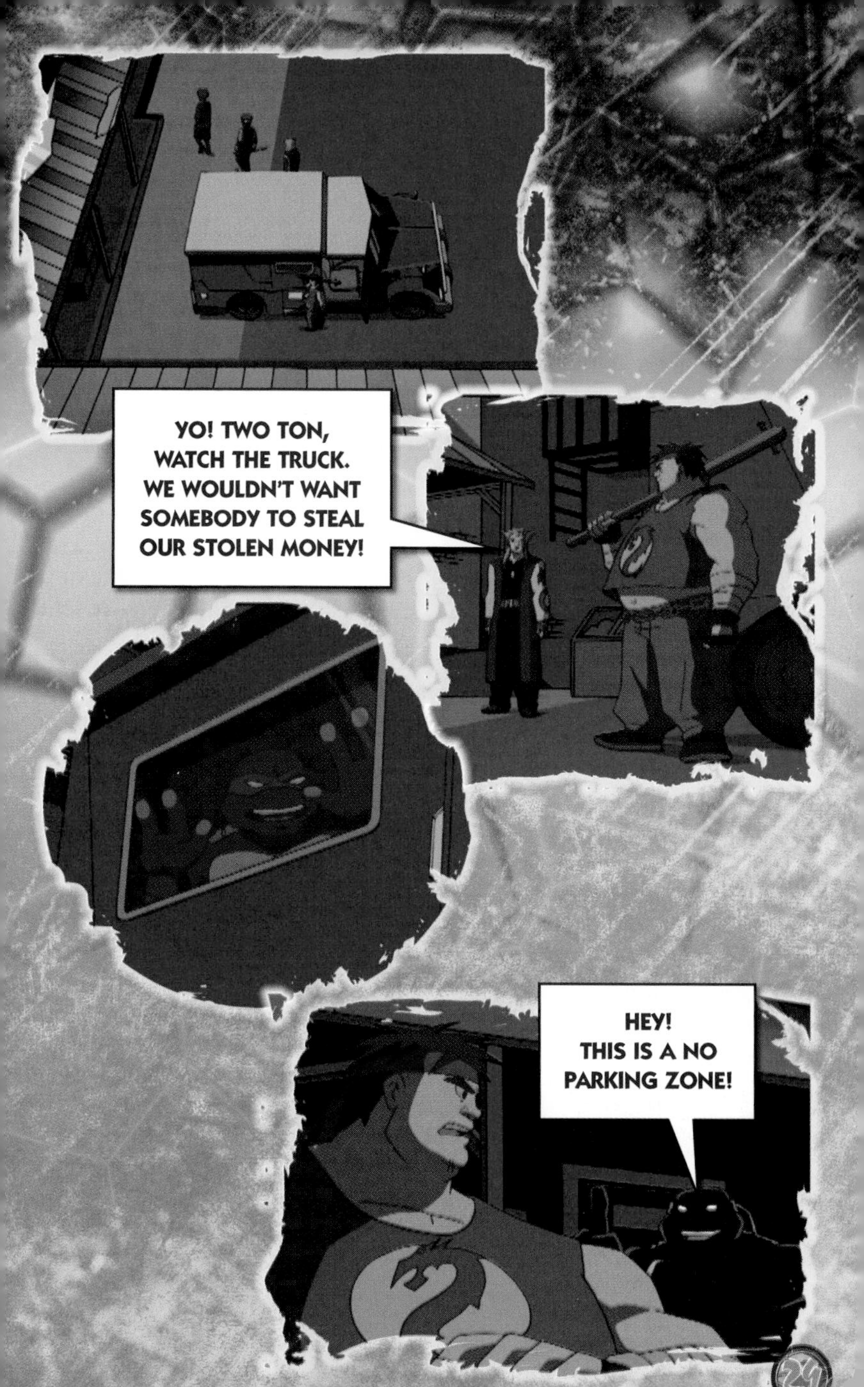
YO! TWO TON, WATCH THE TRUCK. WE WOULDN'T WANT SOMEBODY TO STEAL OUR STOLEN MONEY!
HEY! THIS IS A NO PARKING ZONE!

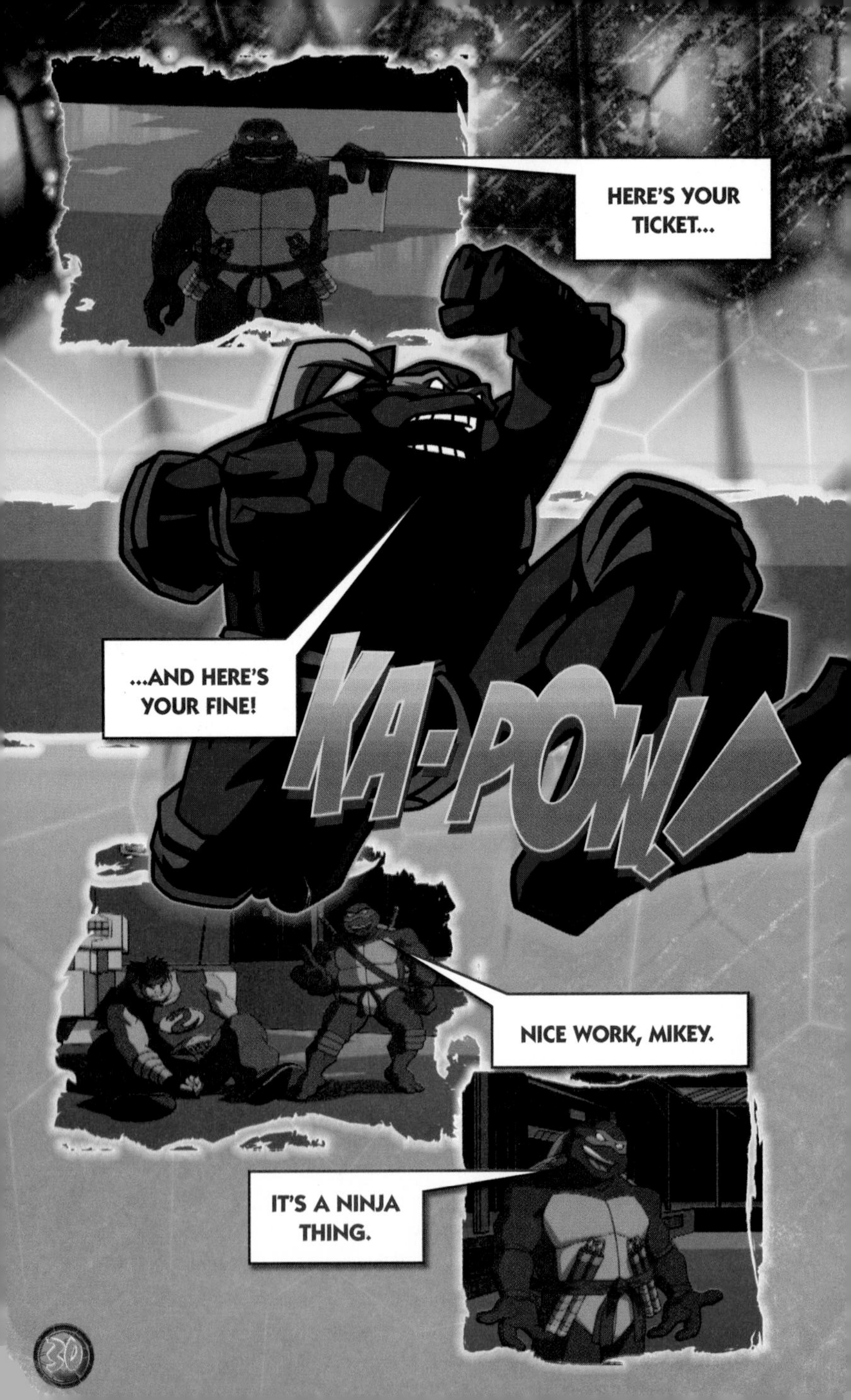
HERE'S YOUR TICKET...
...AND HERE'S YOUR FINE!
KA-POW!
NICE WORK, MIKEY.
IT'S A NINJA THING.

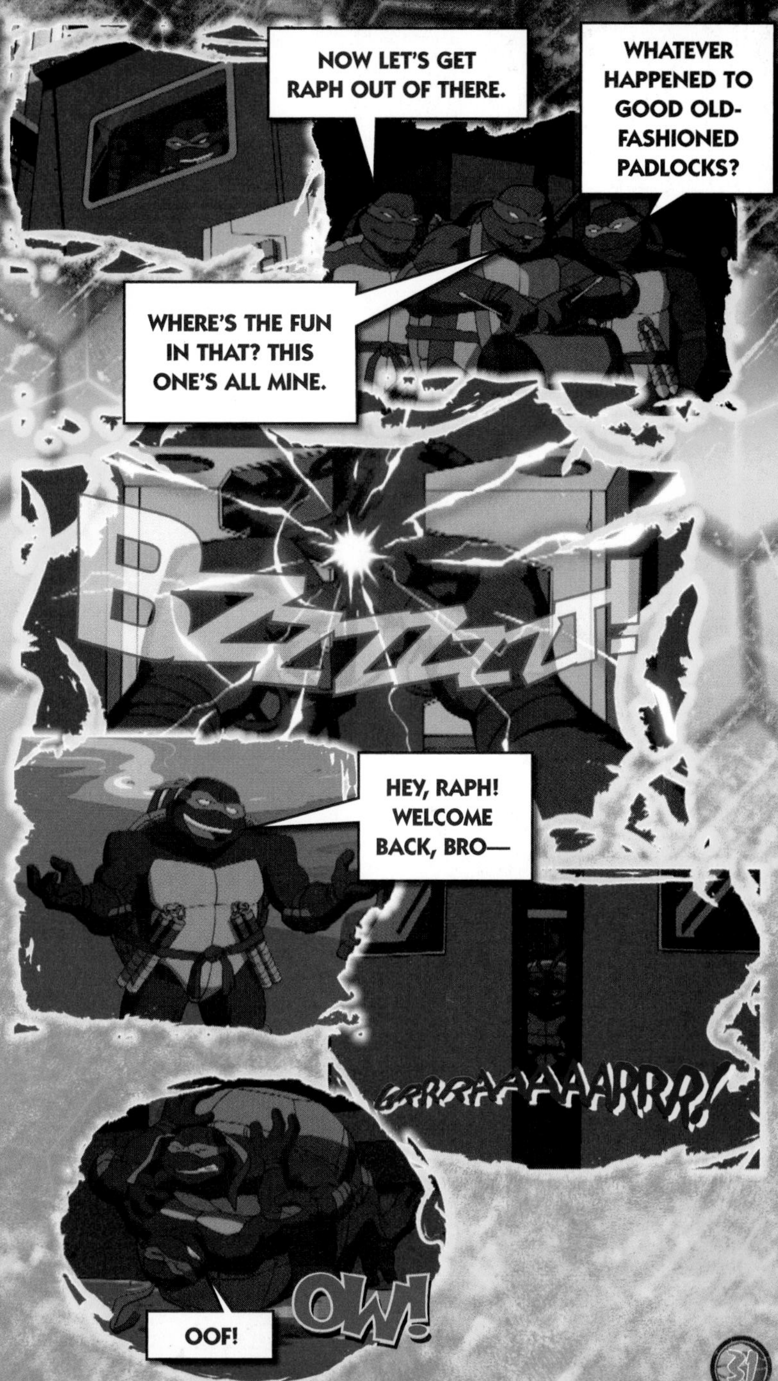
NOW LET'S GET RAPH OUT OF THERE.
WHATEVER HAPPENED TO GOOD OLD-FASHIONED PADLOCKS?
WHERE'S THE FUN IN THAT? THIS ONE'S ALL MINE.
BZZZZT!
HEY, RAPH! WELCOME BACK, BRO—
GRRRRAAAAAARRRR!
OOF!
OW!

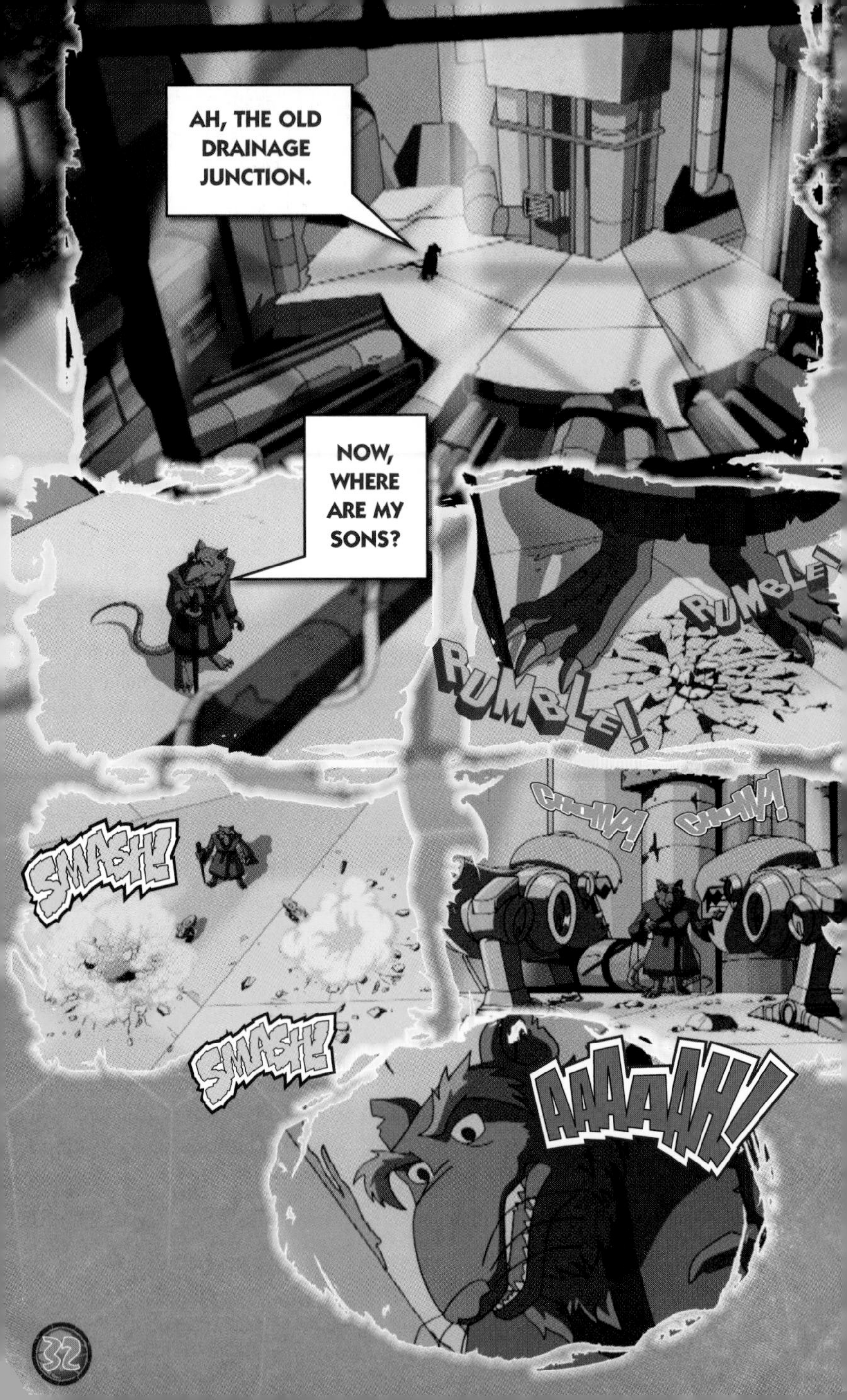
AH, THE OLD DRAINAGE JUNCTION.
NOW, WHERE ARE MY SONS?
RUMBLE!
RUMBLE!
SMASH!
SMASH!
CHOMP!
CHOMP!
AAAAAH!

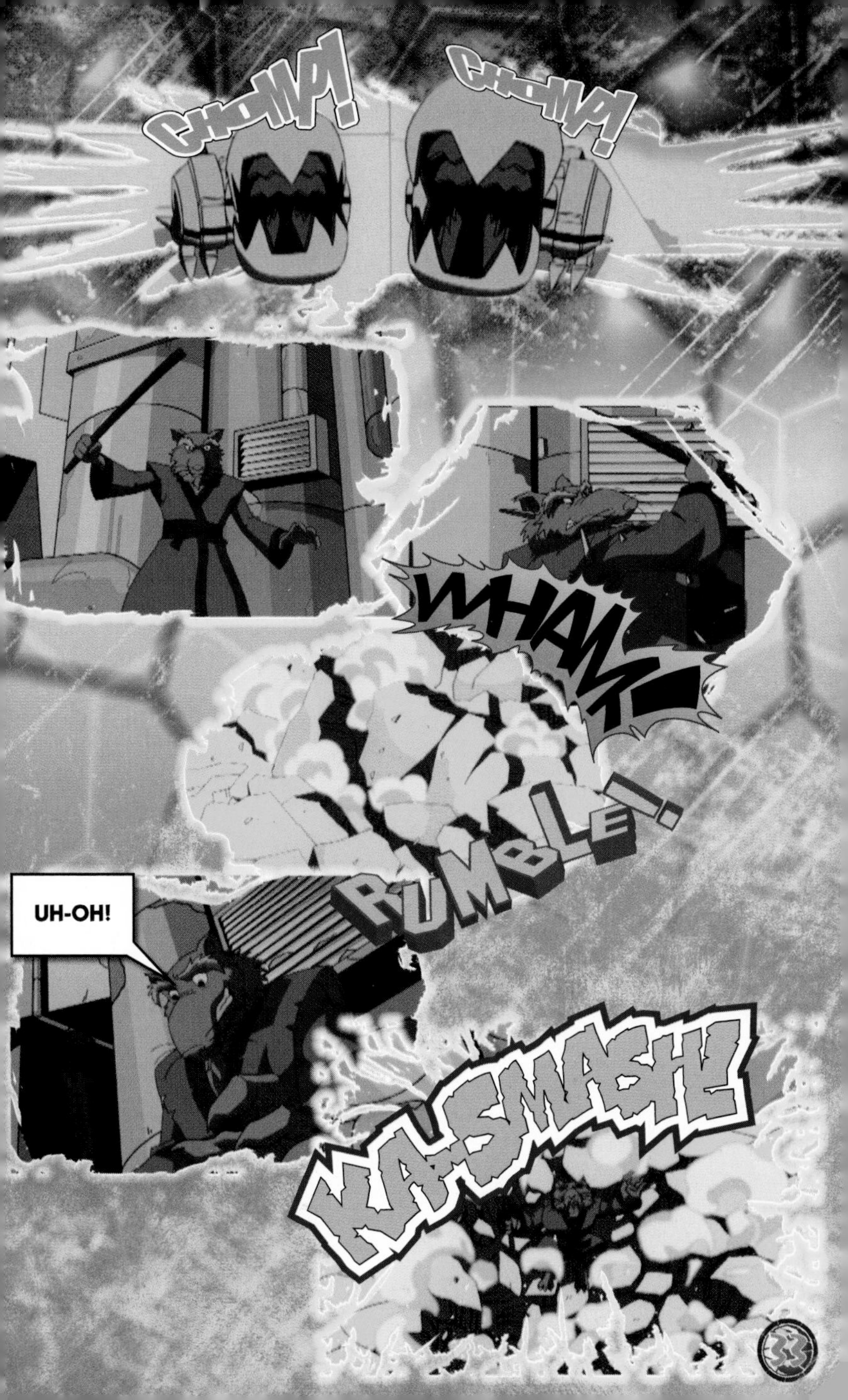
CHOMP!
CHOMP!
WHAM--
RUMBLE!..
UH-OH!
KA-SMASH!

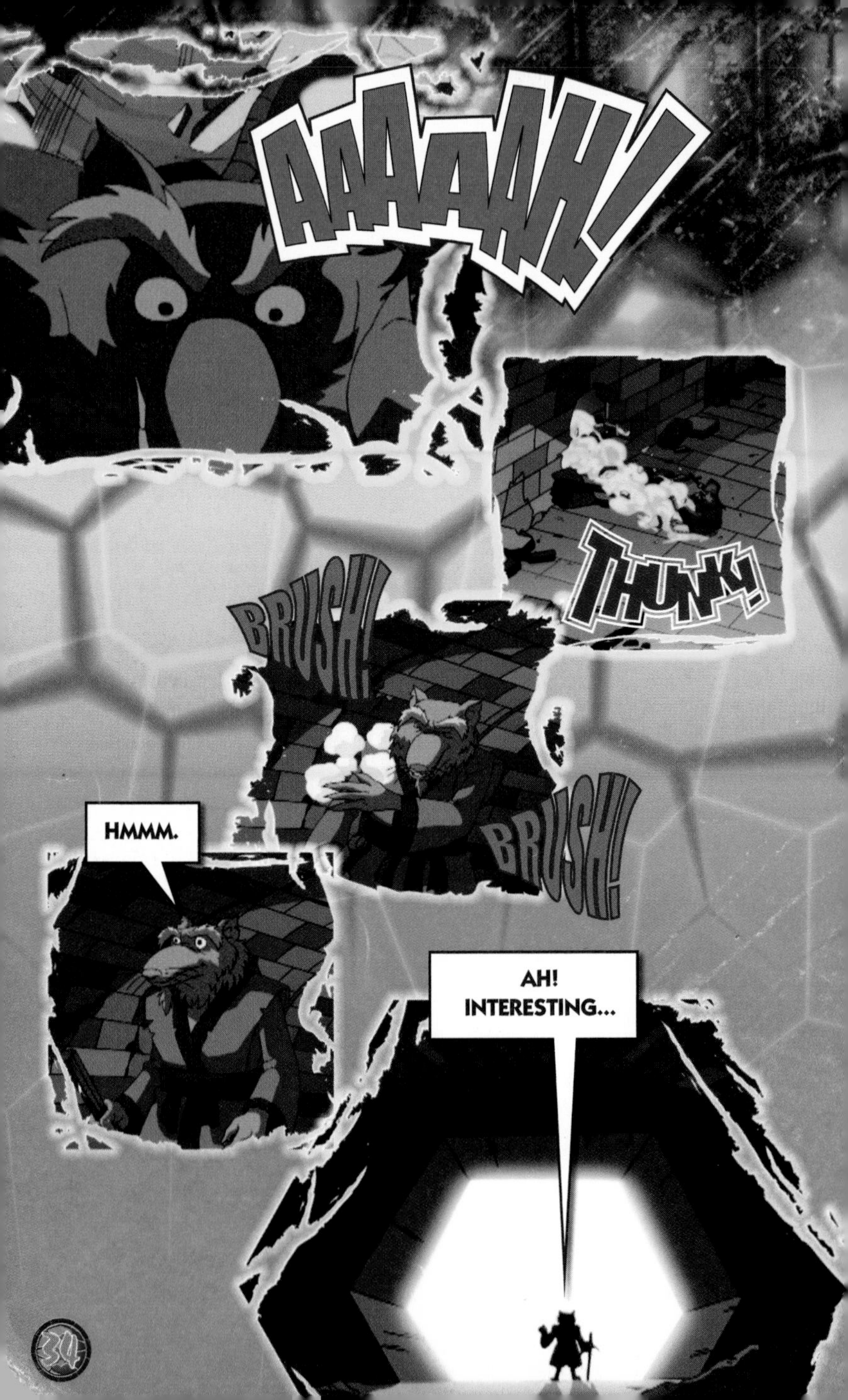
AAAAAAH!
THUNK!
BRUSH!
BRUSH!
HMMM.
AH! INTERESTING...

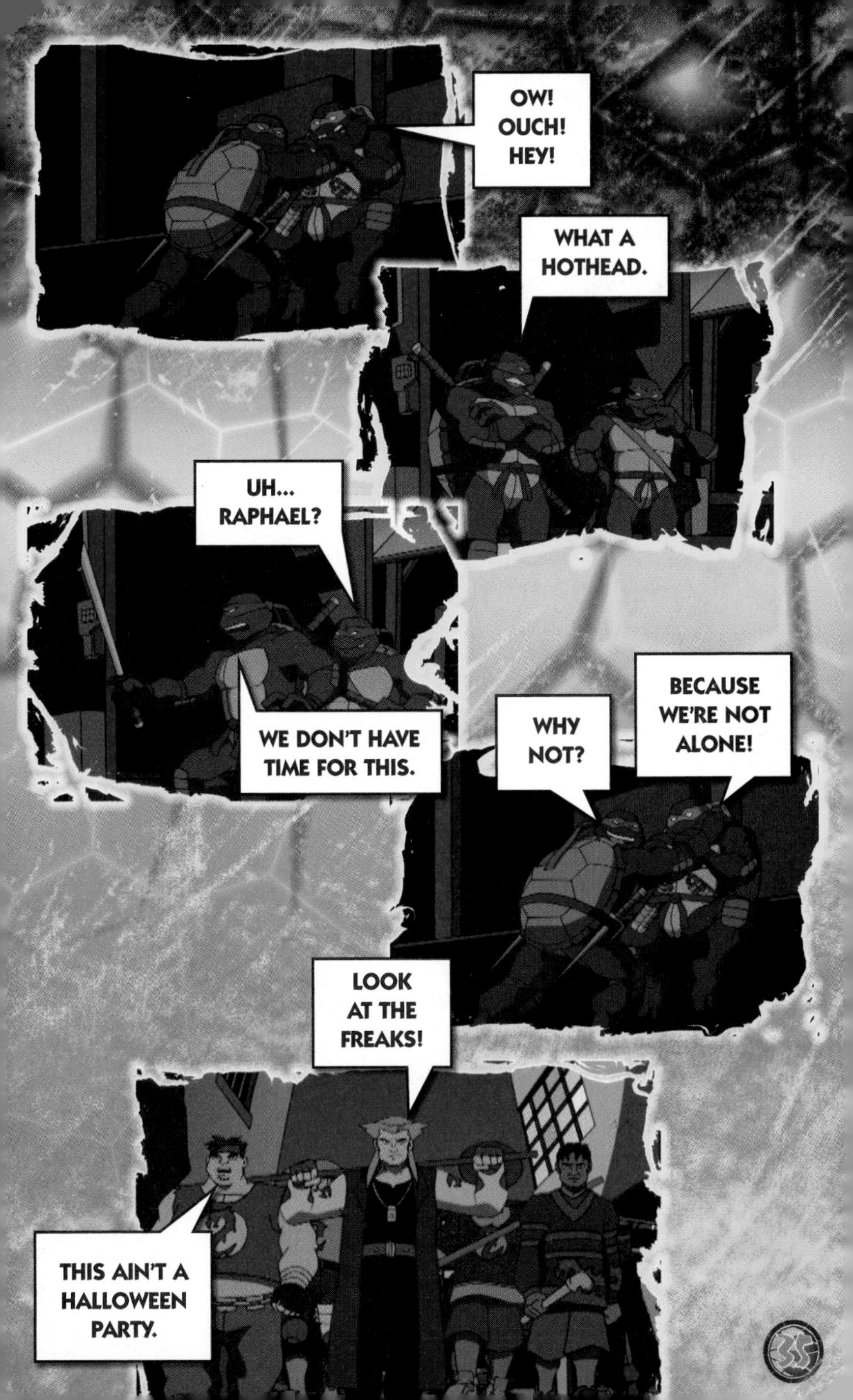
OW! OUCH! HEY!
WHAT A HOTHEAD.
UH... RAPHAEL?
WE DON'T HAVE TIME FOR THIS.
WHY NOT?
BECAUSE WE'RE NOT ALONE!
LOOK AT THE FREAKS!
THIS AIN'T A HALLOWEEN PARTY.

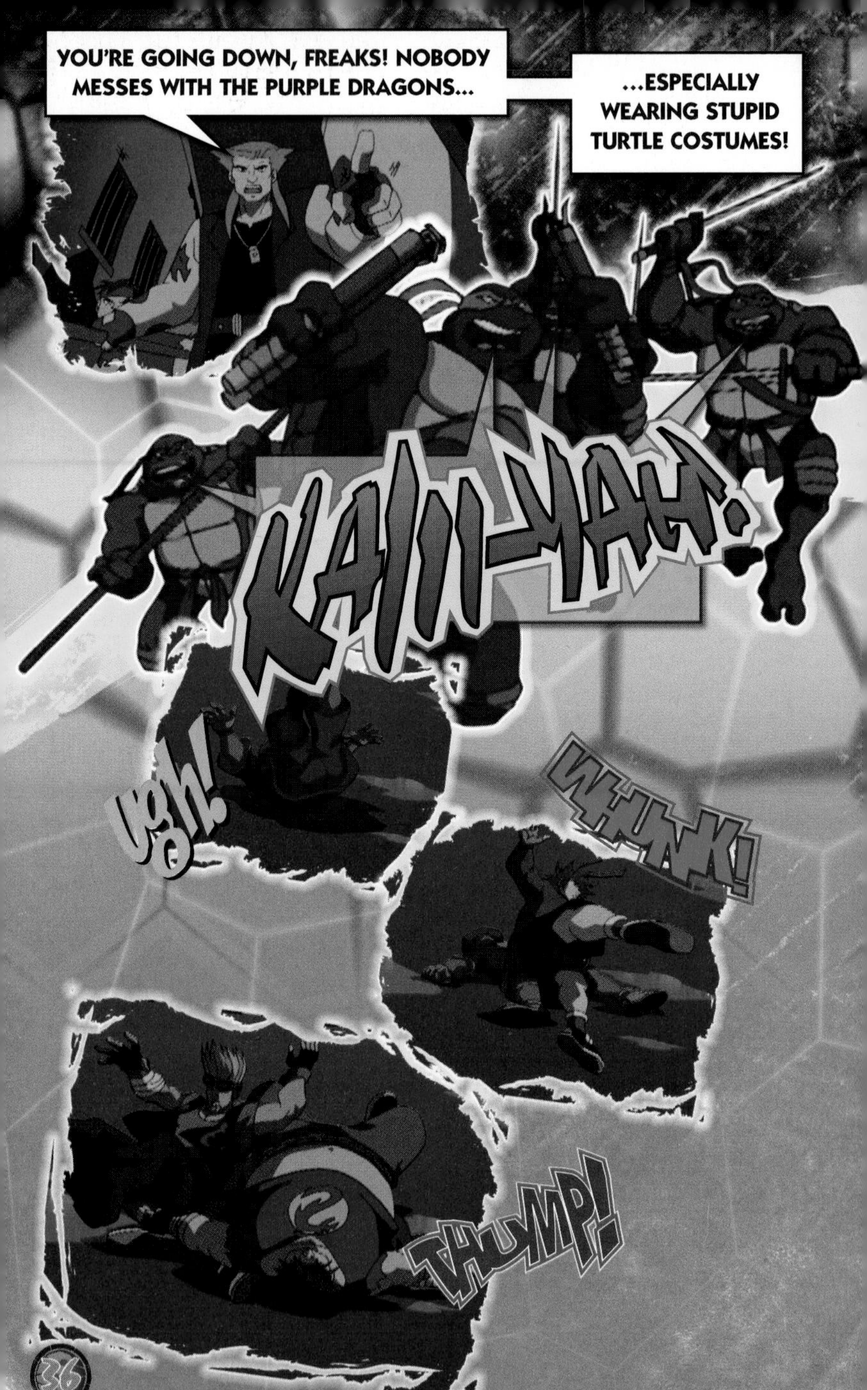
YOU'RE GOING DOWN, FREAKS! NOBODY MESSES WITH THE PURPLE DRAGONS...
...ESPECIALLY WEARING STUPID TURTLE COSTUMES!
KAIII-YAH!
Ugh!
WHUNK!
THUMP!

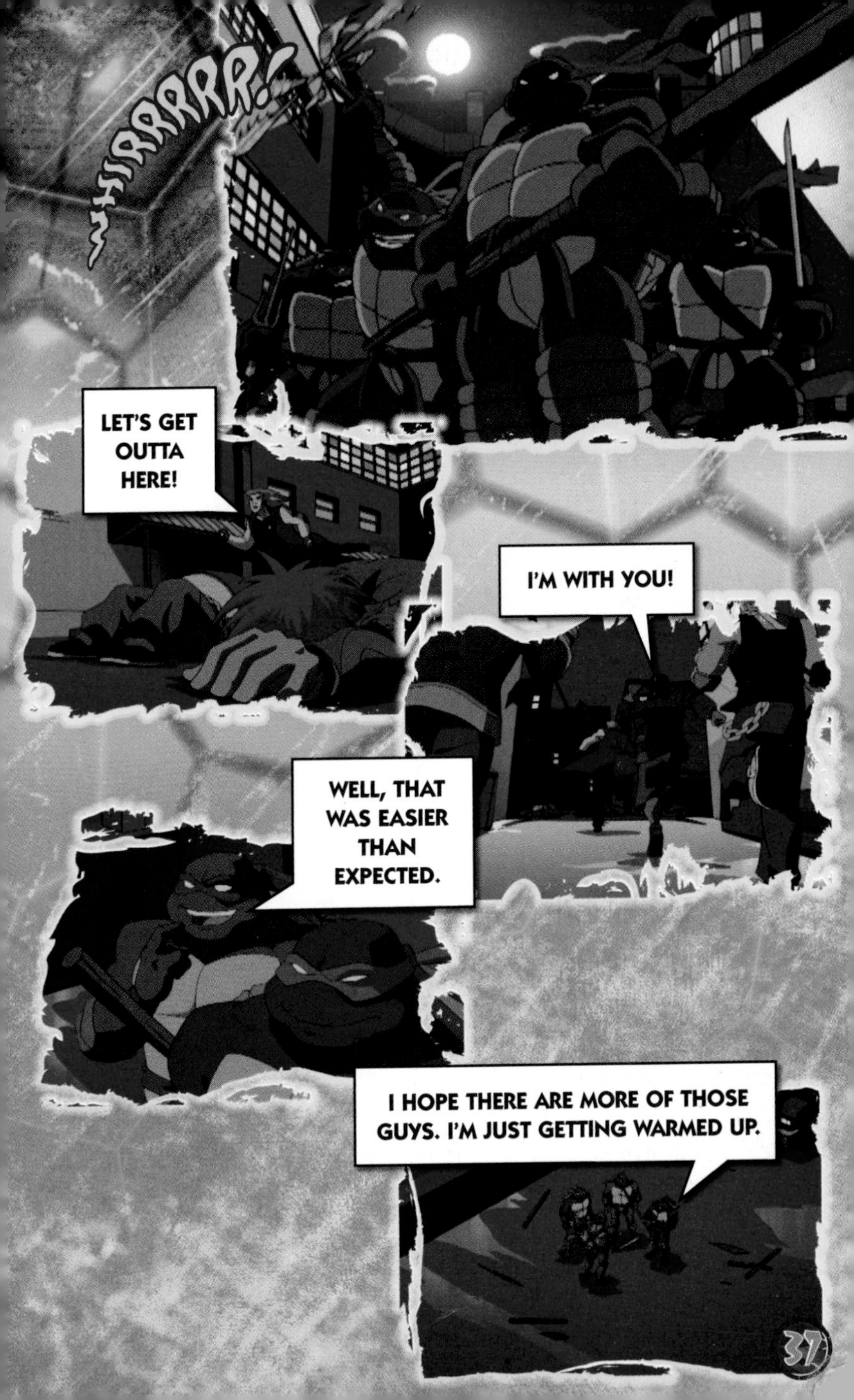
WHIRRRRR!
LET'S GET OUTTA HERE!
I'M WITH YOU!
WELL, THAT WAS EASIER THAN EXPECTED.
I HOPE THERE ARE MORE OF THOSE GUYS. I'M JUST GETTING WARMED UP.

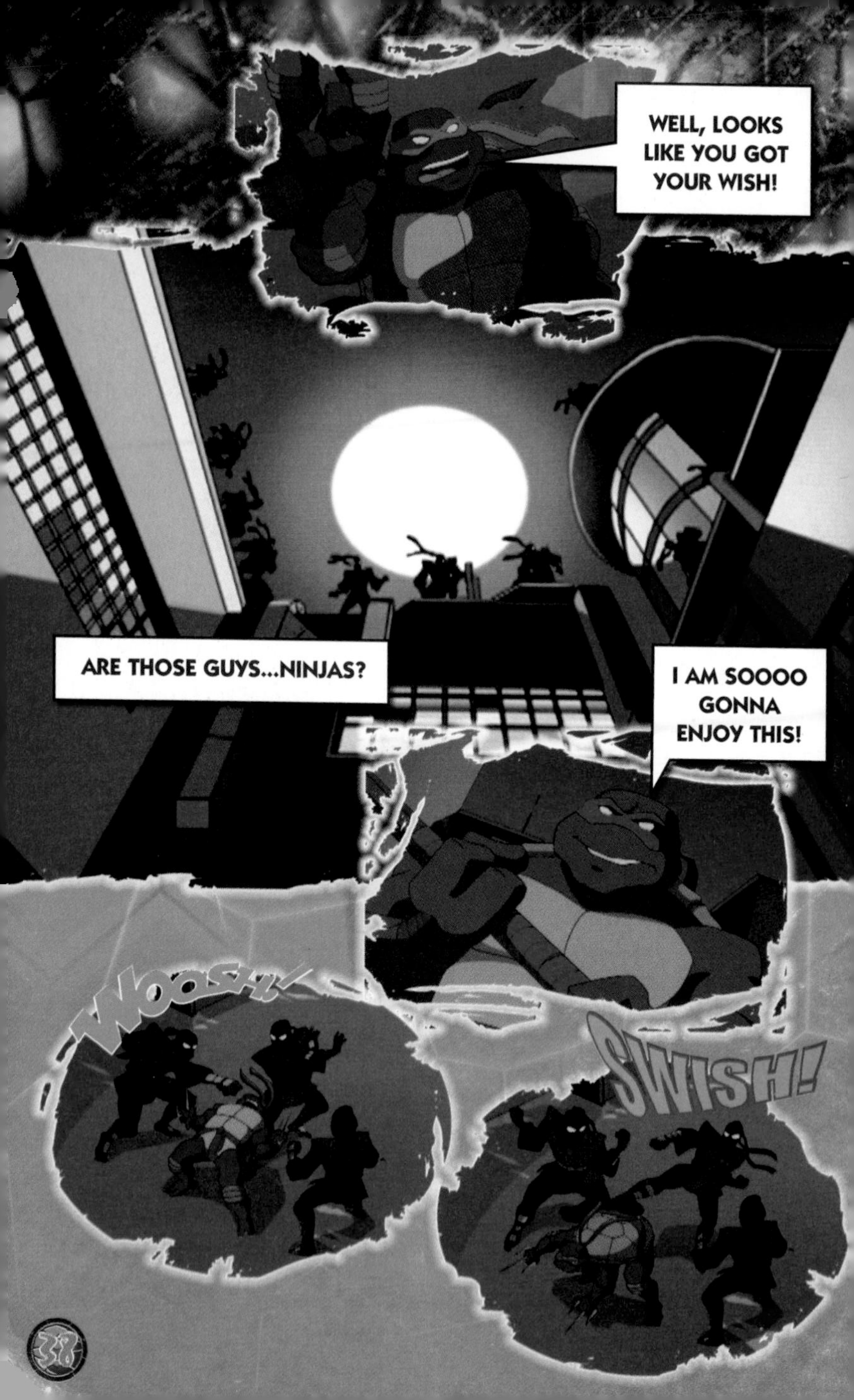
WELL, LOOKS LIKE YOU GOT YOUR WISH!
ARE THOSE GUYS...NINJAS?
I AM SOOOO GONNA ENJOY THIS!
WOOSH!
SWISH!

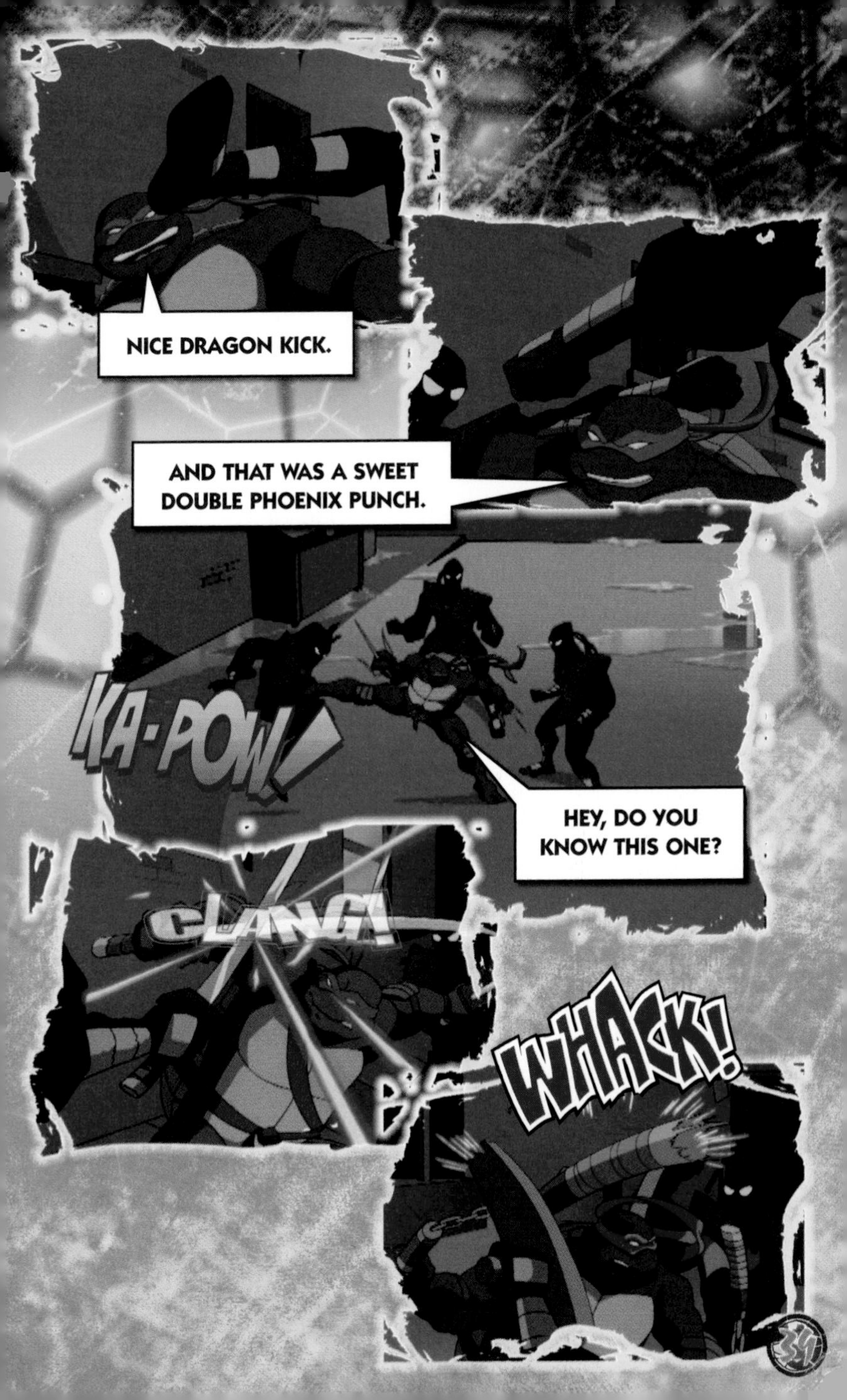
NICE DRAGON KICK.
AND THAT WAS A SWEET DOUBLE PHOENIX PUNCH.
KA-POW!
HEY, DO YOU KNOW THIS ONE?
CLANG!
WHACK!

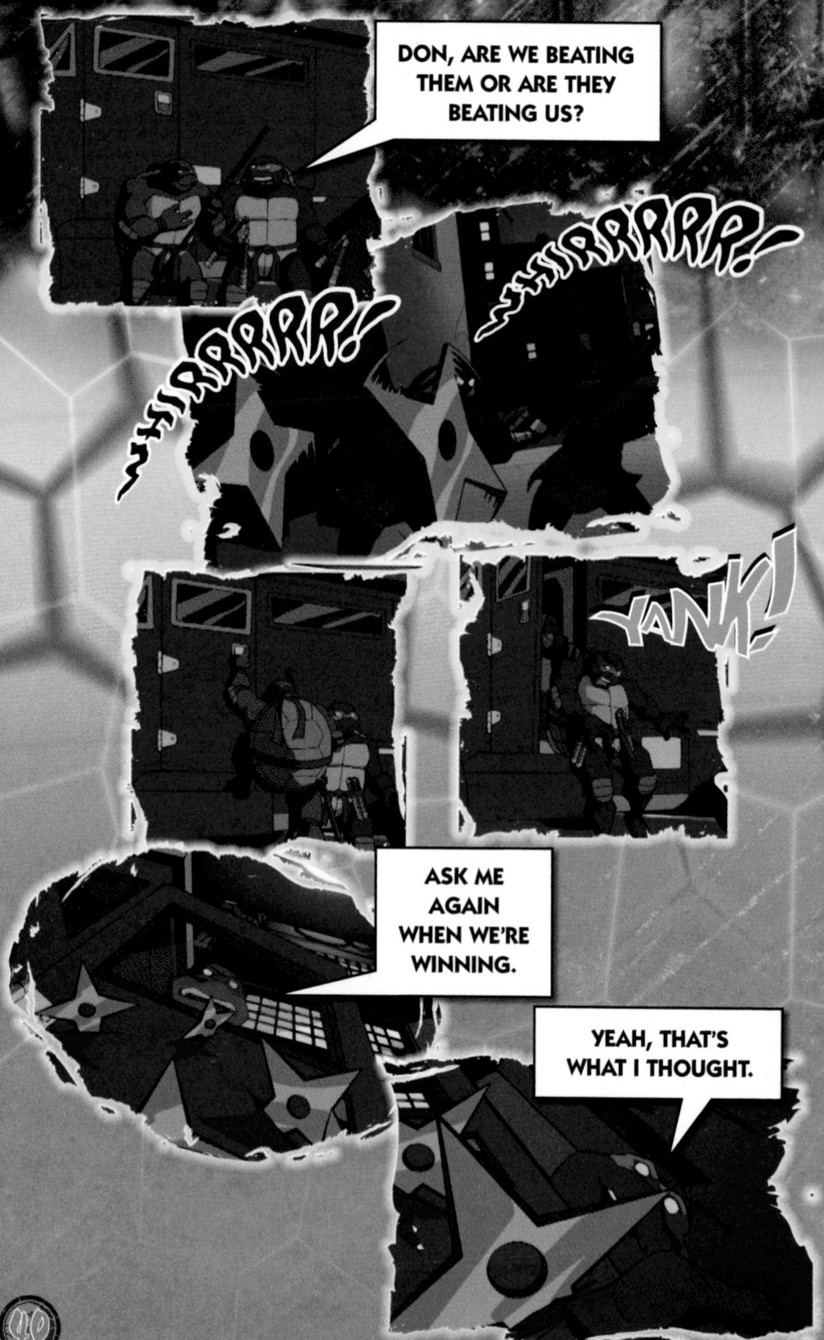
DON, ARE WE BEATING THEM OR ARE THEY BEATING US?
WHIRRRRR!
WHIRRRRRR!
YANK!
ASK ME AGAIN WHEN WE'RE WINNING.
YEAH, THAT'S WHAT I THOUGHT.

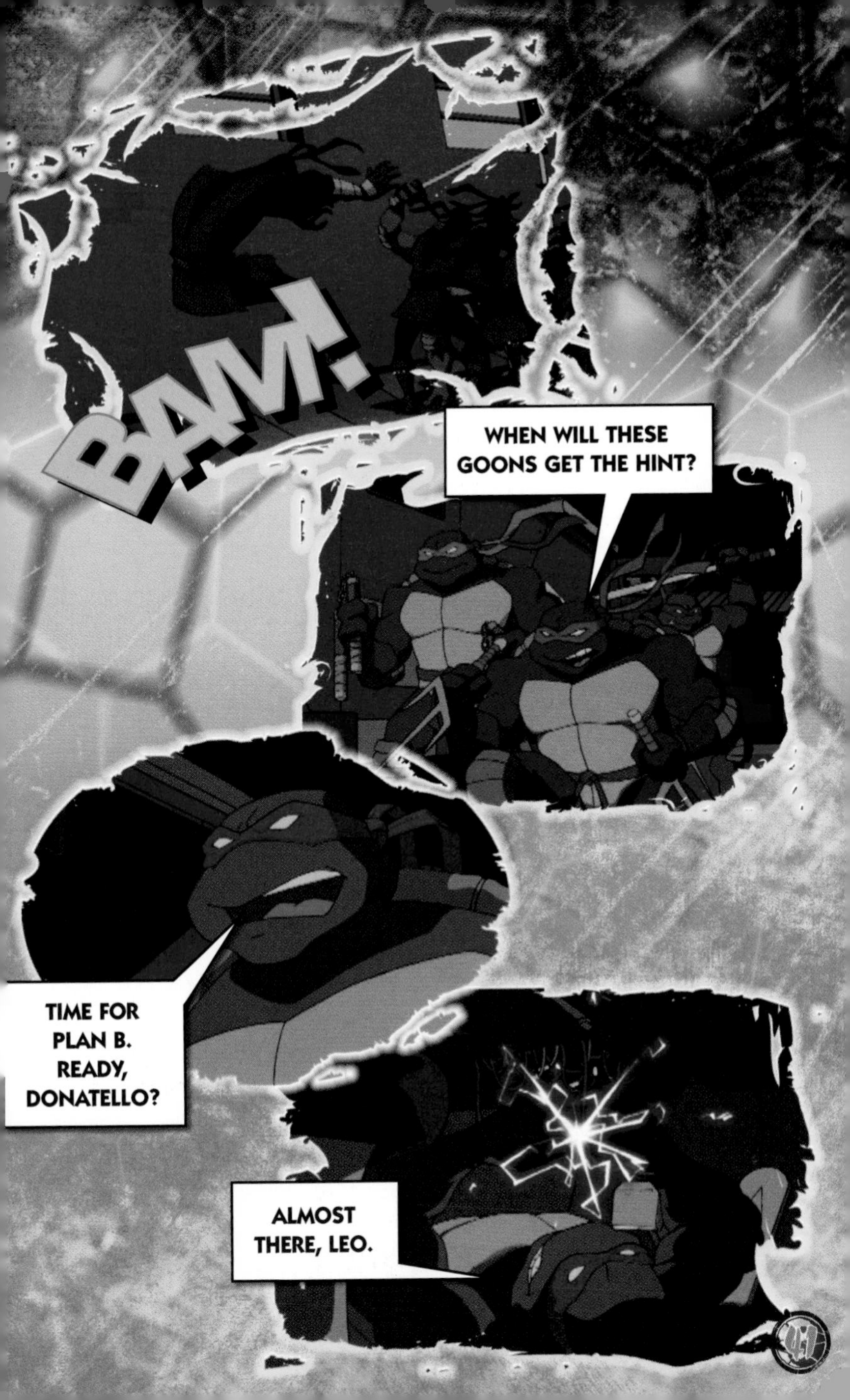
BAM!
WHEN WILL THESE GOONS GET THE HINT?
TIME FOR PLAN B. READY, DONATELLO?
ALMOST THERE, LEO.

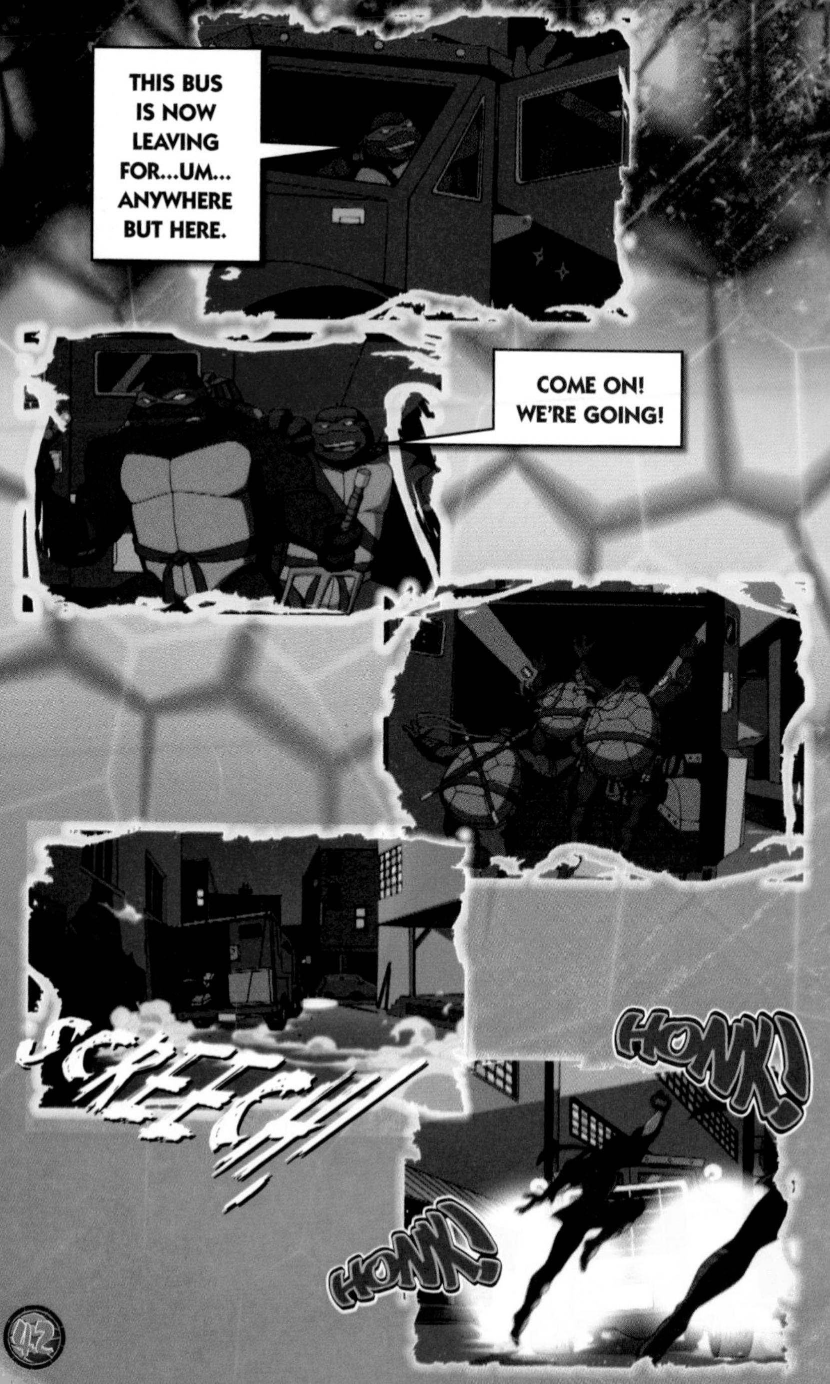
THIS BUS IS NOW LEAVING FOR...UM... ANYWHERE BUT HERE.
COME ON! WE'RE GOING!
SCREECH!
HONK!
HONK!

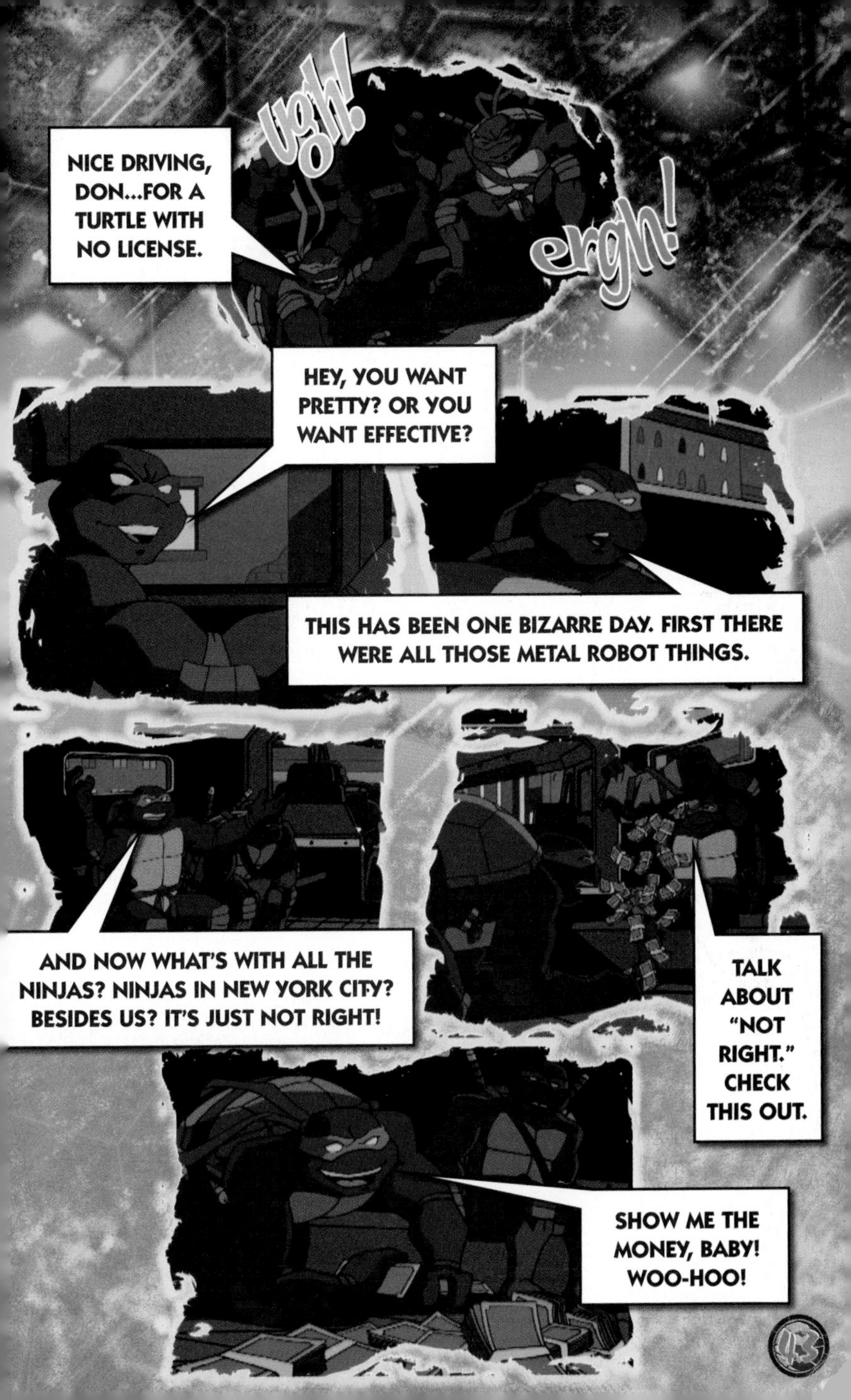
NICE DRIVING, DON...FOR A TURTLE WITH NO LICENSE.
ugh!
ergh!
HEY, YOU WANT PRETTY? OR YOU WANT EFFECTIVE?
THIS HAS BEEN ONE BIZARRE DAY. FIRST THERE WERE ALL THOSE METAL ROBOT THINGS.
AND NOW WHAT'S WITH ALL THE NINJAS? NINJAS IN NEW YORK CITY? BESIDES US? IT'S JUST NOT RIGHT!
TALK ABOUT "NOT RIGHT." CHECK THIS OUT.
SHOW ME THE MONEY, BABY! WOO-HOO!

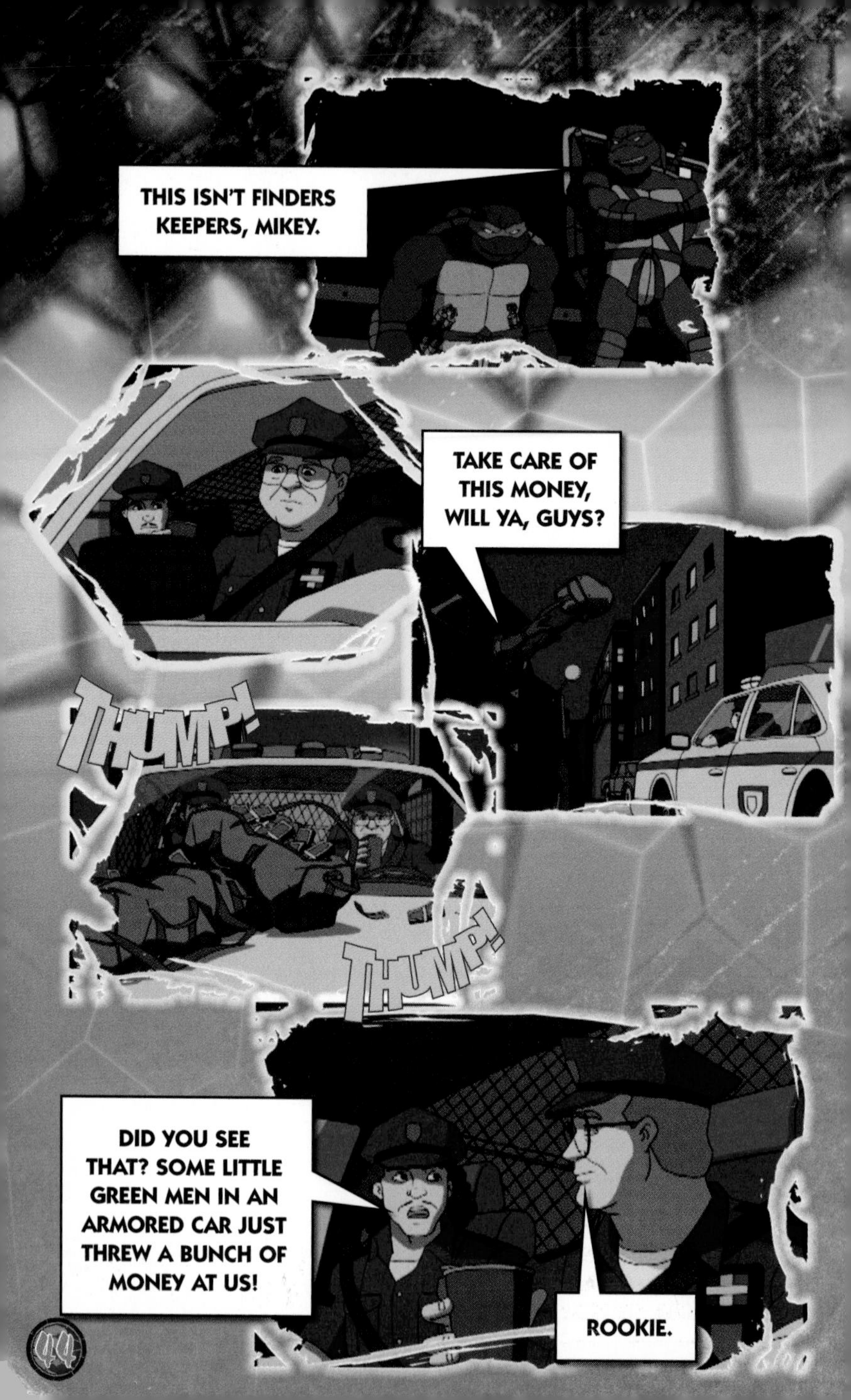
THIS ISN'T FINDERS KEEPERS, MIKEY.
TAKE CARE OF THIS MONEY, WILL YA, GUYS?
THUMP!
THUMP!
DID YOU SEE THAT? SOME LITTLE GREEN MEN IN AN ARMORED CAR JUST THREW A BUNCH OF MONEY AT US!
ROOKIE.

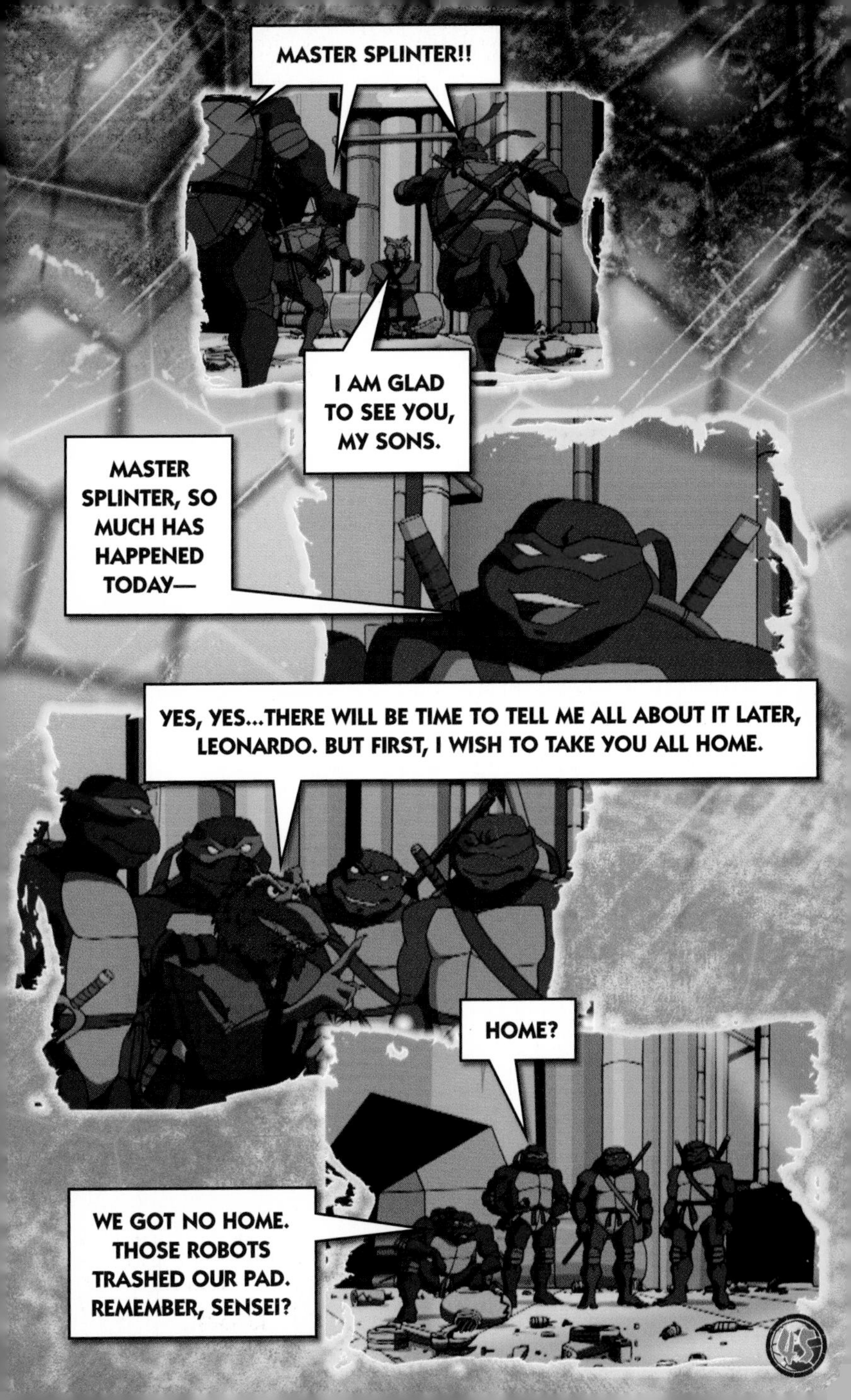
MASTER SPLINTER!!
I AM GLAD TO SEE YOU, MY SONS.
MASTER SPLINTER, SO MUCH HAS HAPPENED TODAY—
YES, YES...THERE WILL BE TIME TO TELL ME ALL ABOUT IT LATER, LEONARDO. BUT FIRST, I WISH TO TAKE YOU ALL HOME.
HOME?
WE GOT NO HOME. THOSE ROBOTS TRASHED OUR PAD. REMEMBER, SENSEI?

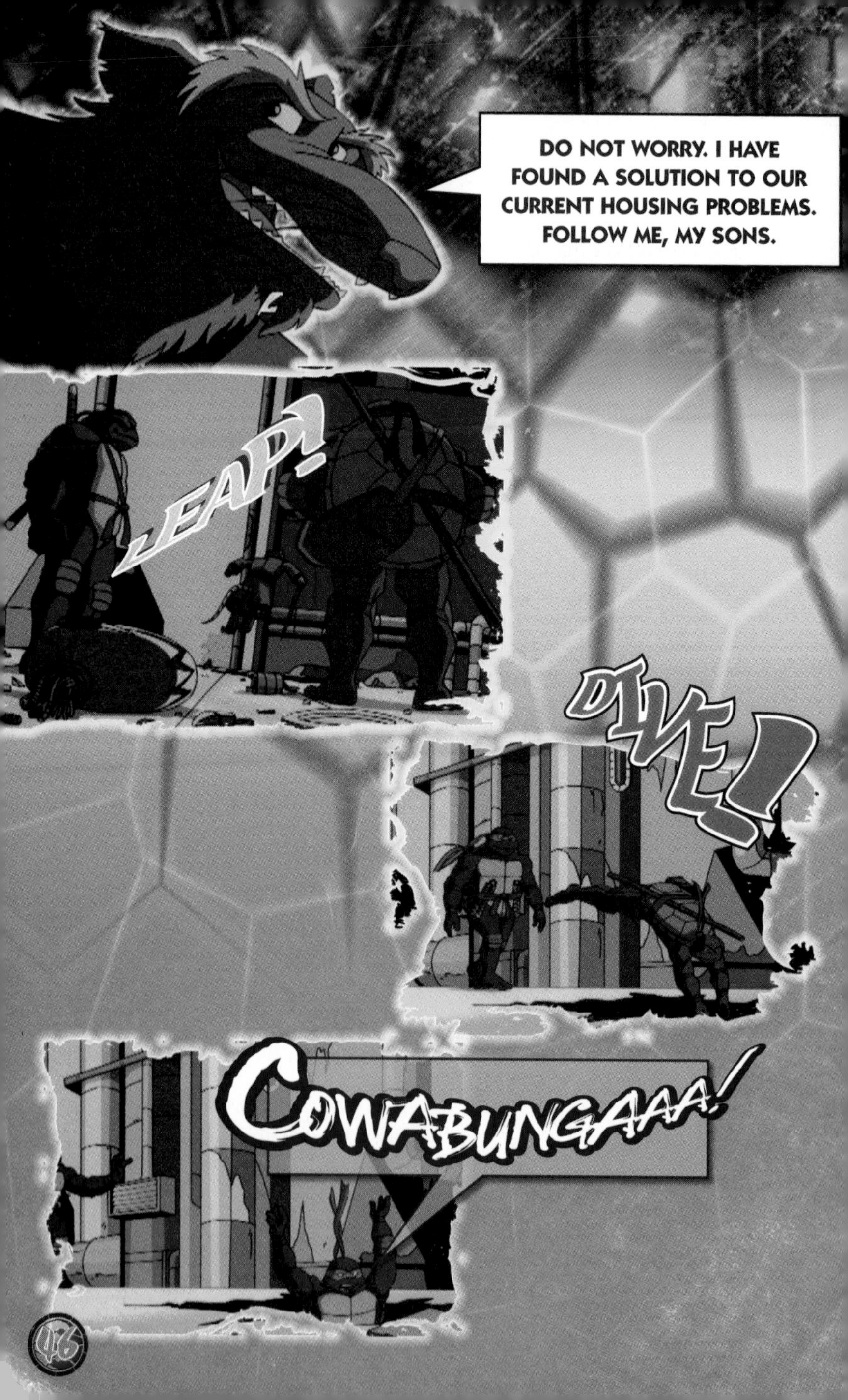
DO NOT WORRY. I HAVE FOUND A SOLUTION TO OUR CURRENT HOUSING PROBLEMS. FOLLOW ME, MY SONS.
LEAP!
DIVE!
COWABUNGAAA!

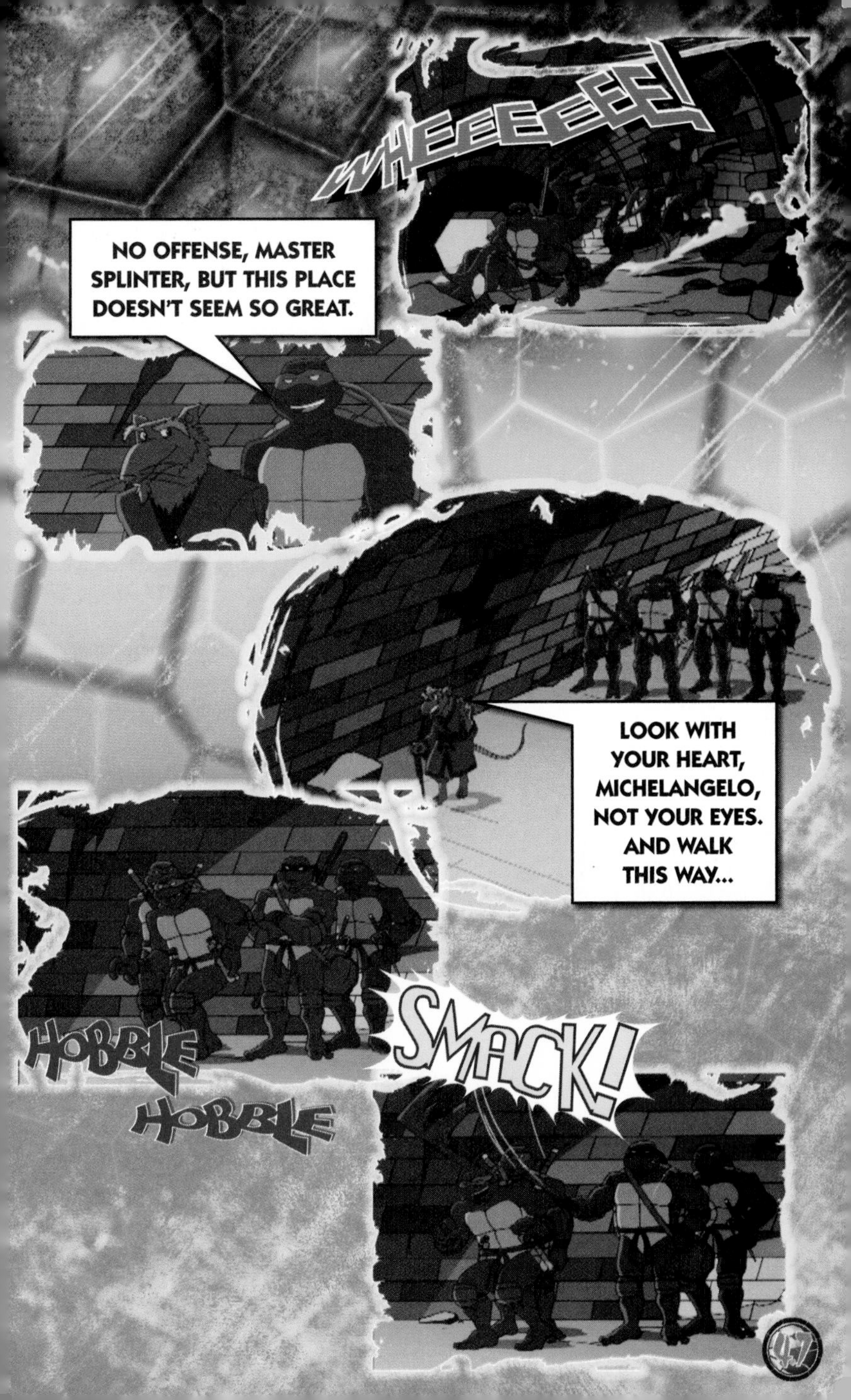
WHEEEEEEE!
NO OFFENSE, MASTER SPLINTER, BUT THIS PLACE DOESN'T SEEM SO GREAT.
LOOK WITH YOUR HEART, MICHELANGELO, NOT YOUR EYES. AND WALK THIS WAY...
HOBBLE
HOBBLE
SMACK!

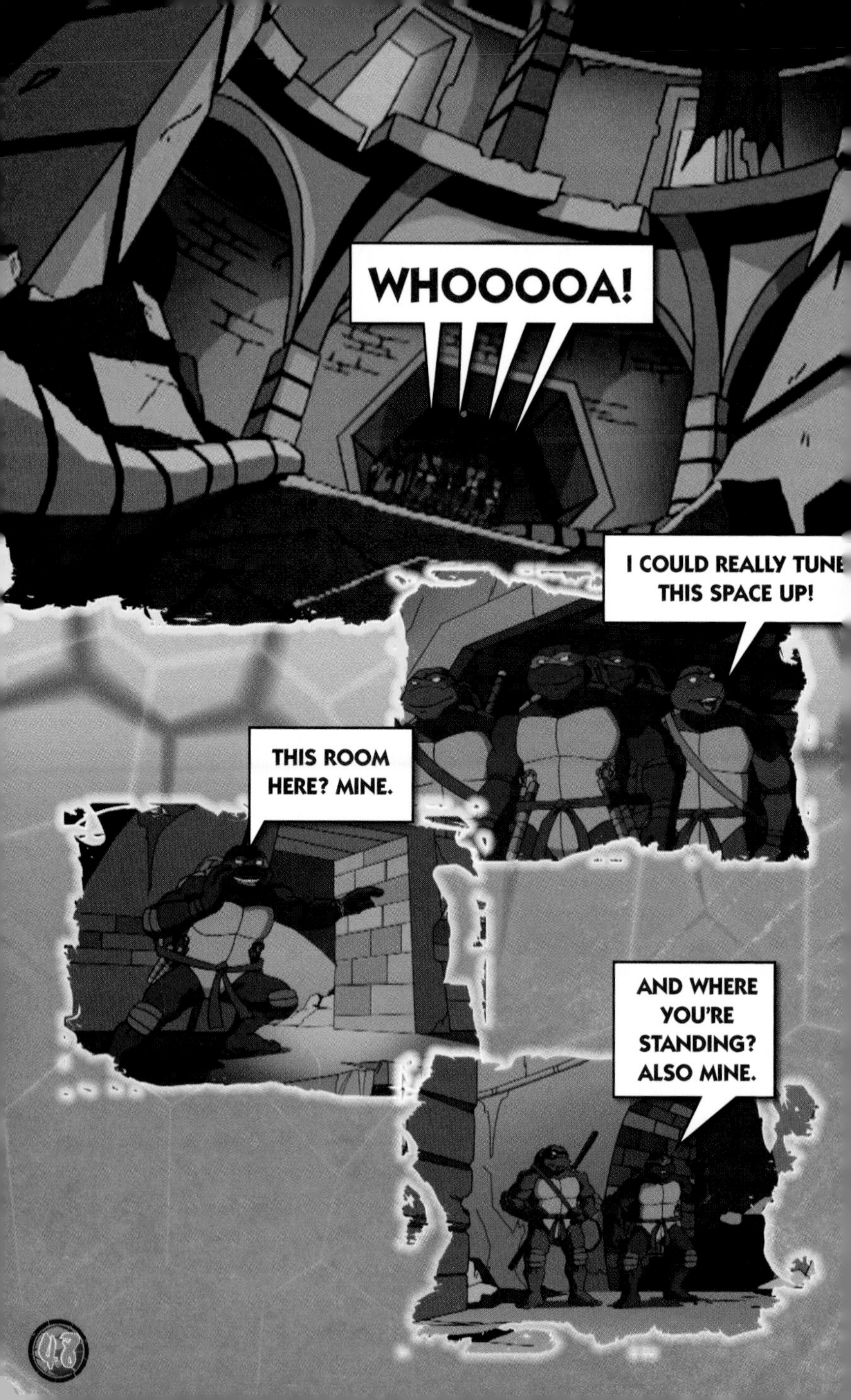
WHOOOOA!
I COULD REALLY TUNE THIS SPACE UP!
THIS ROOM HERE? MINE.
AND WHERE YOU'RE STANDING? ALSO MINE.

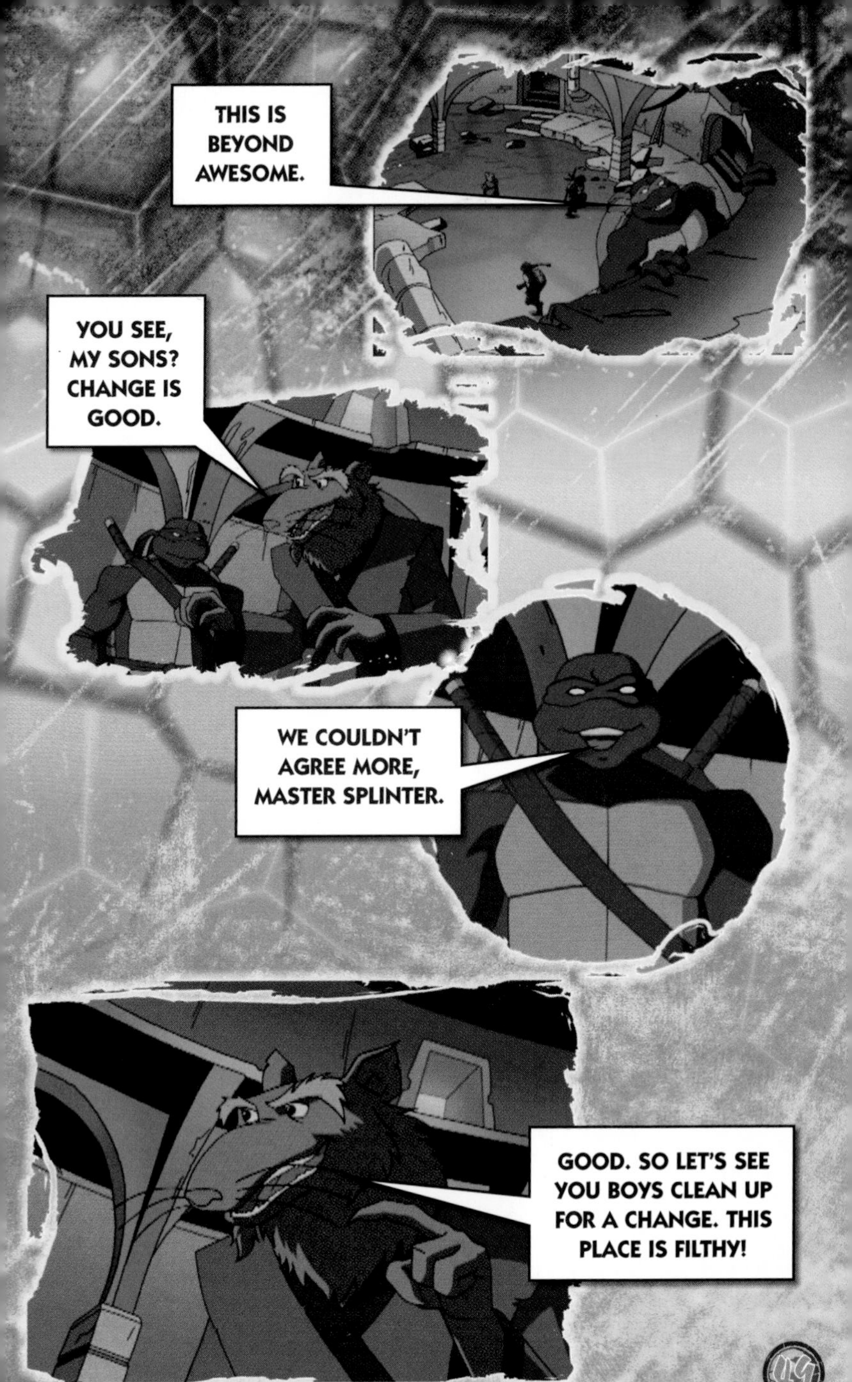
THIS IS BEYOND AWESOME.
YOU SEE, MY SONS? CHANGE IS GOOD.
WE COULDN'T AGREE MORE, MASTER SPLINTER.
GOOD. SO LET'S SEE YOU BOYS CLEAN UP FOR A CHANGE. THIS PLACE IS FILTHY!

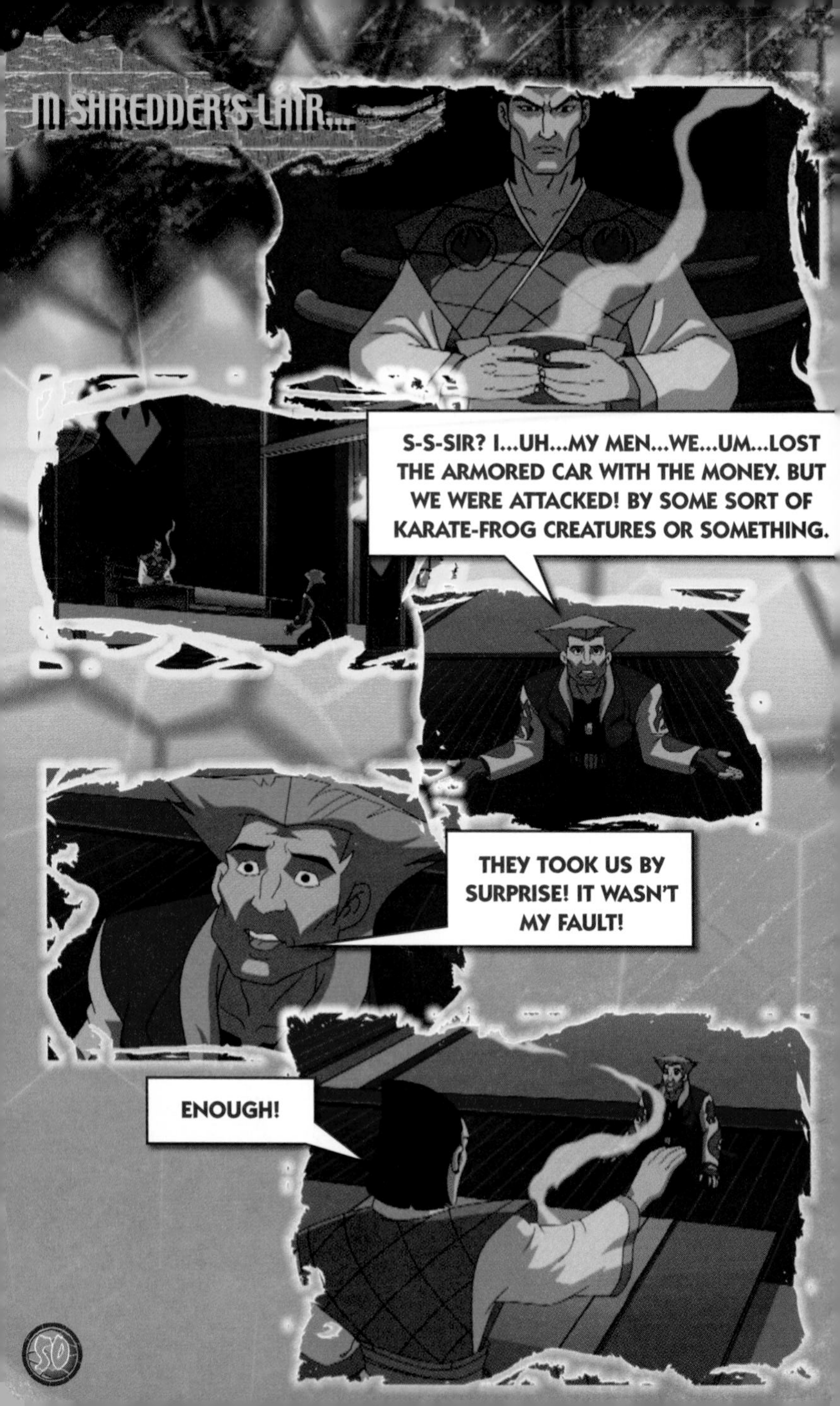
IN SHREDDER'S LAIR...
S-S-SIR? I...UH...MY MEN...WE...UM...LOST THE ARMORED CAR WITH THE MONEY. BUT WE WERE ATTACKED! BY SOME SORT OF KARATE-FROG CREATURES OR SOMETHING.
THEY TOOK US BY SURPRISE! IT WASN'T MY FAULT!
ENOUGH!

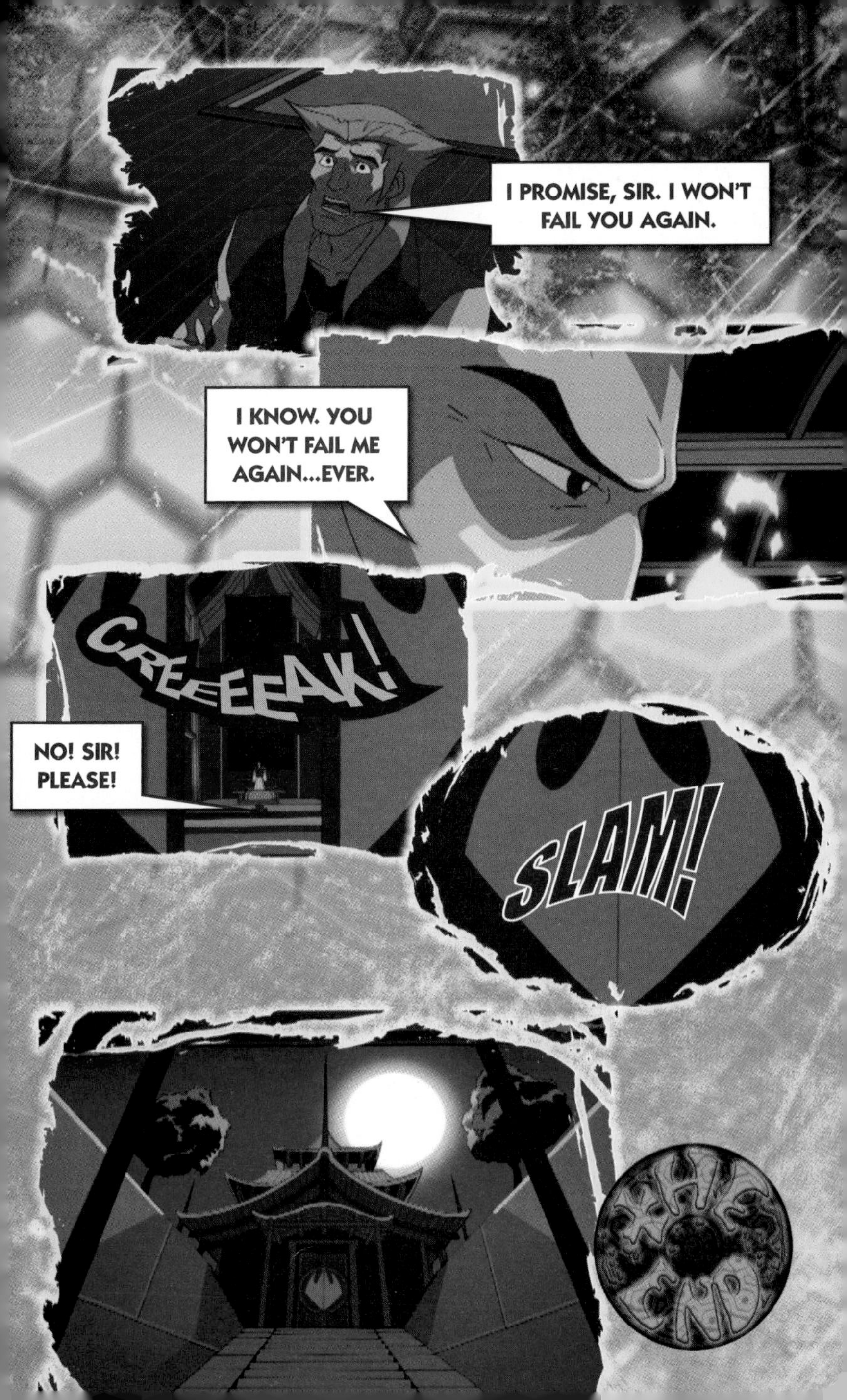
I PROMISE, SIR. I WON'T FAIL YOU AGAIN.
I KNOW. YOU WON'T FAIL ME AGAIN...EVER.
CREEEEAK!
NO! SIR! PLEASE!
SLAM!
THE END

THE UNCONVINCING TURTLE TITAN

WRITTEN BY
MARTY ISENBERG

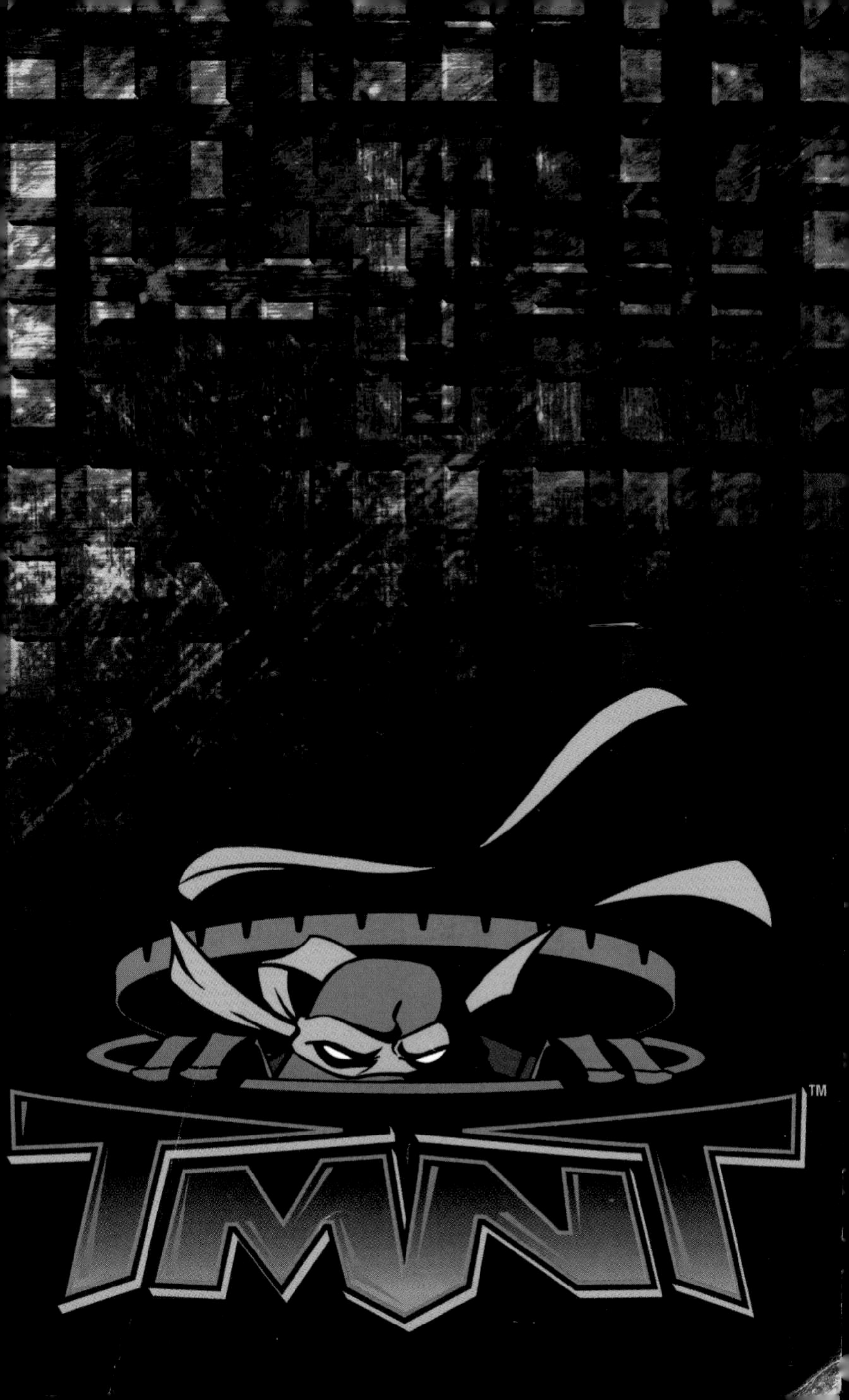
TMNT™

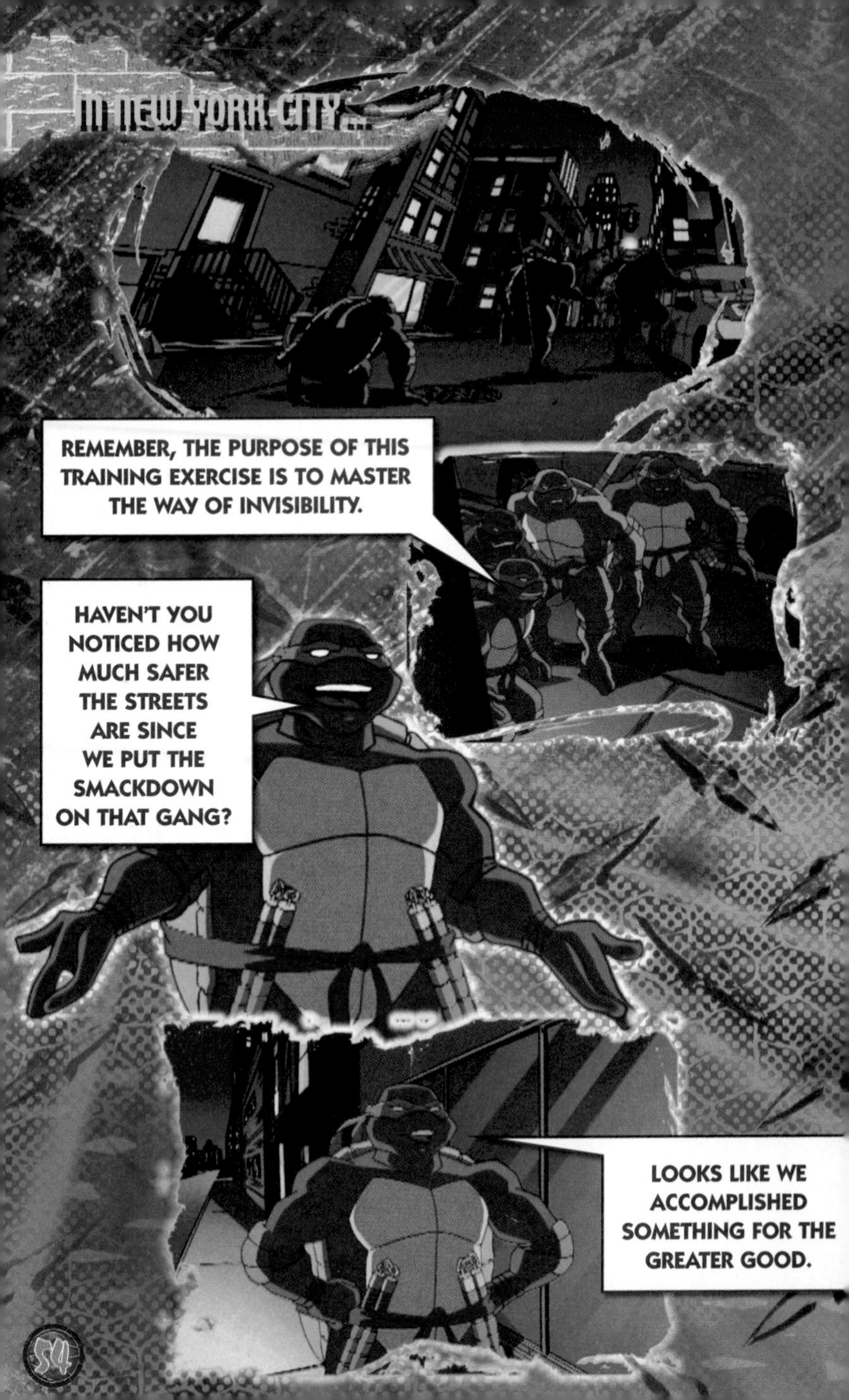
IN NEW YORK CITY...
REMEMBER, THE PURPOSE OF THIS TRAINING EXERCISE IS TO MASTER THE WAY OF INVISIBILITY.
HAVEN'T YOU NOTICED HOW MUCH SAFER THE STREETS ARE SINCE WE PUT THE SMACKDOWN ON THAT GANG?
LOOKS LIKE WE ACCOMPLISHED SOMETHING FOR THE GREATER GOOD.

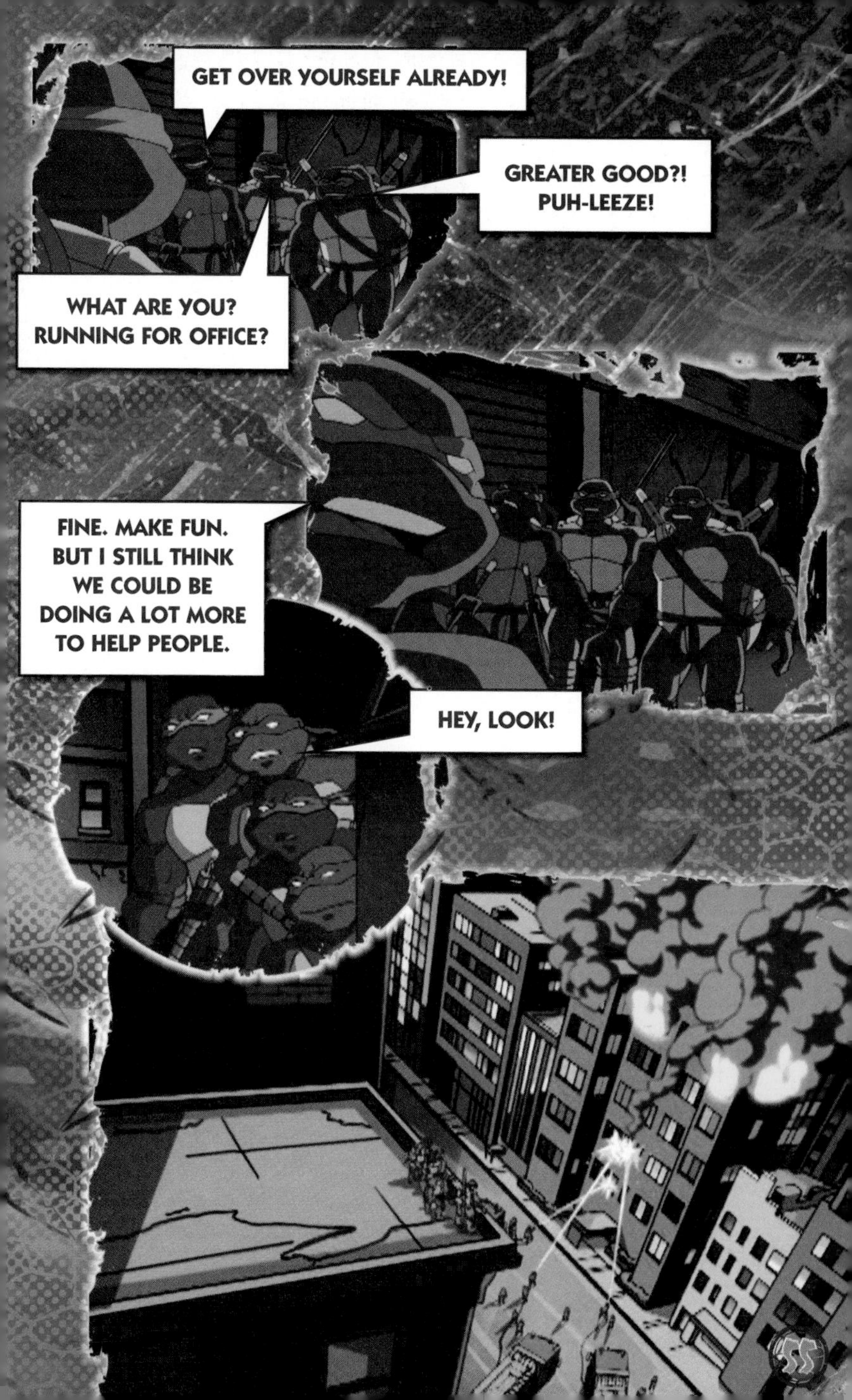
GET OVER YOURSELF ALREADY!
GREATER GOOD?! PUH-LEEZE!
WHAT ARE YOU? RUNNING FOR OFFICE?
FINE. MAKE FUN. BUT I STILL THINK WE COULD BE DOING A LOT MORE TO HELP PEOPLE.
HEY, LOOK!

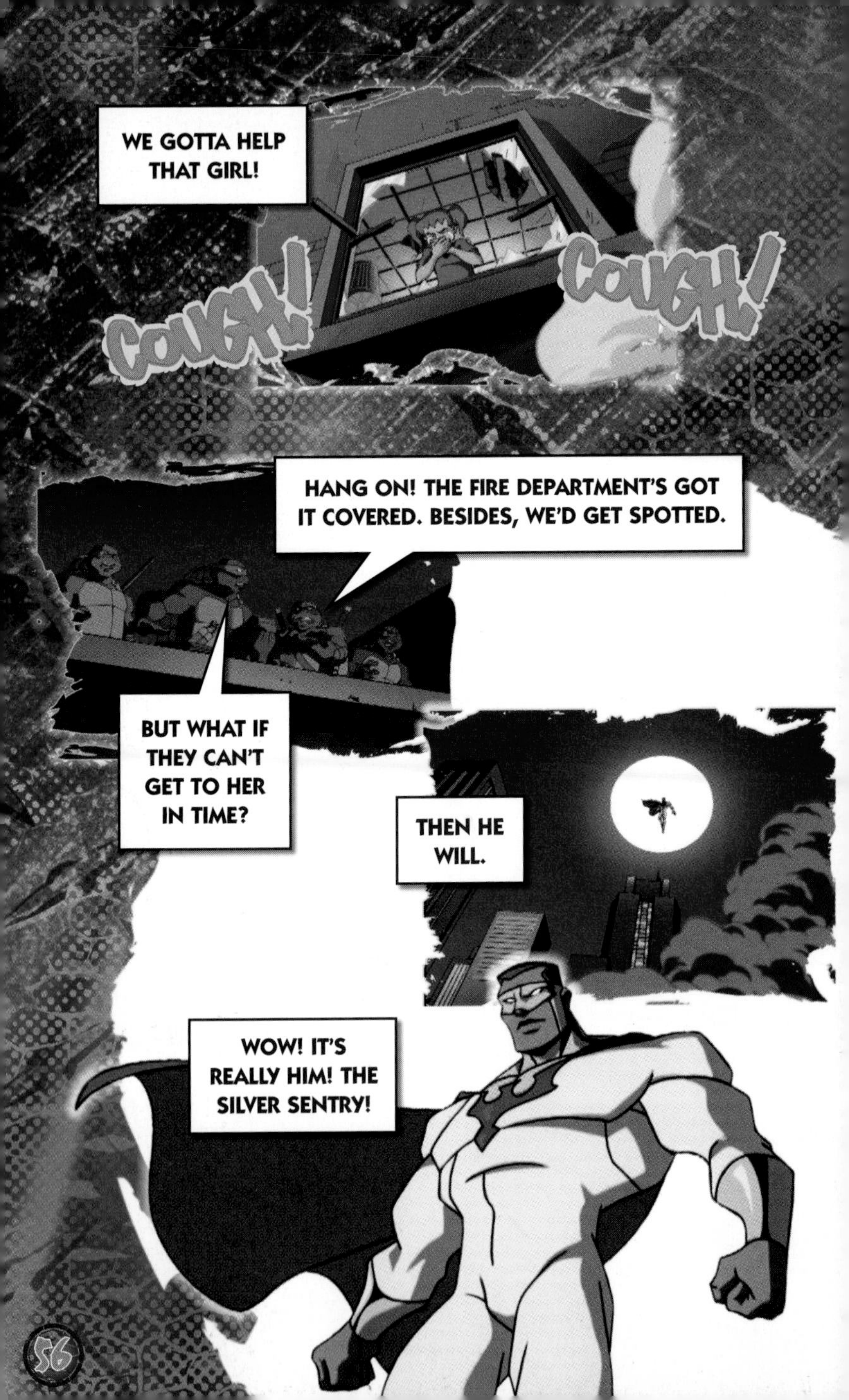
WE GOTTA HELP THAT GIRL!
COUGH!
COUGH!
HANG ON! THE FIRE DEPARTMENT'S GOT IT COVERED. BESIDES, WE'D GET SPOTTED.
BUT WHAT IF THEY CAN'T GET TO HER IN TIME?
THEN HE WILL.
WOW! IT'S REALLY HIM! THE SILVER SENTRY!

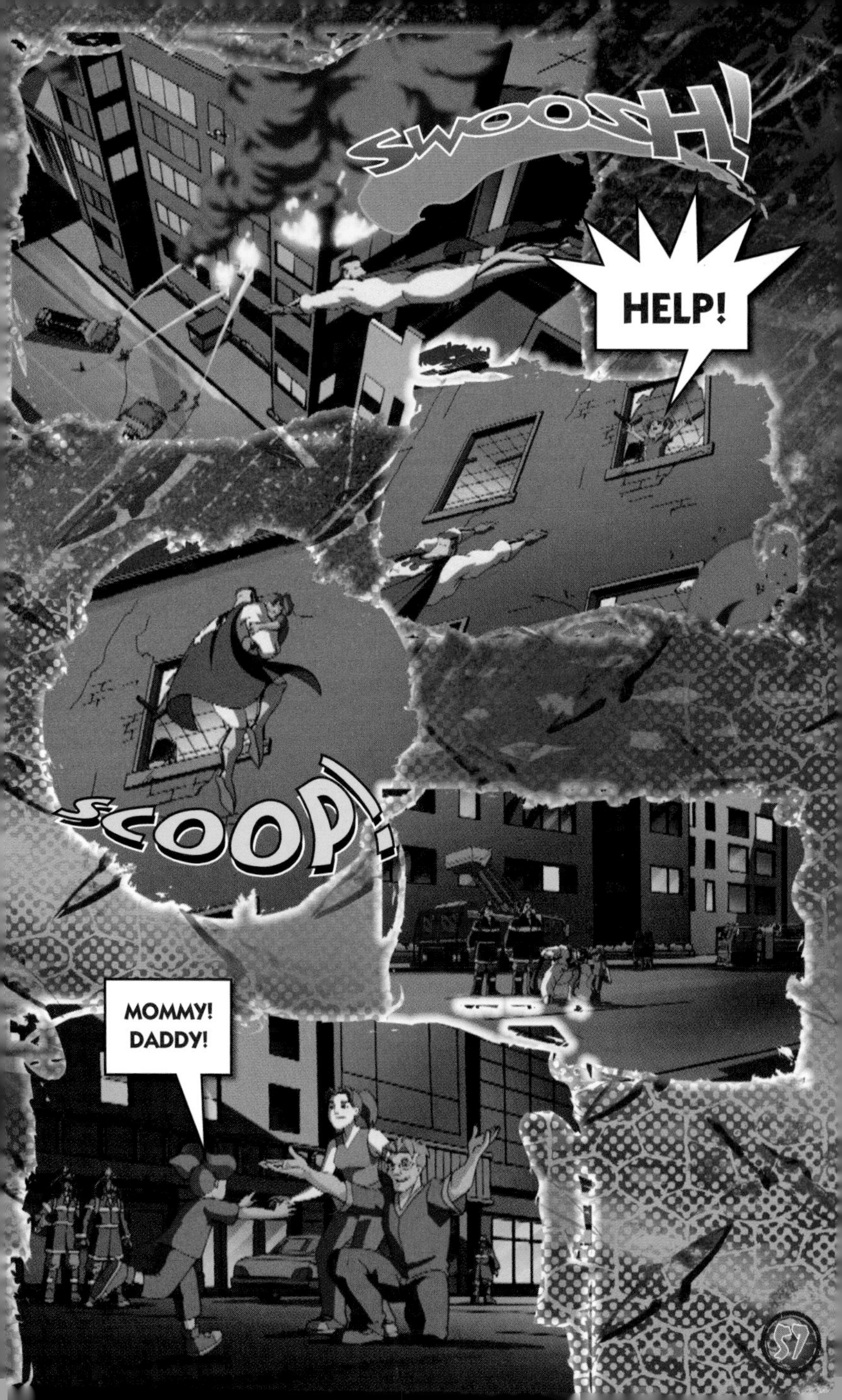

SWOOSH!
HELP!
SCOOP!
MOMMY! DADDY!

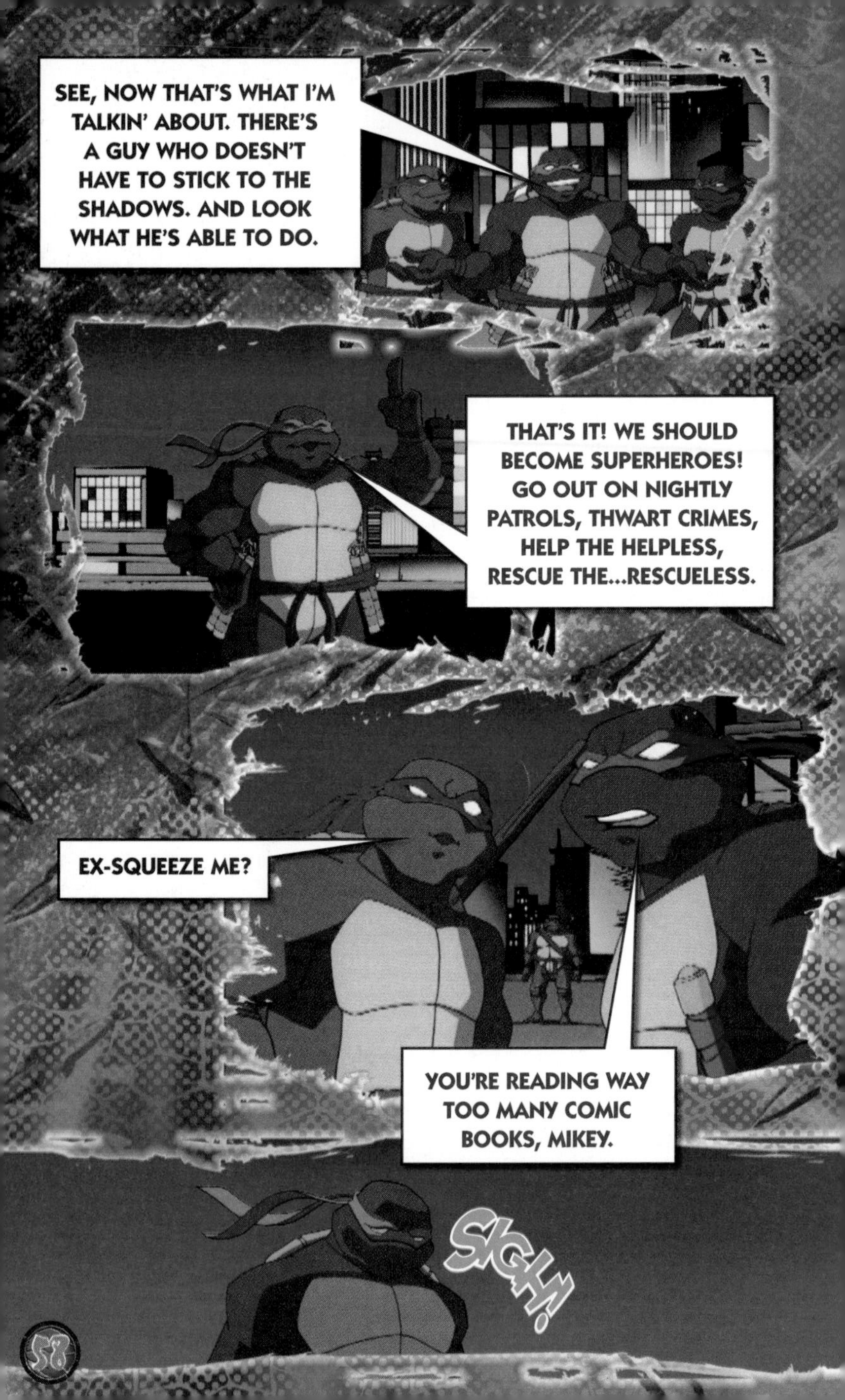
SEE, NOW THAT'S WHAT I'M TALKIN' ABOUT. THERE'S A GUY WHO DOESN'T HAVE TO STICK TO THE SHADOWS. AND LOOK WHAT HE'S ABLE TO DO.
THAT'S IT! WE SHOULD BECOME SUPERHEROES! GO OUT ON NIGHTLY PATROLS, THWART CRIMES, HELP THE HELPLESS, RESCUE THE...RESCUELESS.
EX-SQUEEZE ME?
YOU'RE READING WAY TOO MANY COMIC BOOKS, MIKEY.
SIGH!

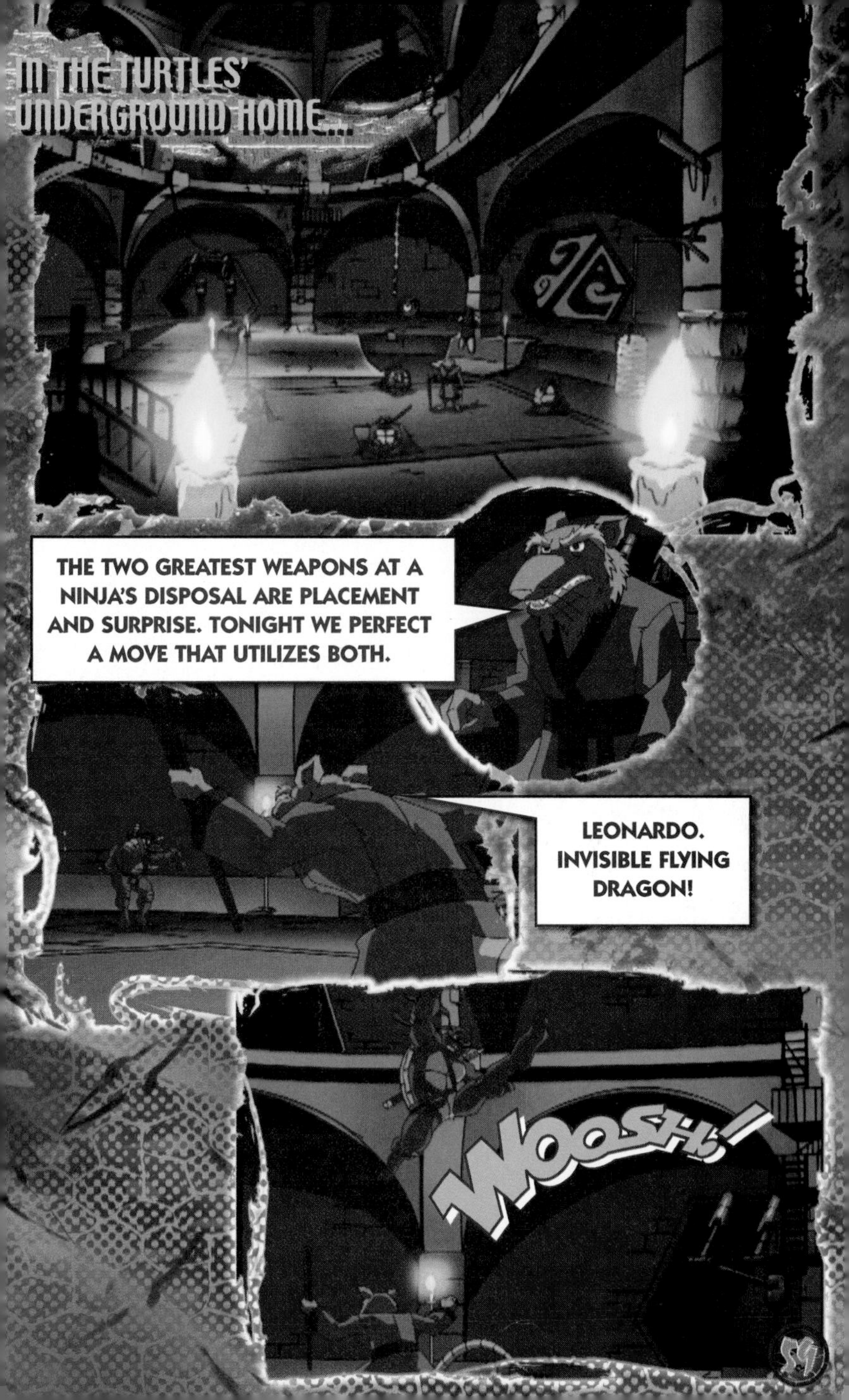
IN THE TURTLES' UNDERGROUND HOME...
THE TWO GREATEST WEAPONS AT A NINJA'S DISPOSAL ARE PLACEMENT AND SURPRISE. TONIGHT WE PERFECT A MOVE THAT UTILIZES BOTH.
LEONARDO. INVISIBLE FLYING DRAGON!
WOOSH!

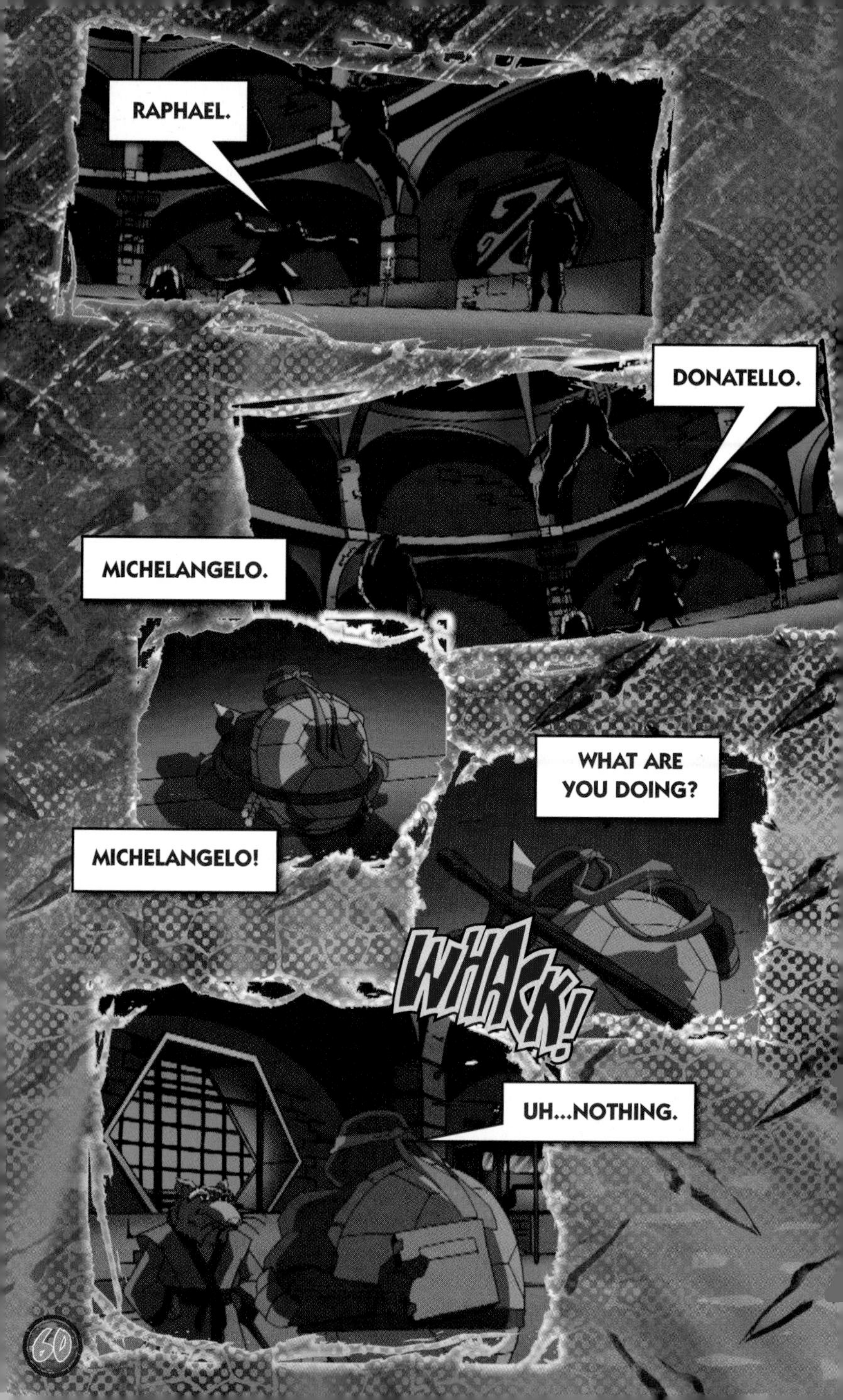
RAPHAEL.
DONATELLO.
MICHELANGELO.
MICHELANGELO!
WHAT ARE YOU DOING?
WHACK!
UH...NOTHING.

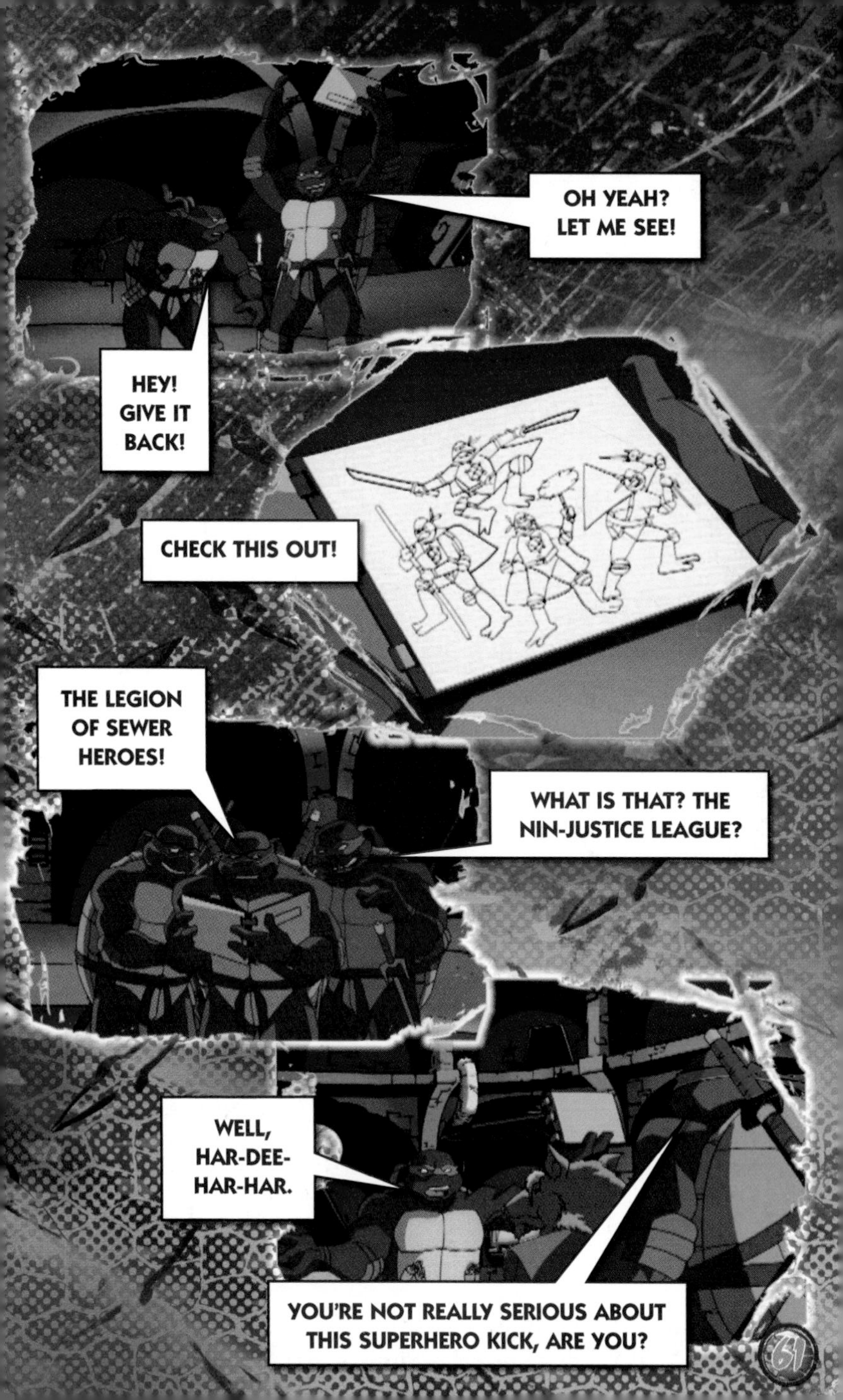
OH YEAH? LET ME SEE!
HEY! GIVE IT BACK!
CHECK THIS OUT!
THE LEGION OF SEWER HEROES!
WHAT IS THAT? THE NIN-JUSTICE LEAGUE?
WELL, HAR-DEE-HAR-HAR.
YOU'RE NOT REALLY SERIOUS ABOUT THIS SUPERHERO KICK, ARE YOU?

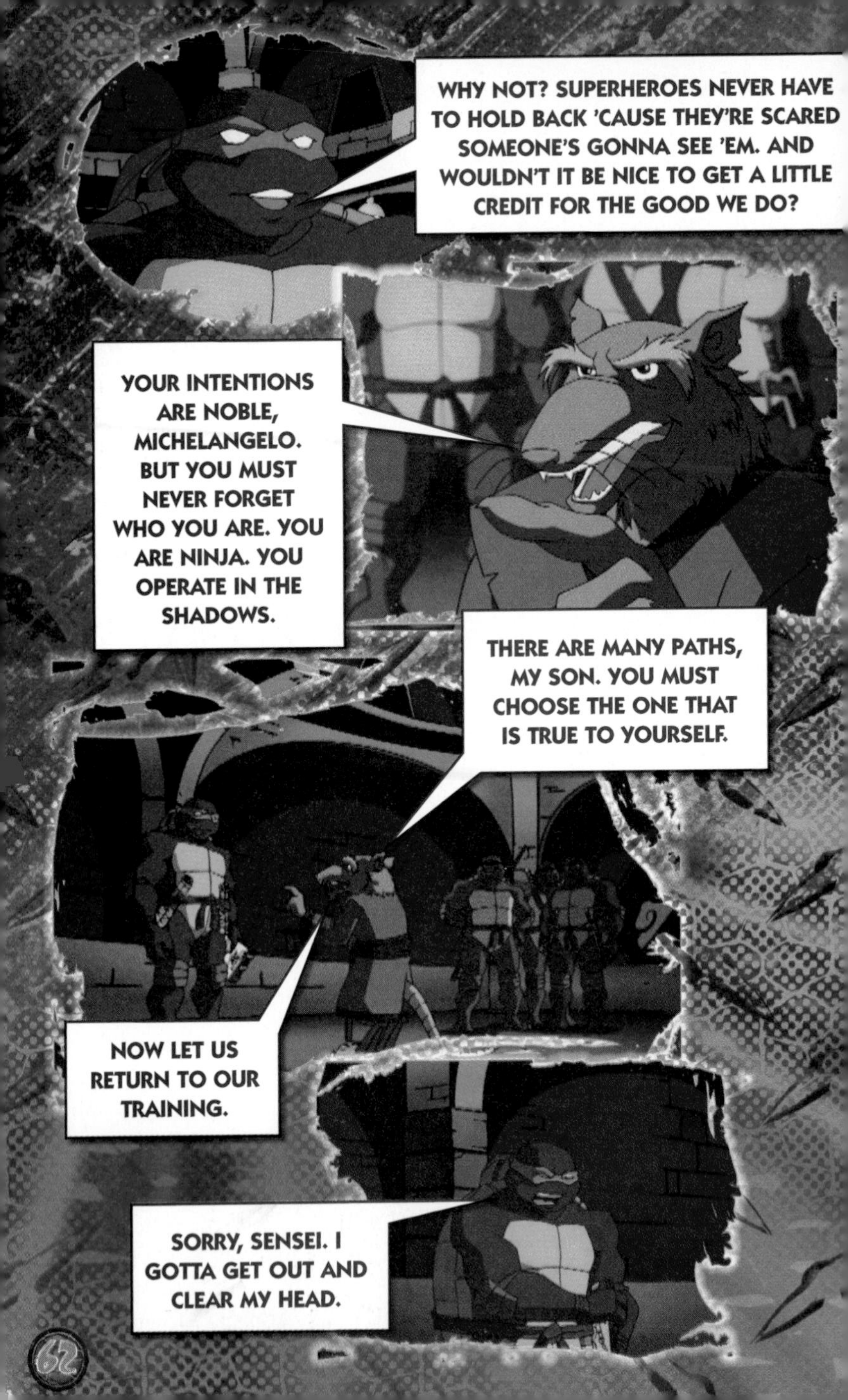

WHY NOT? SUPERHEROES NEVER HAVE TO HOLD BACK 'CAUSE THEY'RE SCARED SOMEONE'S GONNA SEE 'EM. AND WOULDN'T IT BE NICE TO GET A LITTLE CREDIT FOR THE GOOD WE DO?
YOUR INTENTIONS ARE NOBLE, MICHELANGELO. BUT YOU MUST NEVER FORGET WHO YOU ARE. YOU ARE NINJA. YOU OPERATE IN THE SHADOWS.
THERE ARE MANY PATHS, MY SON. YOU MUST CHOOSE THE ONE THAT IS TRUE TO YOURSELF.
NOW LET US RETURN TO OUR TRAINING.
SORRY, SENSEI. I GOTTA GET OUT AND CLEAR MY HEAD.

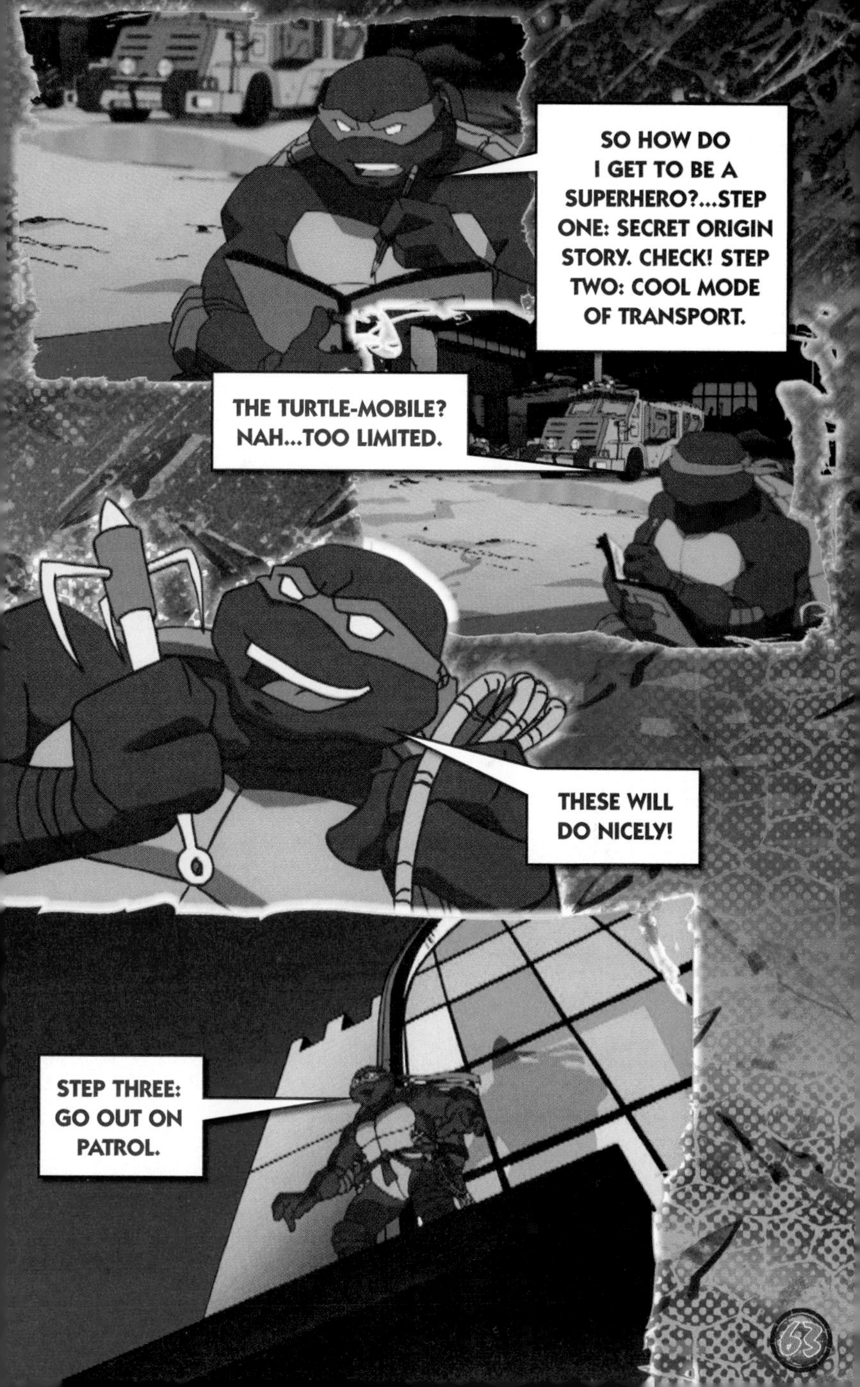
SO HOW DO I GET TO BE A SUPERHERO?...STEP ONE: SECRET ORIGIN STORY. CHECK! STEP TWO: COOL MODE OF TRANSPORT.
THE TURTLE-MOBILE? NAH...TOO LIMITED.
THESE WILL DO NICELY!
STEP THREE: GO OUT ON PATROL.

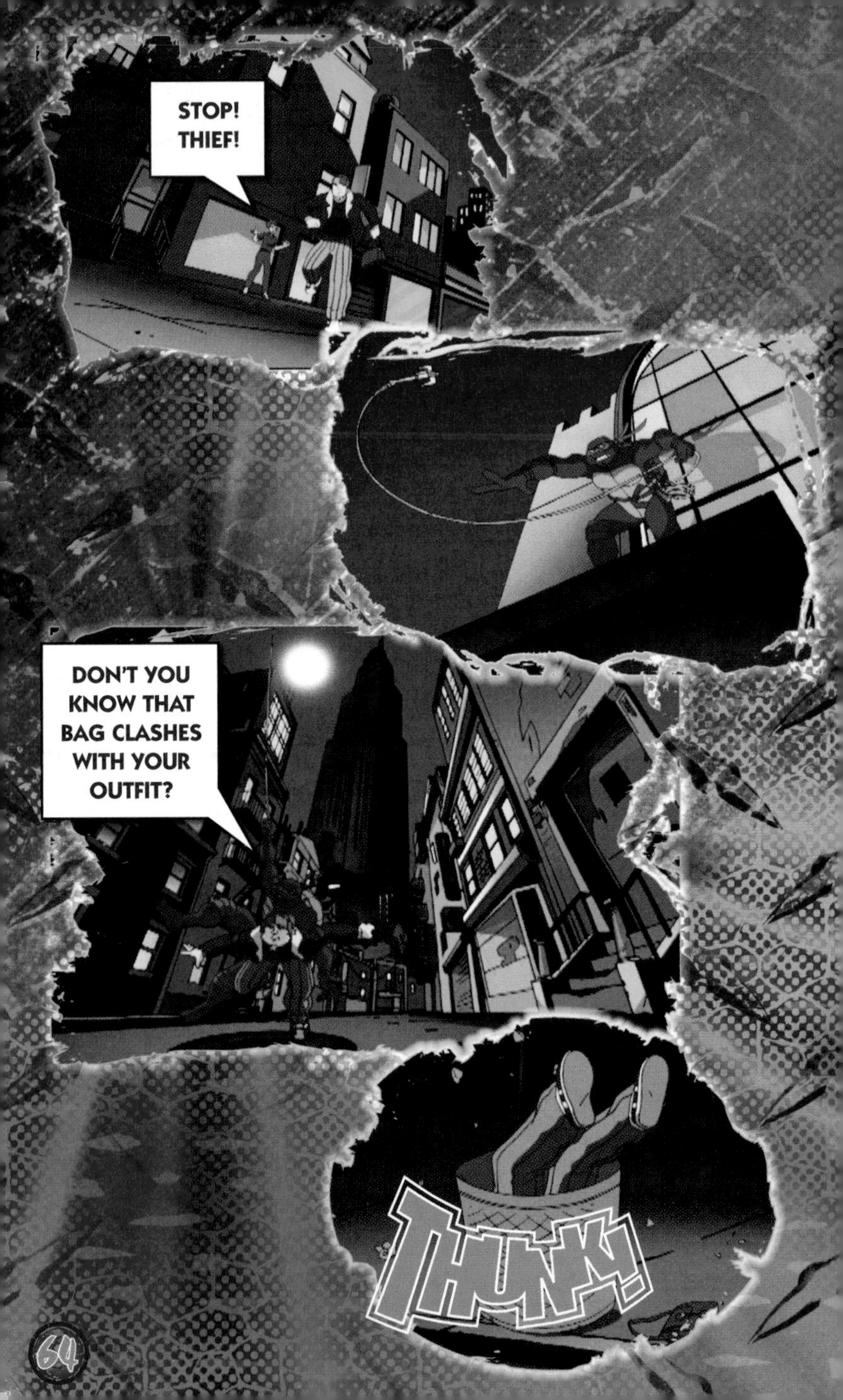
STOP! THIEF!
DON'T YOU KNOW THAT BAG CLASHES WITH YOUR OUTFIT?
THUNK!

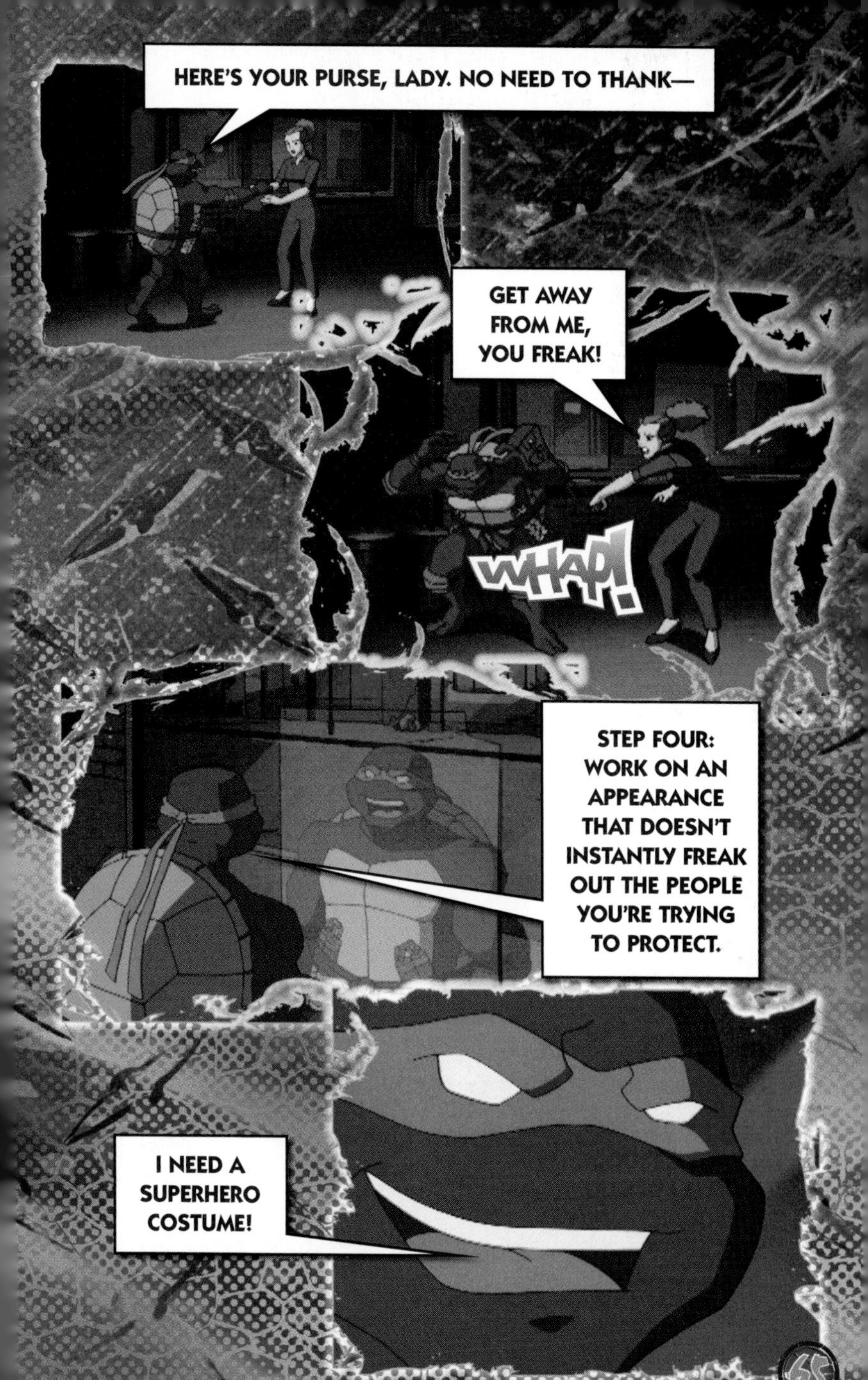

HERE'S YOUR PURSE, LADY. NO NEED TO THANK—
GET AWAY FROM ME, YOU FREAK!
WHAP!
STEP FOUR: WORK ON AN APPEARANCE THAT DOESN'T INSTANTLY FREAK OUT THE PEOPLE YOU'RE TRYING TO PROTECT.
I NEED A SUPERHERO COSTUME!

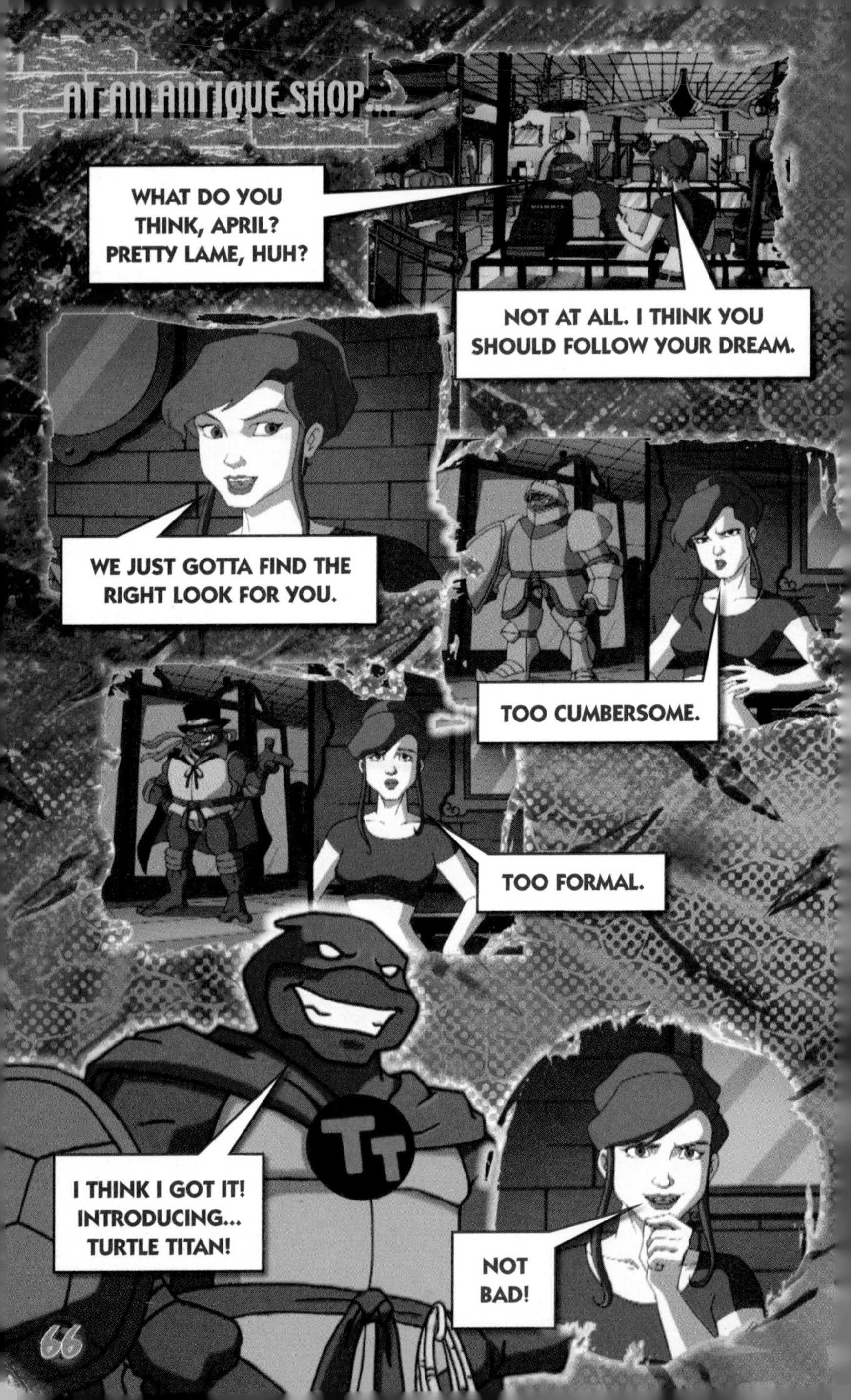
AT AN ANTIQUE SHOP...
WHAT DO YOU THINK, APRIL? PRETTY LAME, HUH?
NOT AT ALL. I THINK YOU SHOULD FOLLOW YOUR DREAM.
WE JUST GOTTA FIND THE RIGHT LOOK FOR YOU.
TOO CUMBERSOME.
TOO FORMAL.
I THINK I GOT IT! INTRODUCING... TURTLE TITAN!
NOT BAD!

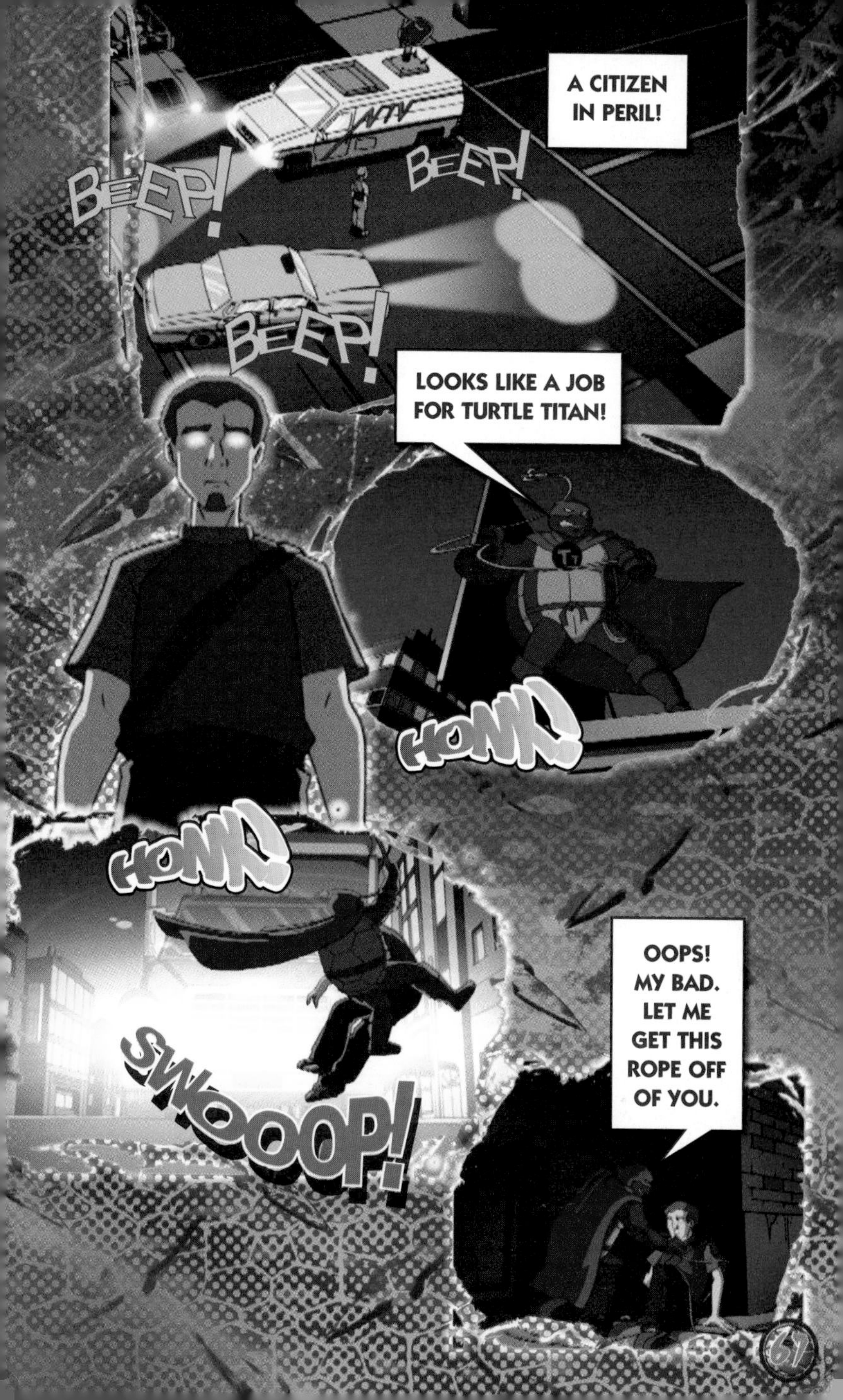
A CITIZEN IN PERIL!
BEEP!
BEEP!
BEEP!
LOOKS LIKE A JOB FOR TURTLE TITAN!
HONK!
HONK!
SWOOOP!
OOPS! MY BAD. LET ME GET THIS ROPE OFF OF YOU.

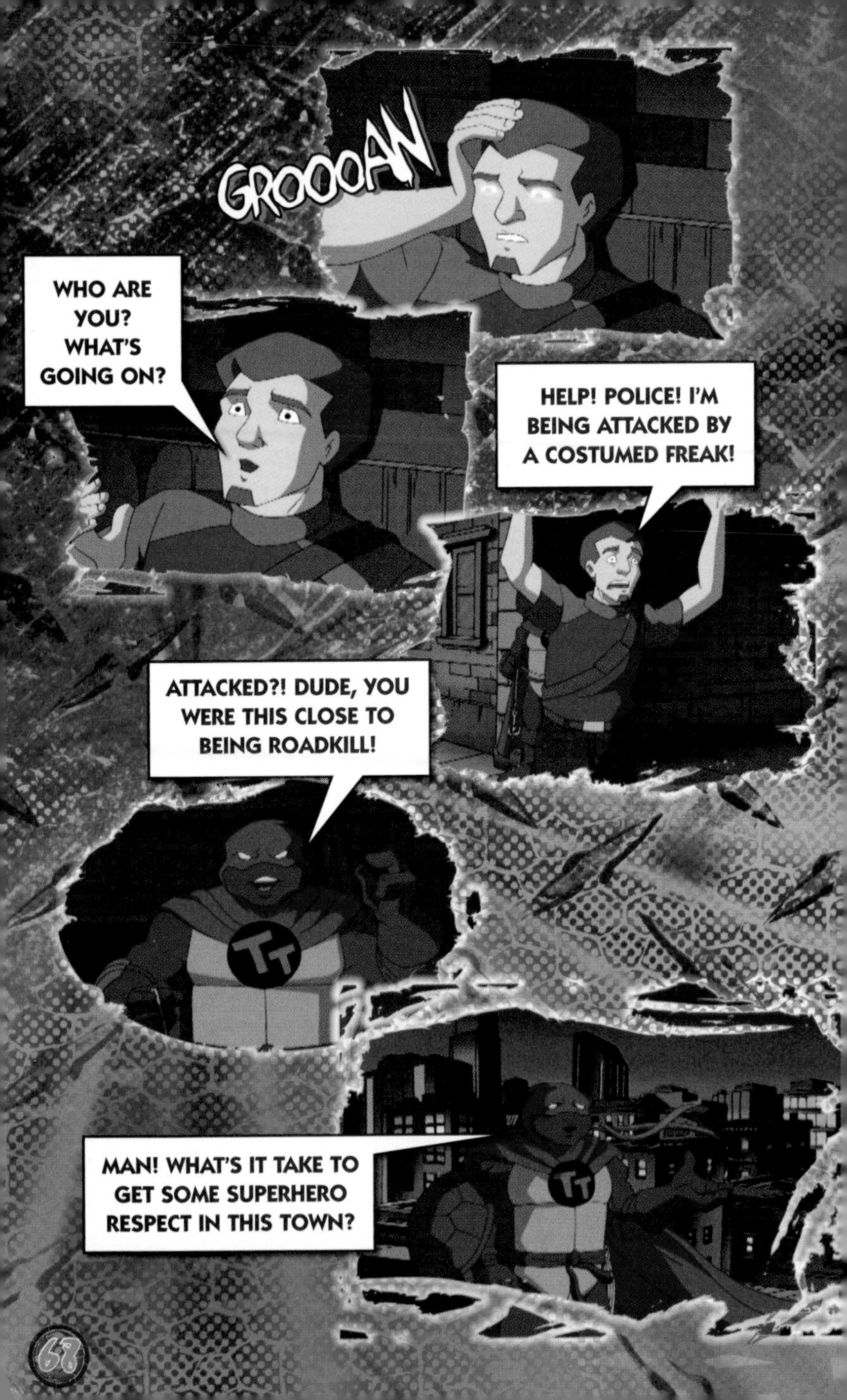
GROOOAN
WHO ARE YOU? WHAT'S GOING ON?
HELP! POLICE! I'M BEING ATTACKED BY A COSTUMED FREAK!
ATTACKED?! DUDE, YOU WERE THIS CLOSE TO BEING ROADKILL!
MAN! WHAT'S IT TAKE TO GET SOME SUPERHERO RESPECT IN THIS TOWN?

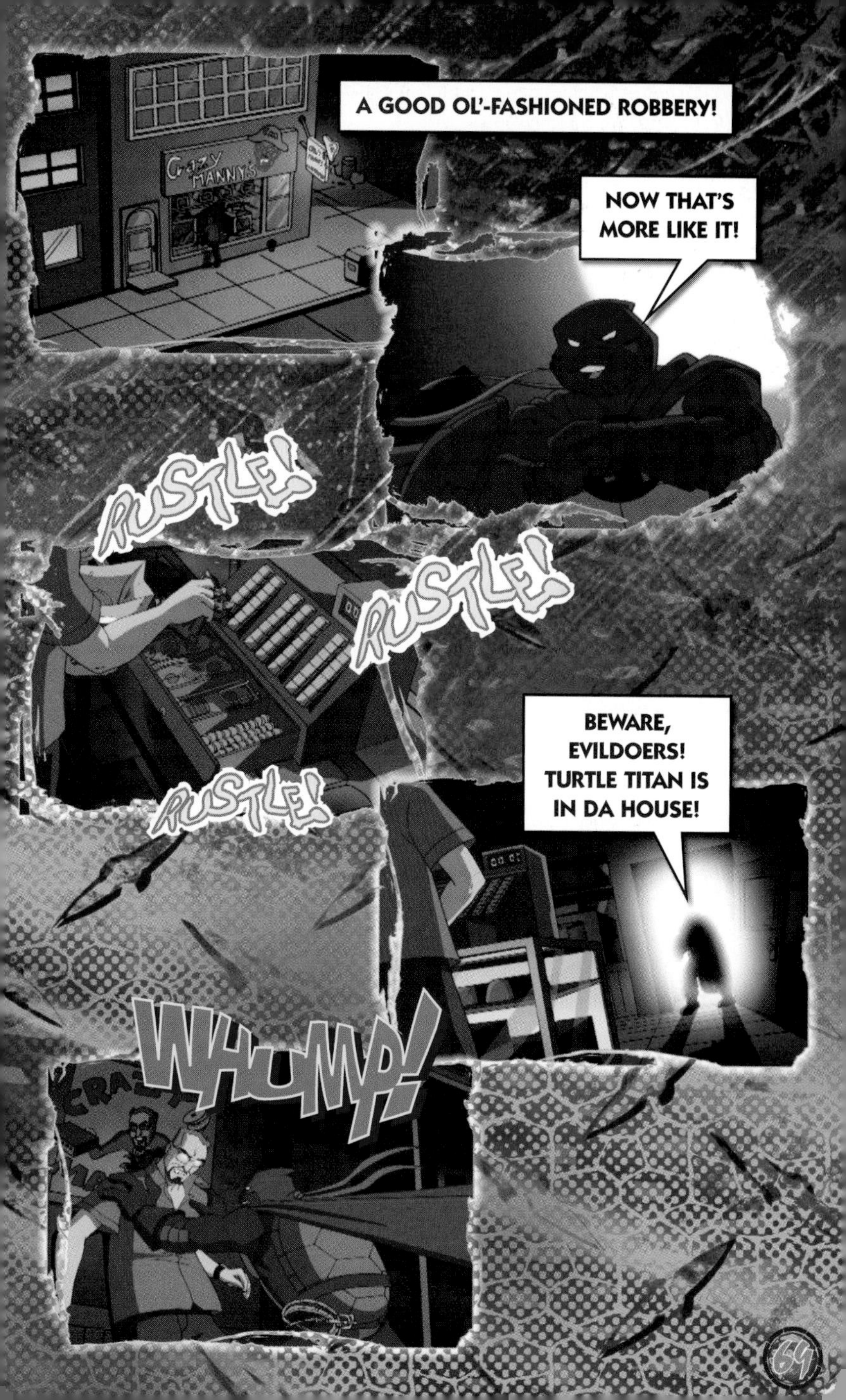
A GOOD OL'-FASHIONED ROBBERY!
NOW THAT'S MORE LIKE IT!
RUSTLE!
RUSTLE!
RUSTLE!
BEWARE, EVILDOERS! TURTLE TITAN IS IN DA HOUSE!
WHUMP!

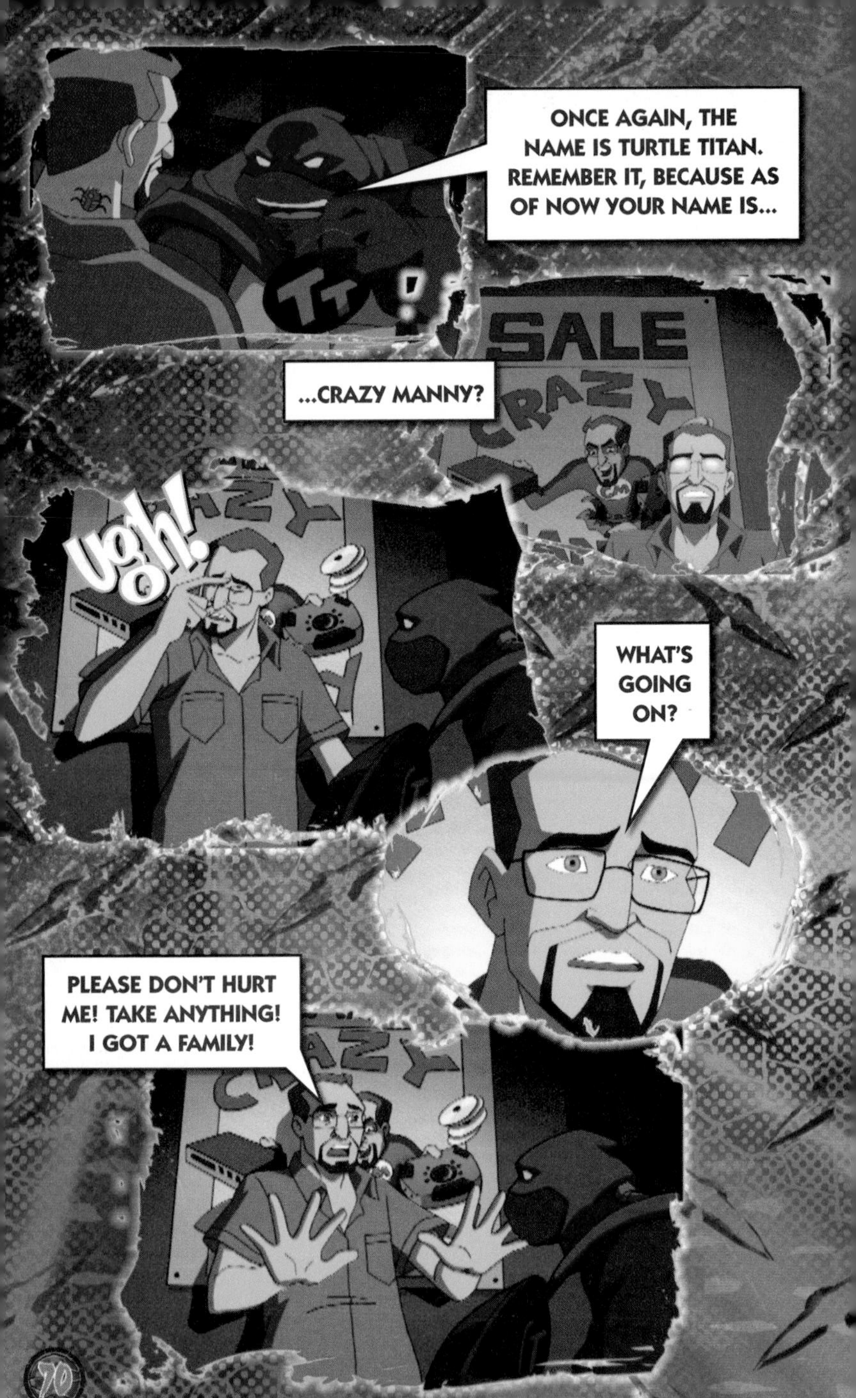
ONCE AGAIN, THE NAME IS TURTLE TITAN. REMEMBER IT, BECAUSE AS OF NOW YOUR NAME IS...
TT
SALE
...CRAZY MANNY?
CRAZY
Ugh!
WHAT'S GOING ON?
PLEASE DON'T HURT ME! TAKE ANYTHING! I GOT A FAMILY!

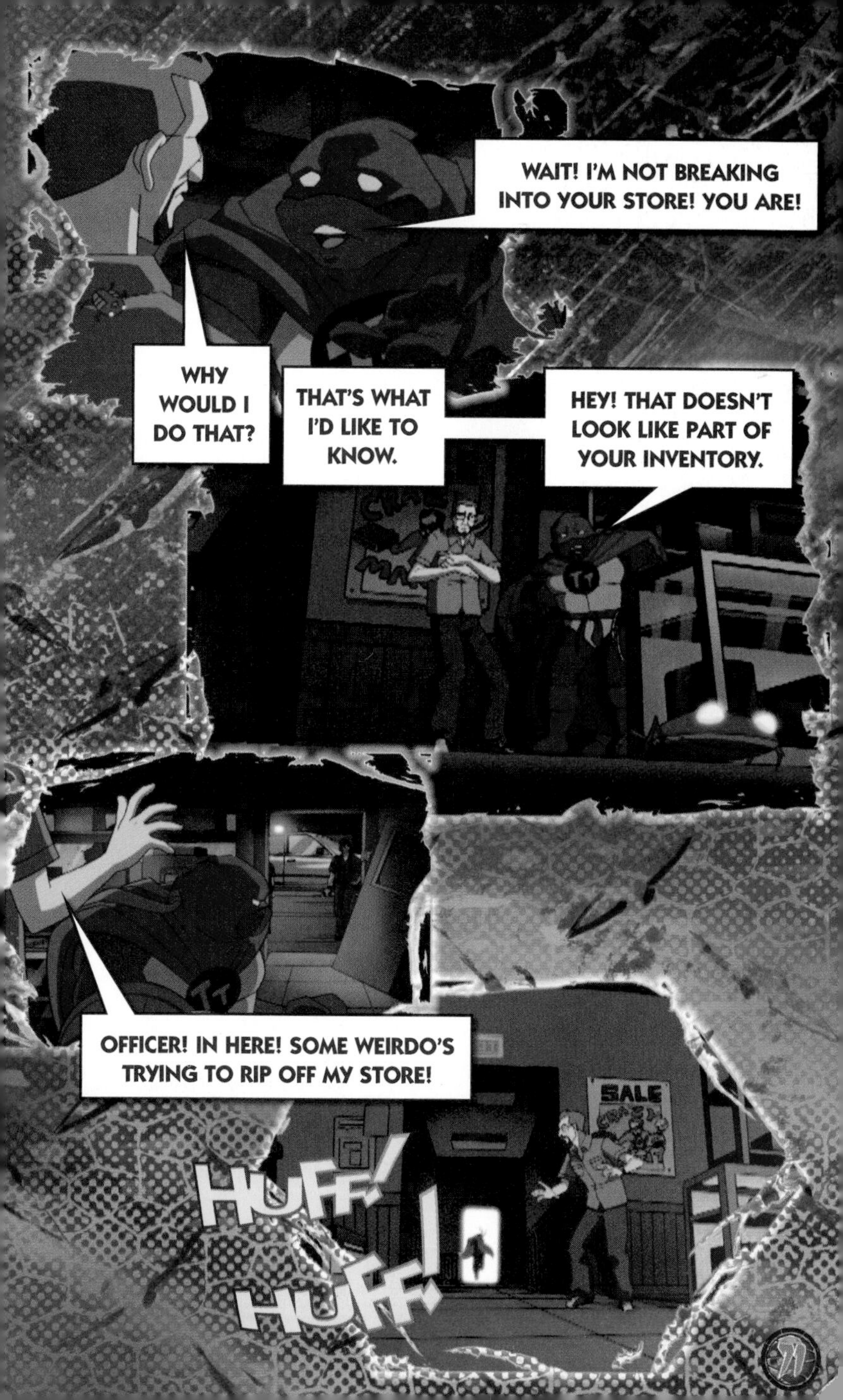

WAIT! I'M NOT BREAKING INTO YOUR STORE! YOU ARE!
WHY WOULD I DO THAT?
THAT'S WHAT I'D LIKE TO KNOW.
HEY! THAT DOESN'T LOOK LIKE PART OF YOUR INVENTORY.
OFFICER! IN HERE! SOME WEIRDO'S TRYING TO RIP OFF MY STORE!
SALE
HUFF! HUFF!

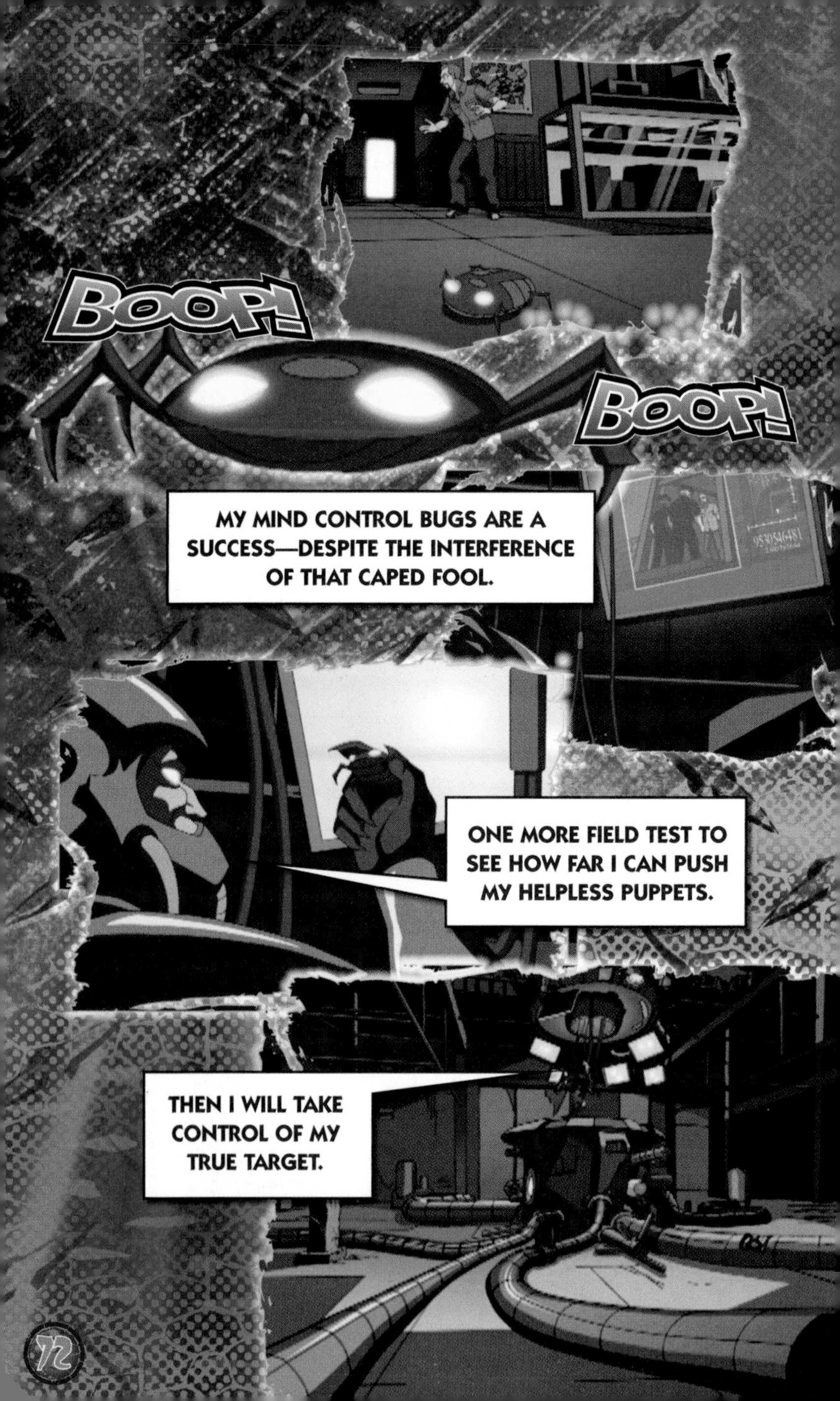
BOOP!
BOOP!
MY MIND CONTROL BUGS ARE A SUCCESS—DESPITE THE INTERFERENCE OF THAT CAPED FOOL.
ONE MORE FIELD TEST TO SEE HOW FAR I CAN PUSH MY HELPLESS PUPPETS.
THEN I WILL TAKE CONTROL OF MY TRUE TARGET.

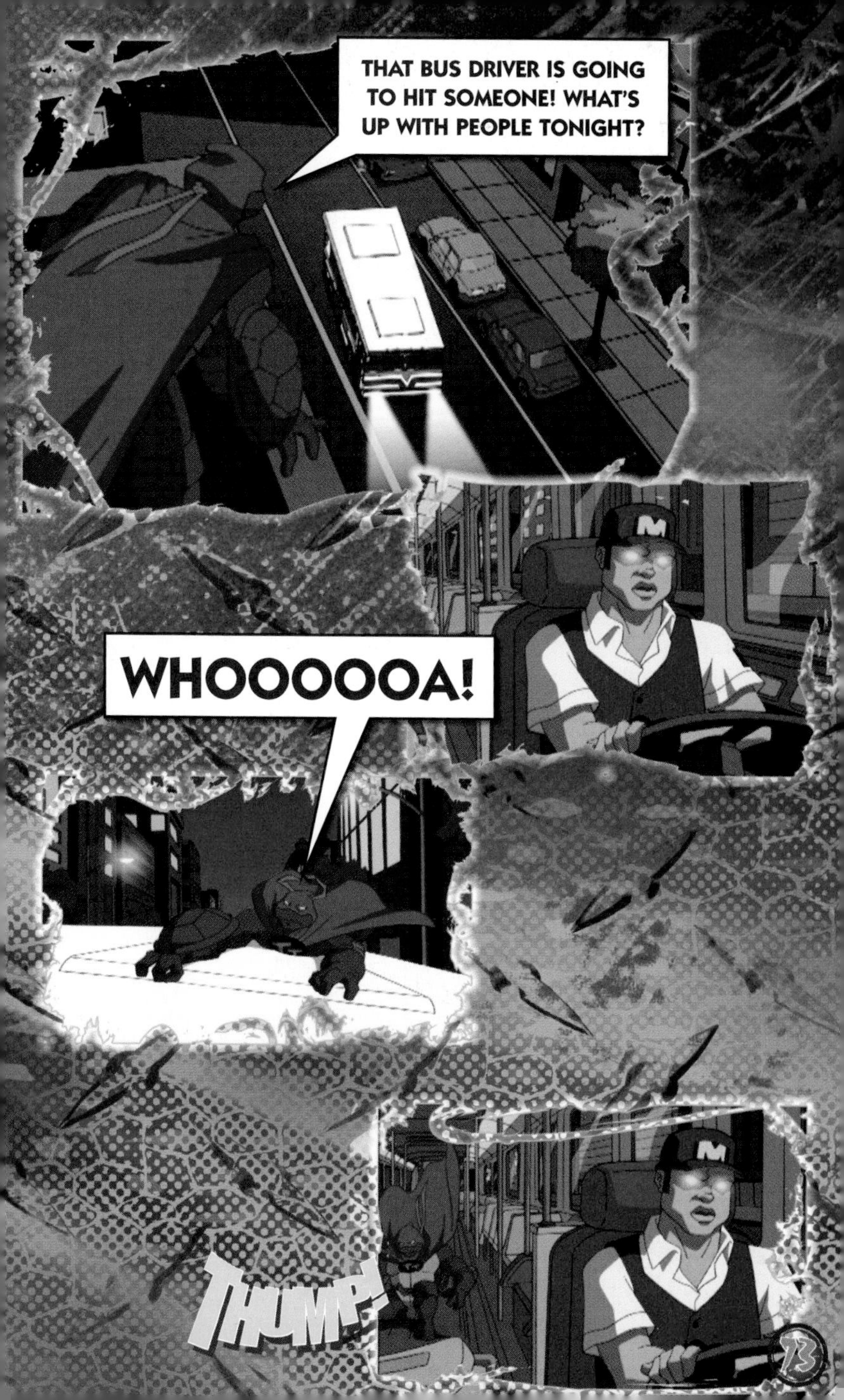
THAT BUS DRIVER IS GOING TO HIT SOMEONE! WHAT'S UP WITH PEOPLE TONIGHT?
M
WHOOOOOA!
THUMP!
M

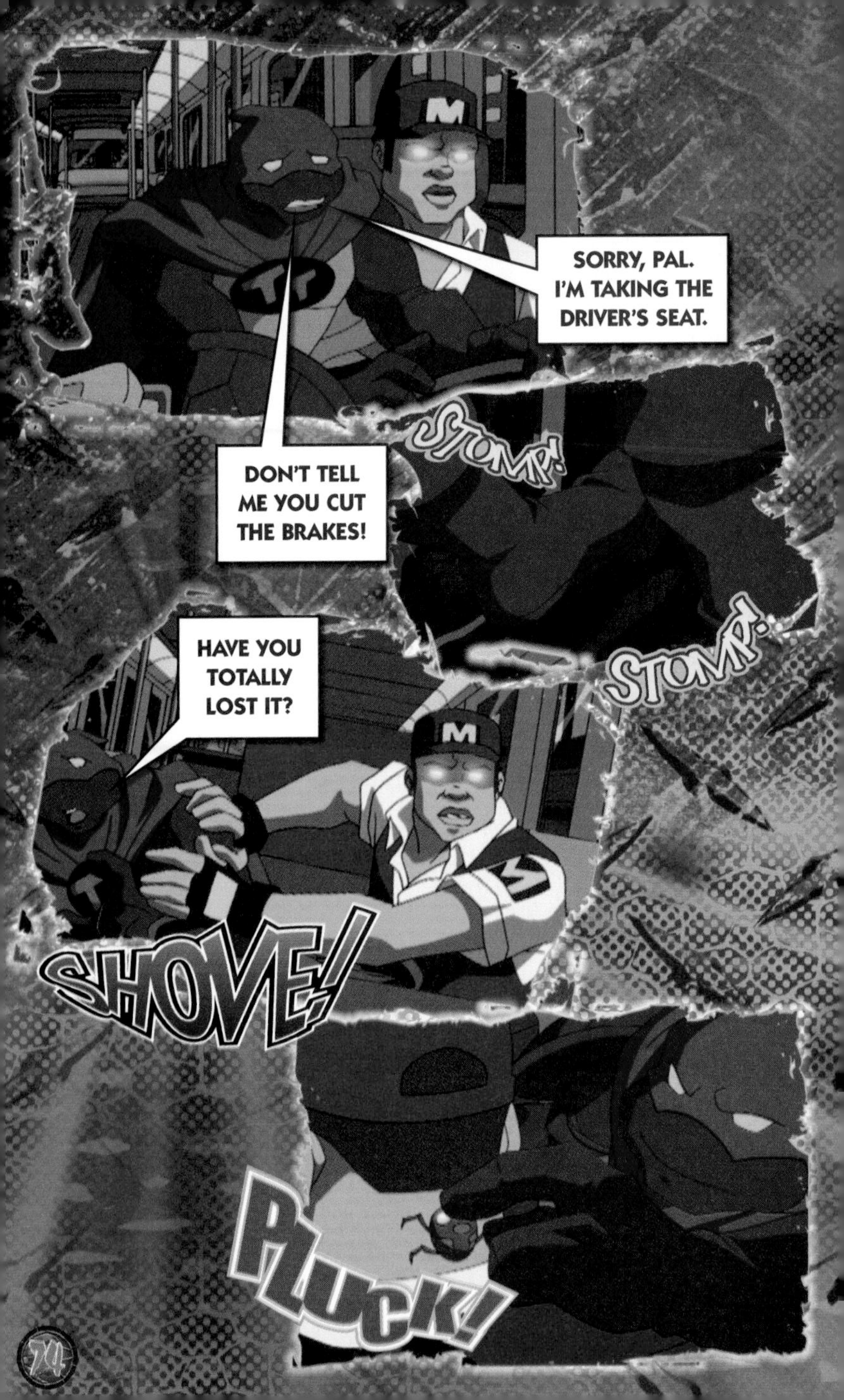
SORRY, PAL. I'M TAKING THE DRIVER'S SEAT.
DON'T TELL ME YOU CUT THE BRAKES!
STOMP!
STOMP!
HAVE YOU TOTALLY LOST IT?
SHOVE!
PLUCK!

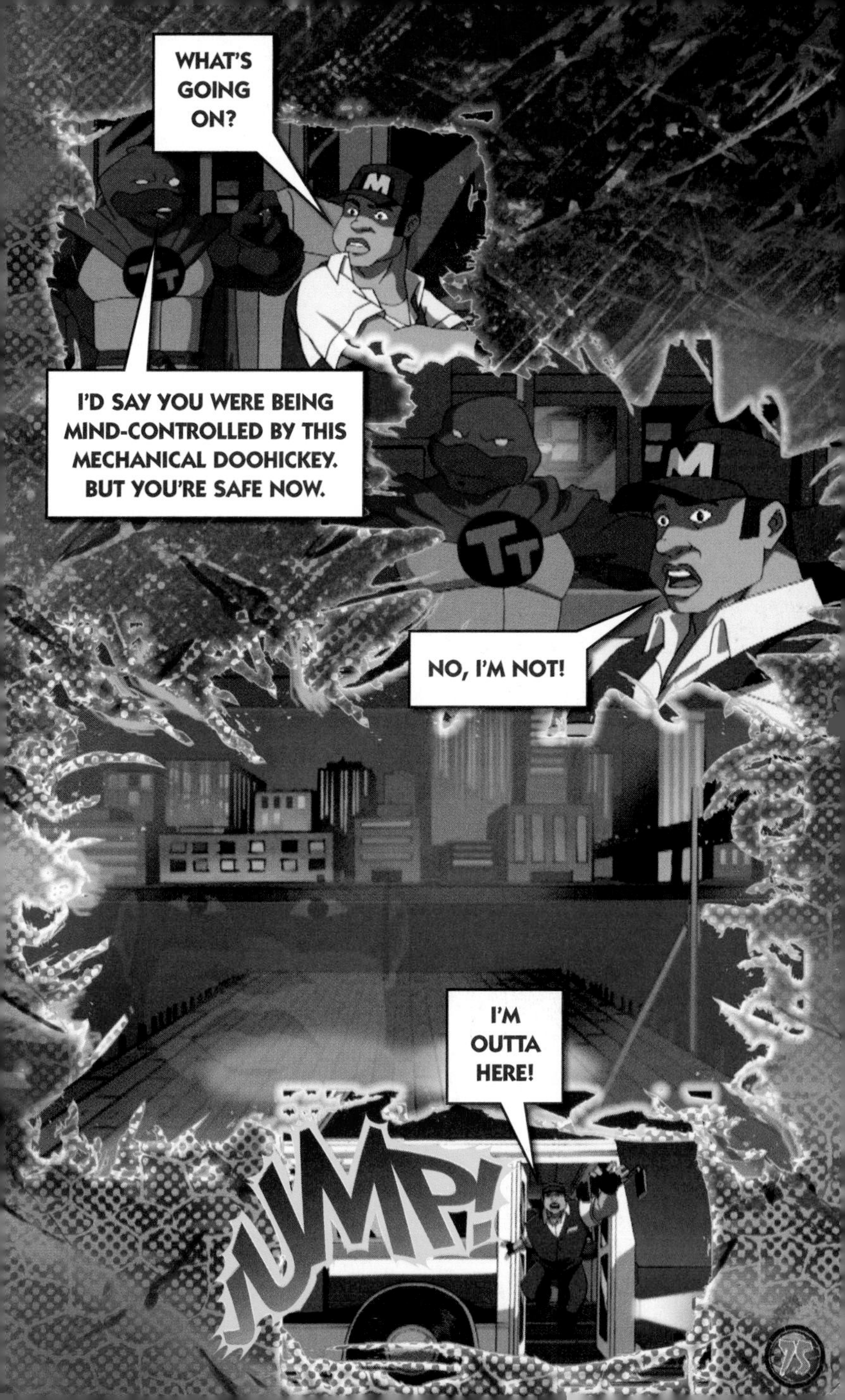
WHAT'S GOING ON?
I'D SAY YOU WERE BEING MIND-CONTROLLED BY THIS MECHANICAL DOOHICKEY. BUT YOU'RE SAFE NOW.
NO, I'M NOT!
I'M OUTTA HERE!
JUMP!

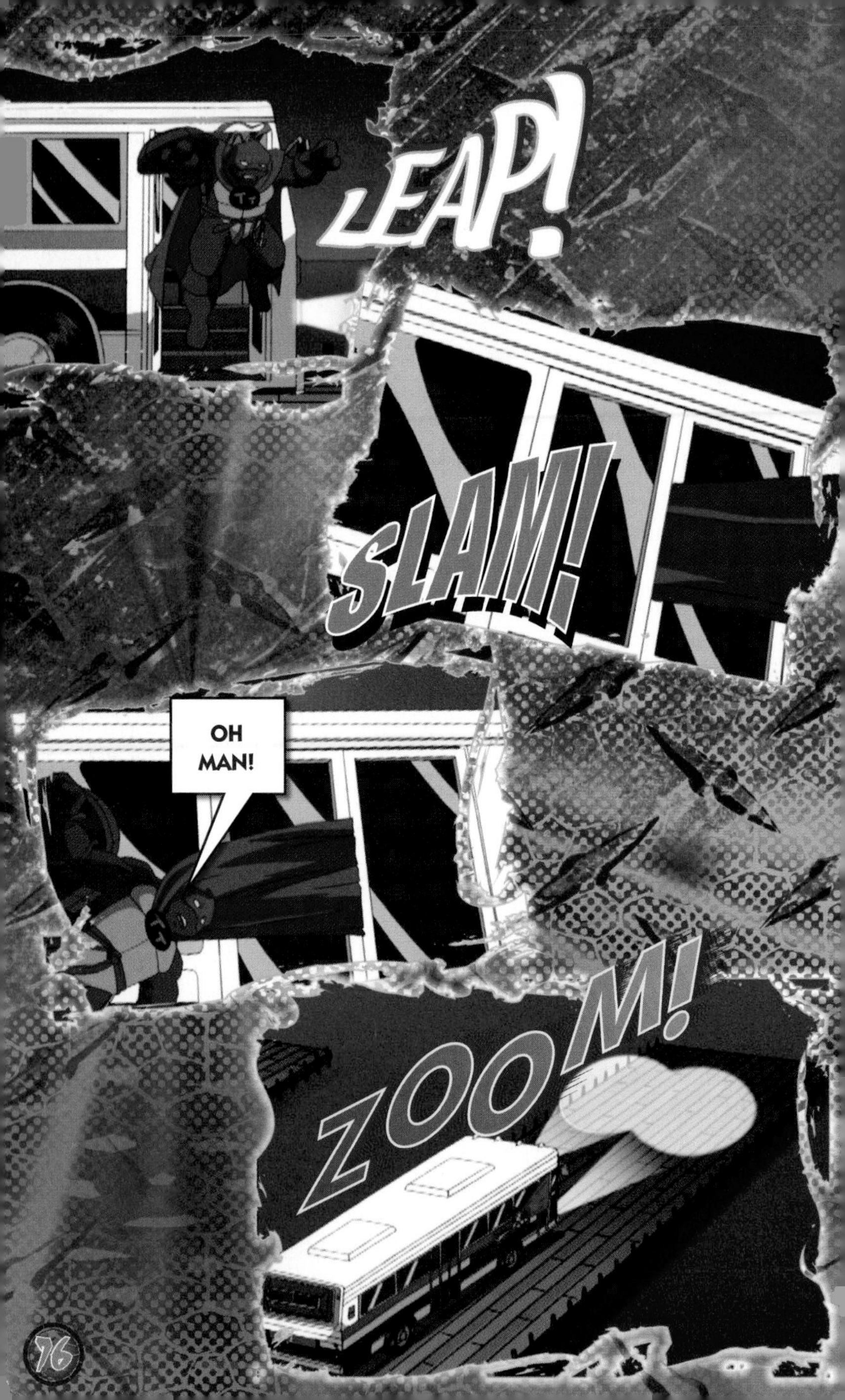
LEAP!
SLAM!
OH MAN!
ZOOOM!

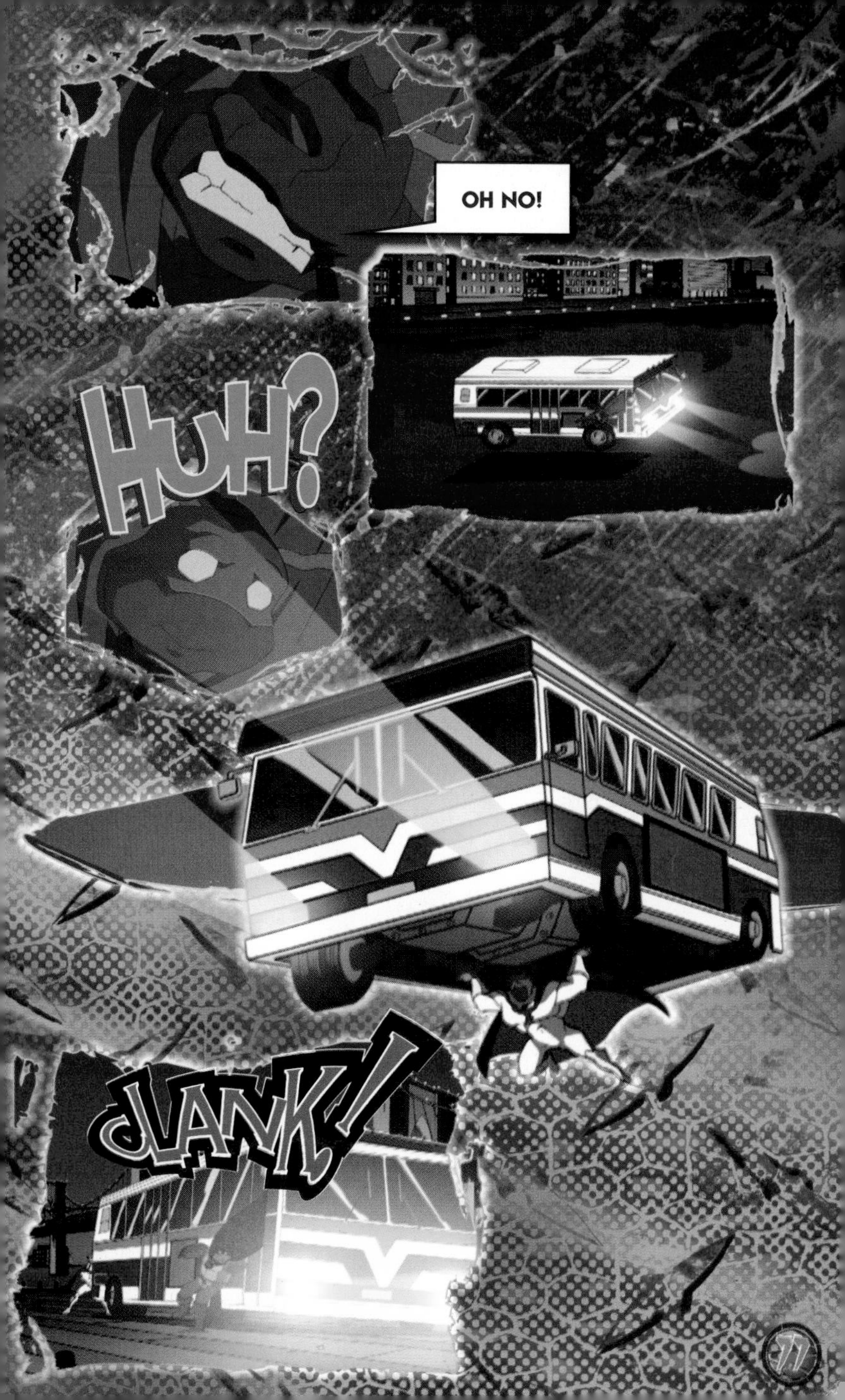
OH NO!
HUH?
CLANK!!

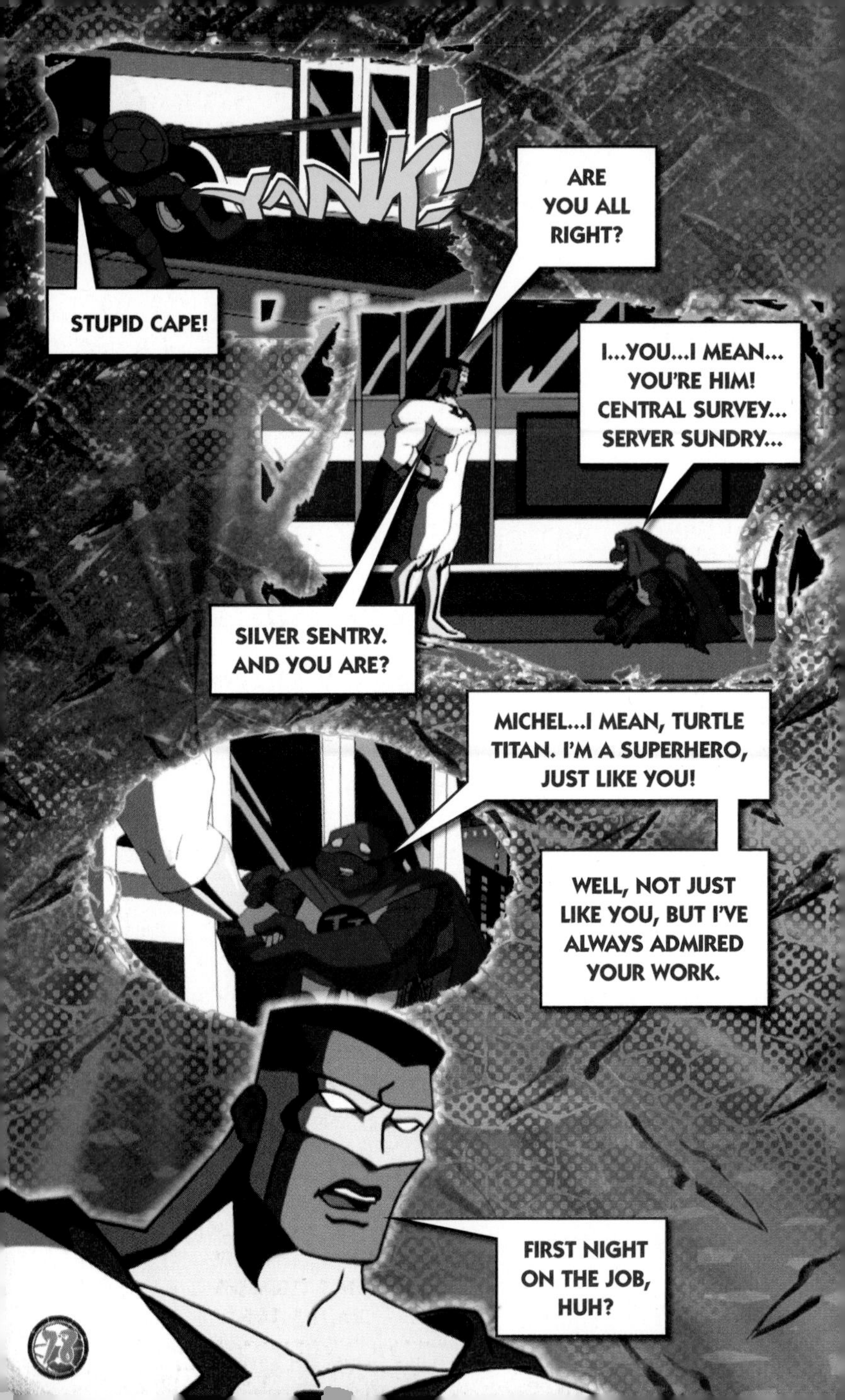
YANK!
STUPID CAPE!
ARE YOU ALL RIGHT?
I...YOU...I MEAN... YOU'RE HIM! CENTRAL SURVEY... SERVER SUNDRY...
SILVER SENTRY. AND YOU ARE?
MICHEL...I MEAN, TURTLE TITAN. I'M A SUPERHERO, JUST LIKE YOU!
WELL, NOT JUST LIKE YOU, BUT I'VE ALWAYS ADMIRED YOUR WORK.
FIRST NIGHT ON THE JOB, HUH?

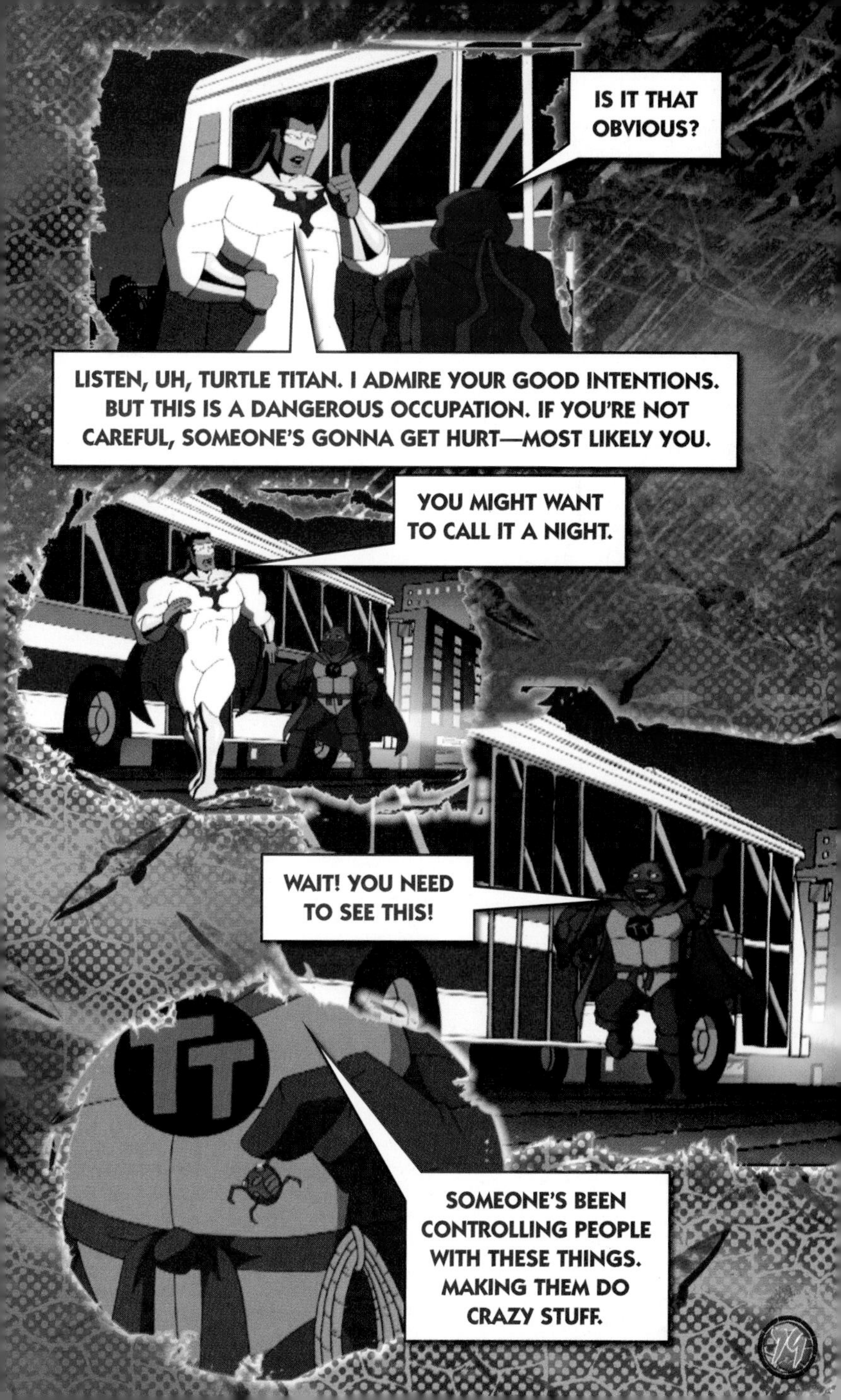
IS IT THAT OBVIOUS?
LISTEN, UH, TURTLE TITAN. I ADMIRE YOUR GOOD INTENTIONS. BUT THIS IS A DANGEROUS OCCUPATION. IF YOU'RE NOT CAREFUL, SOMEONE'S GONNA GET HURT—MOST LIKELY YOU.
YOU MIGHT WANT TO CALL IT A NIGHT.
WAIT! YOU NEED TO SEE THIS!
SOMEONE'S BEEN CONTROLLING PEOPLE WITH THESE THINGS. MAKING THEM DO CRAZY STUFF.

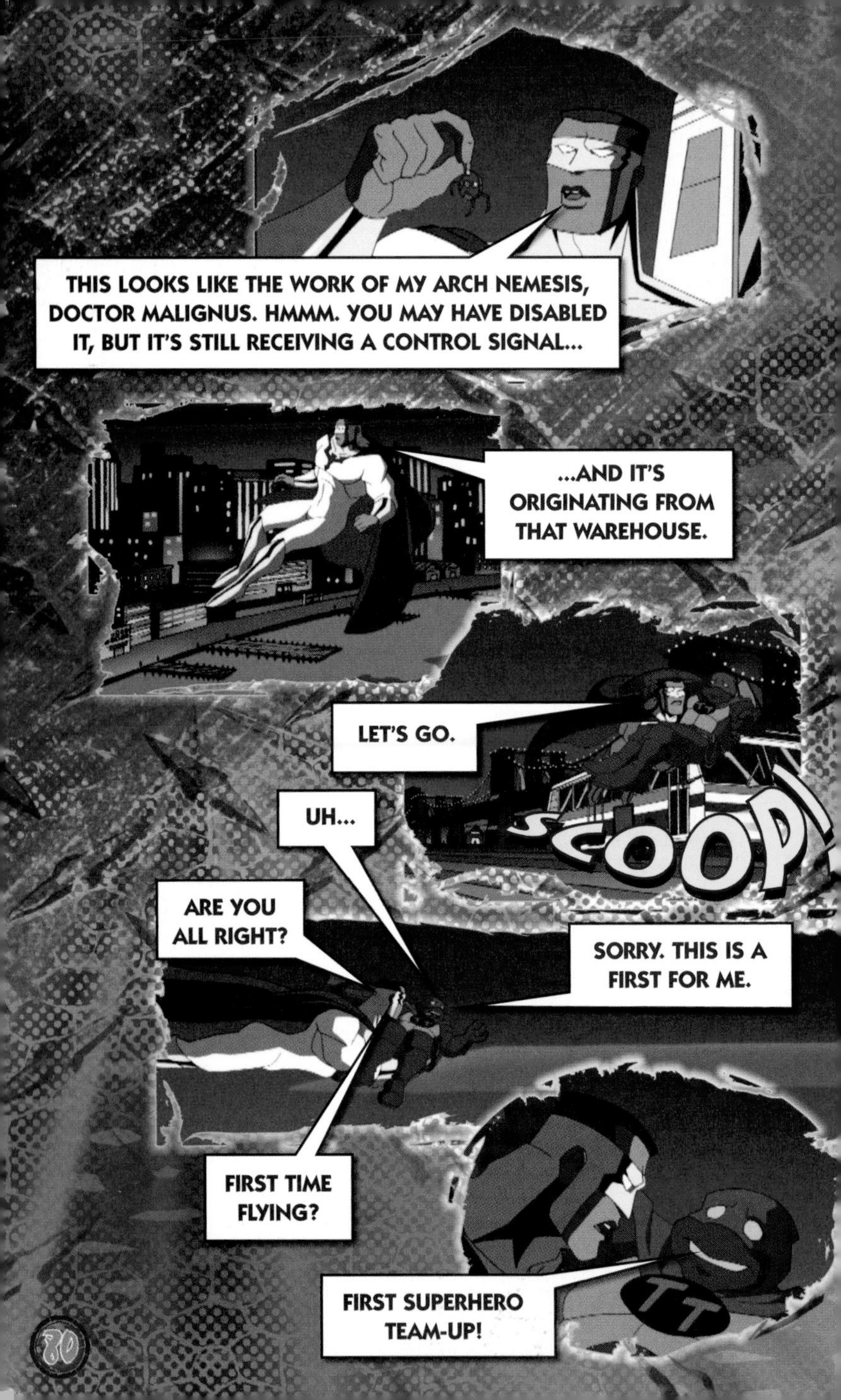
THIS LOOKS LIKE THE WORK OF MY ARCH NEMESIS, DOCTOR MALIGNUS. HMMM. YOU MAY HAVE DISABLED IT, BUT IT'S STILL RECEIVING A CONTROL SIGNAL...
...AND IT'S ORIGINATING FROM THAT WAREHOUSE.
LET'S GO.
SCOOP!
UH...
ARE YOU ALL RIGHT?
SORRY. THIS IS A FIRST FOR ME.
FIRST TIME FLYING?
FIRST SUPERHERO TEAM-UP!

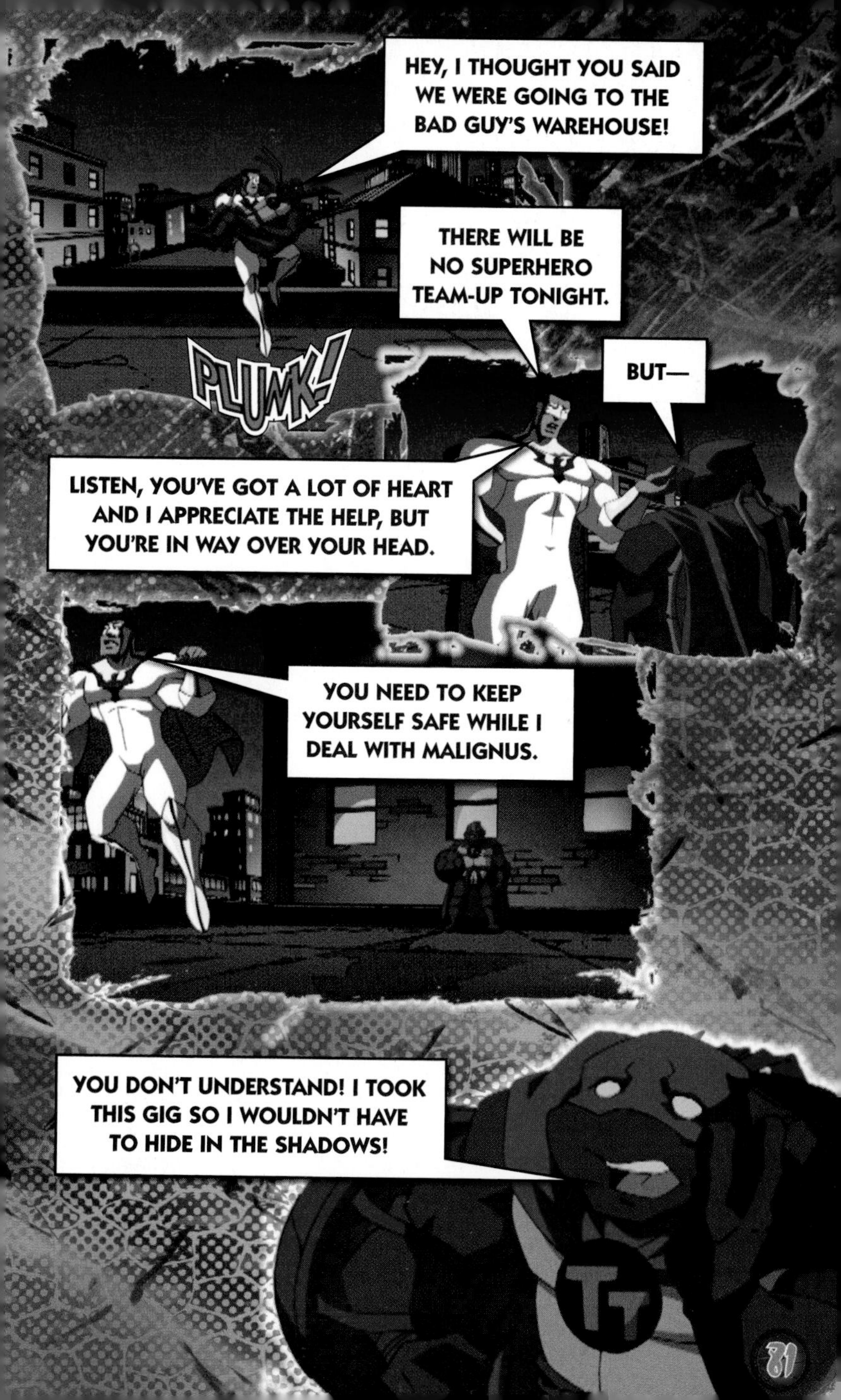
HEY, I THOUGHT YOU SAID WE WERE GOING TO THE BAD GUY'S WAREHOUSE!
PLUNK!
THERE WILL BE NO SUPERHERO TEAM-UP TONIGHT.
BUT—
LISTEN, YOU'VE GOT A LOT OF HEART AND I APPRECIATE THE HELP, BUT YOU'RE IN WAY OVER YOUR HEAD.
YOU NEED TO KEEP YOURSELF SAFE WHILE I DEAL WITH MALIGNUS.
YOU DON'T UNDERSTAND! I TOOK THIS GIG SO I WOULDN'T HAVE TO HIDE IN THE SHADOWS!

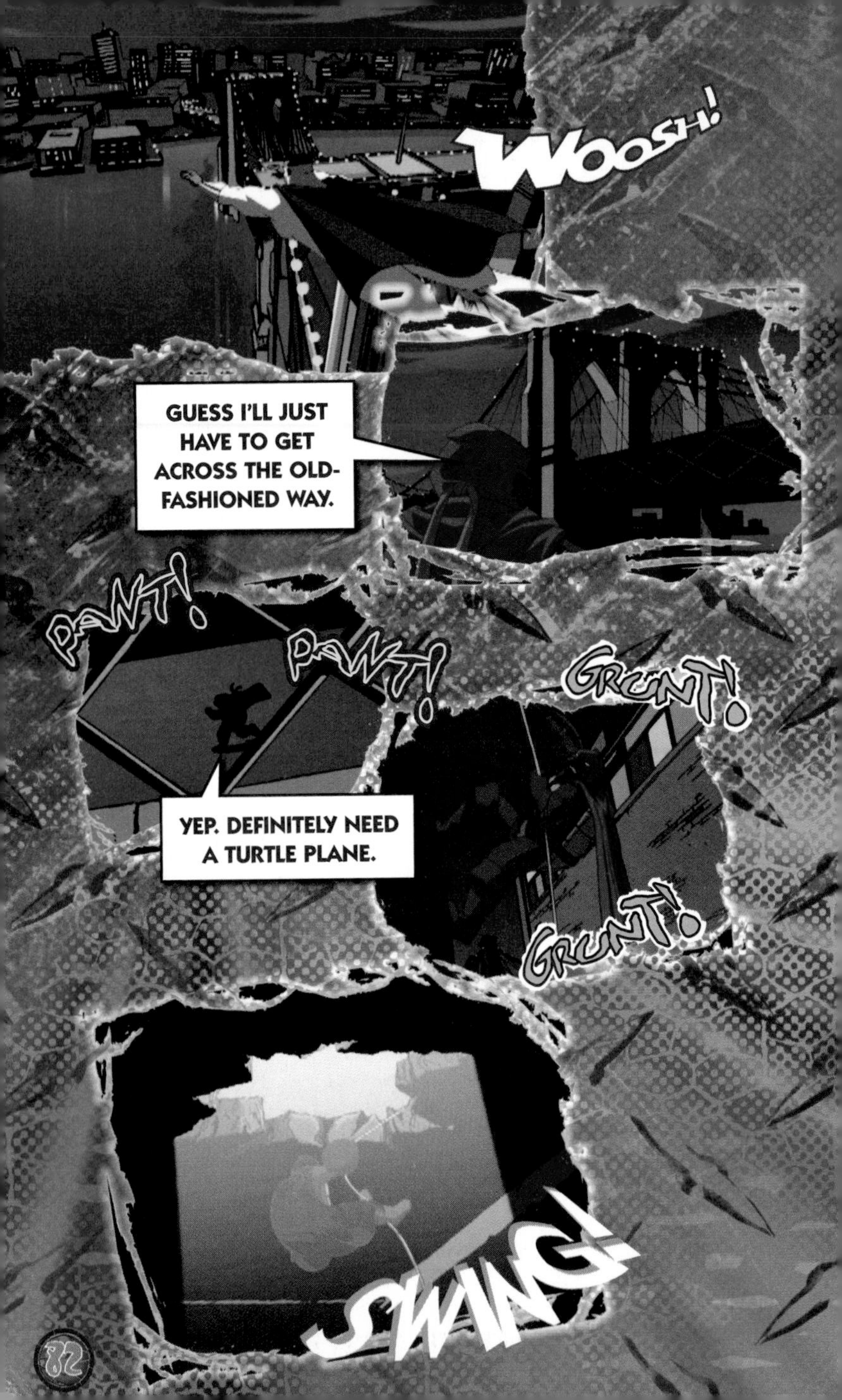
WOOSH!
GUESS I'LL JUST HAVE TO GET ACROSS THE OLD-FASHIONED WAY.
PANT!
PANT!
YEP. DEFINITELY NEED A TURTLE PLANE.
GRUNT!
GRUNT!
SWING!

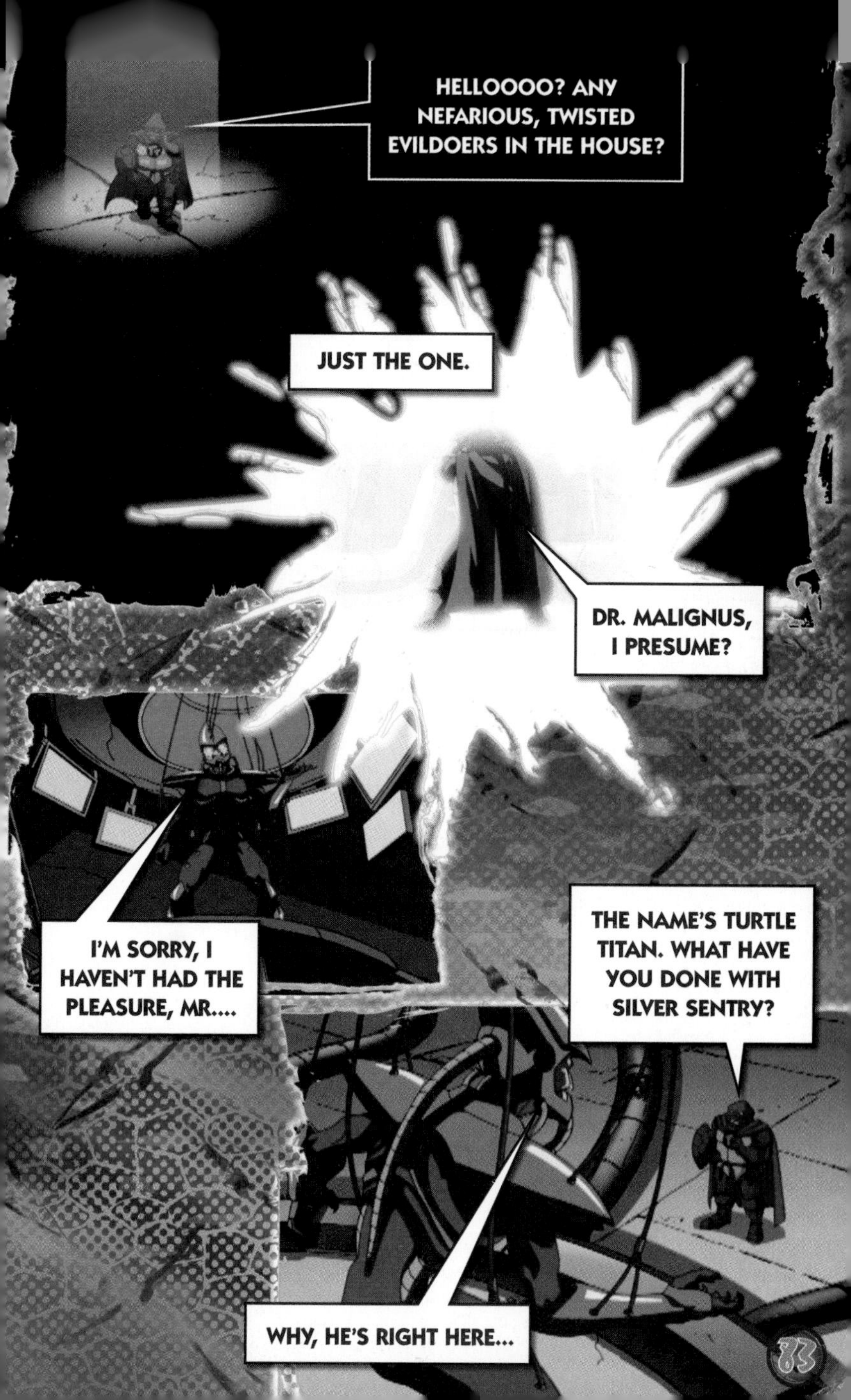
HELLOOOO? ANY NEFARIOUS, TWISTED EVILDOERS IN THE HOUSE?
JUST THE ONE.
DR. MALIGNUS, I PRESUME?
I'M SORRY, I HAVEN'T HAD THE PLEASURE, MR....
THE NAME'S TURTLE TITAN. WHAT HAVE YOU DONE WITH SILVER SENTRY?
WHY, HE'S RIGHT HERE...

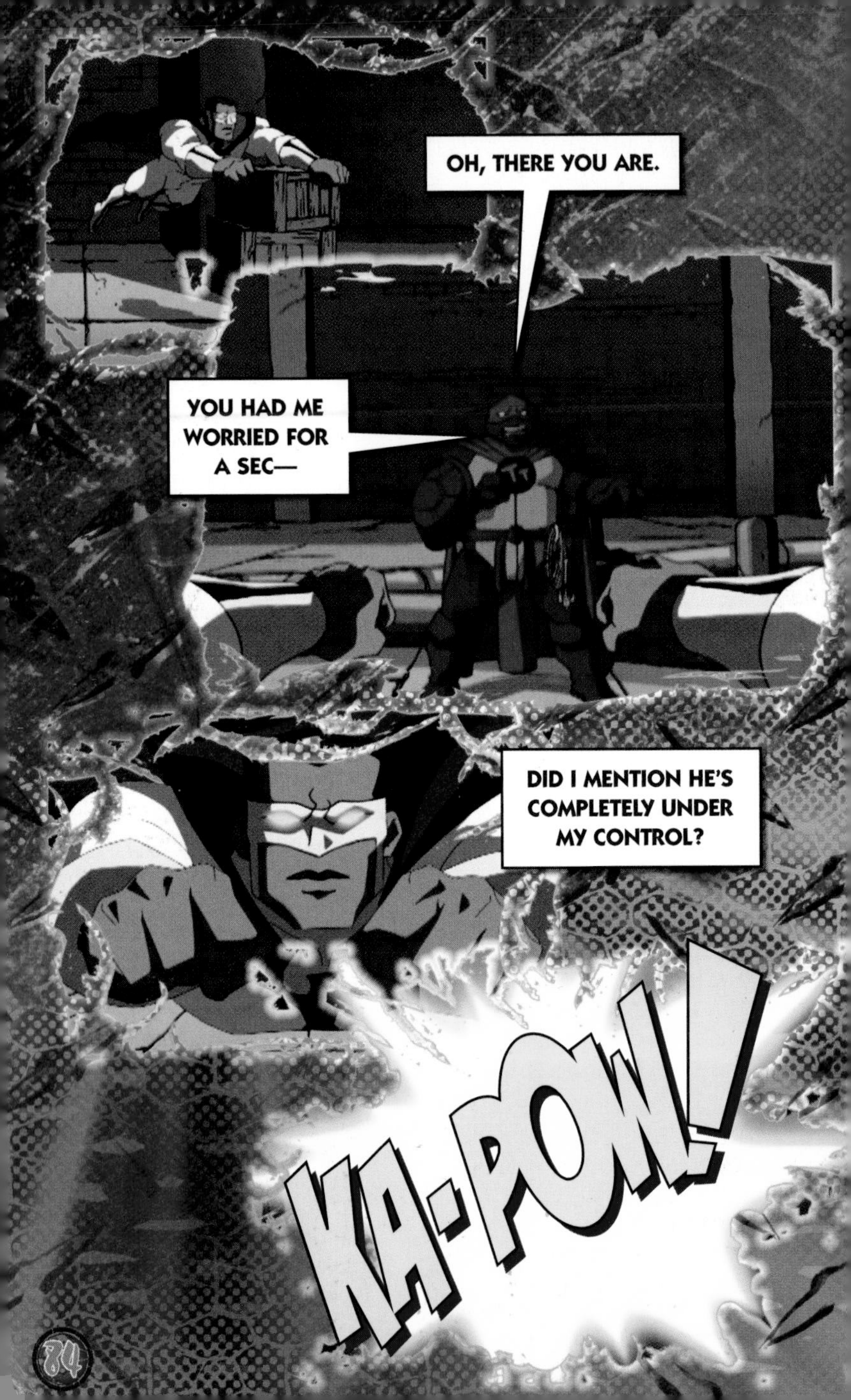
OH, THERE YOU ARE.
YOU HAD ME WORRIED FOR A SEC—
DID I MENTION HE'S COMPLETELY UNDER MY CONTROL?
KA-POW!

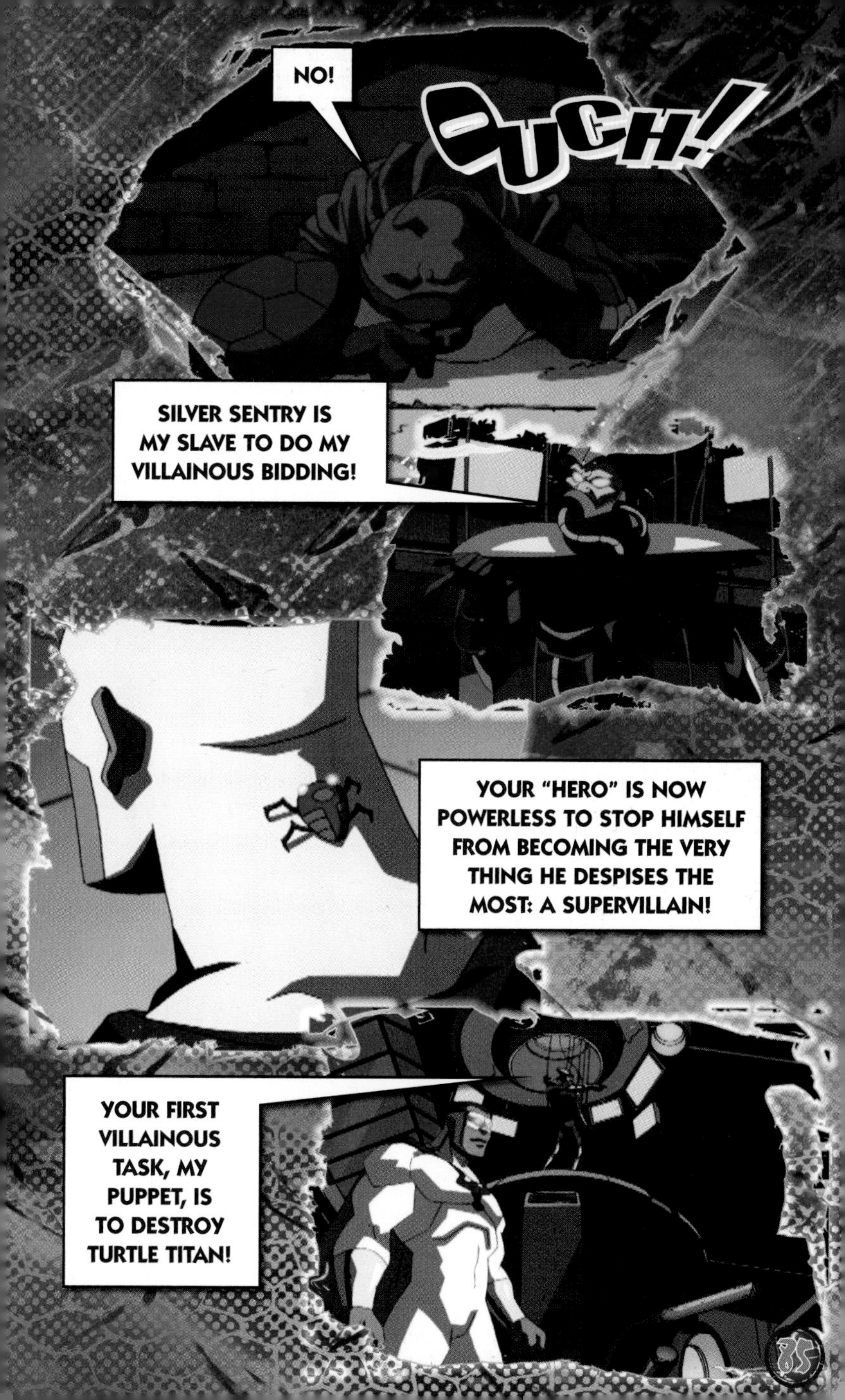
NO!
OUCH!
SILVER SENTRY IS MY SLAVE TO DO MY VILLAINOUS BIDDING!
YOUR "HERO" IS NOW POWERLESS TO STOP HIMSELF FROM BECOMING THE VERY THING HE DESPISES THE MOST: A SUPERVILLAIN!
YOUR FIRST VILLAINOUS TASK, MY PUPPET, IS TO DESTROY TURTLE TITAN!

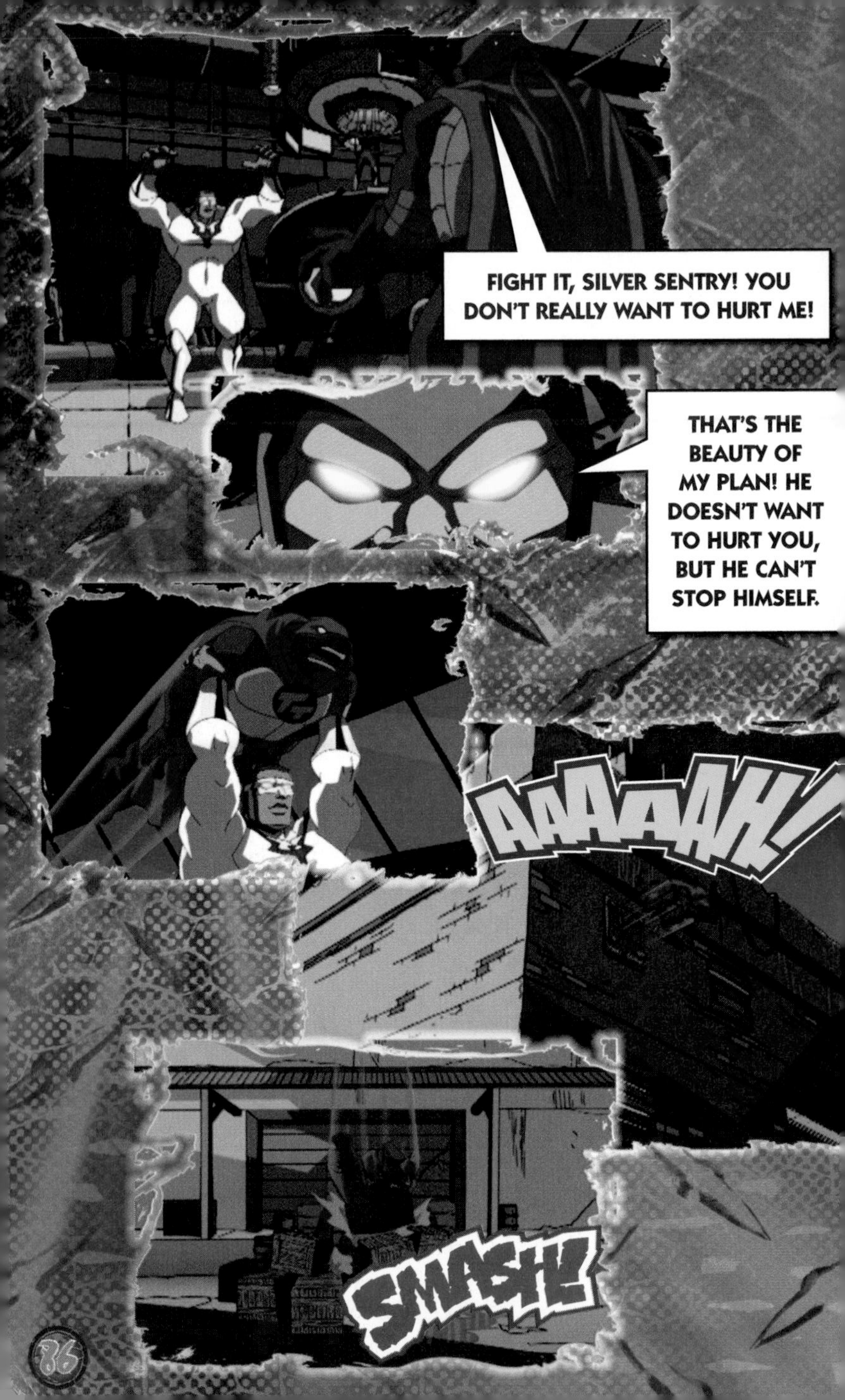
FIGHT IT, SILVER SENTRY! YOU DON'T REALLY WANT TO HURT ME!
THAT'S THE BEAUTY OF MY PLAN! HE DOESN'T WANT TO HURT YOU, BUT HE CAN'T STOP HIMSELF.
AAAAAH!
SMASH!

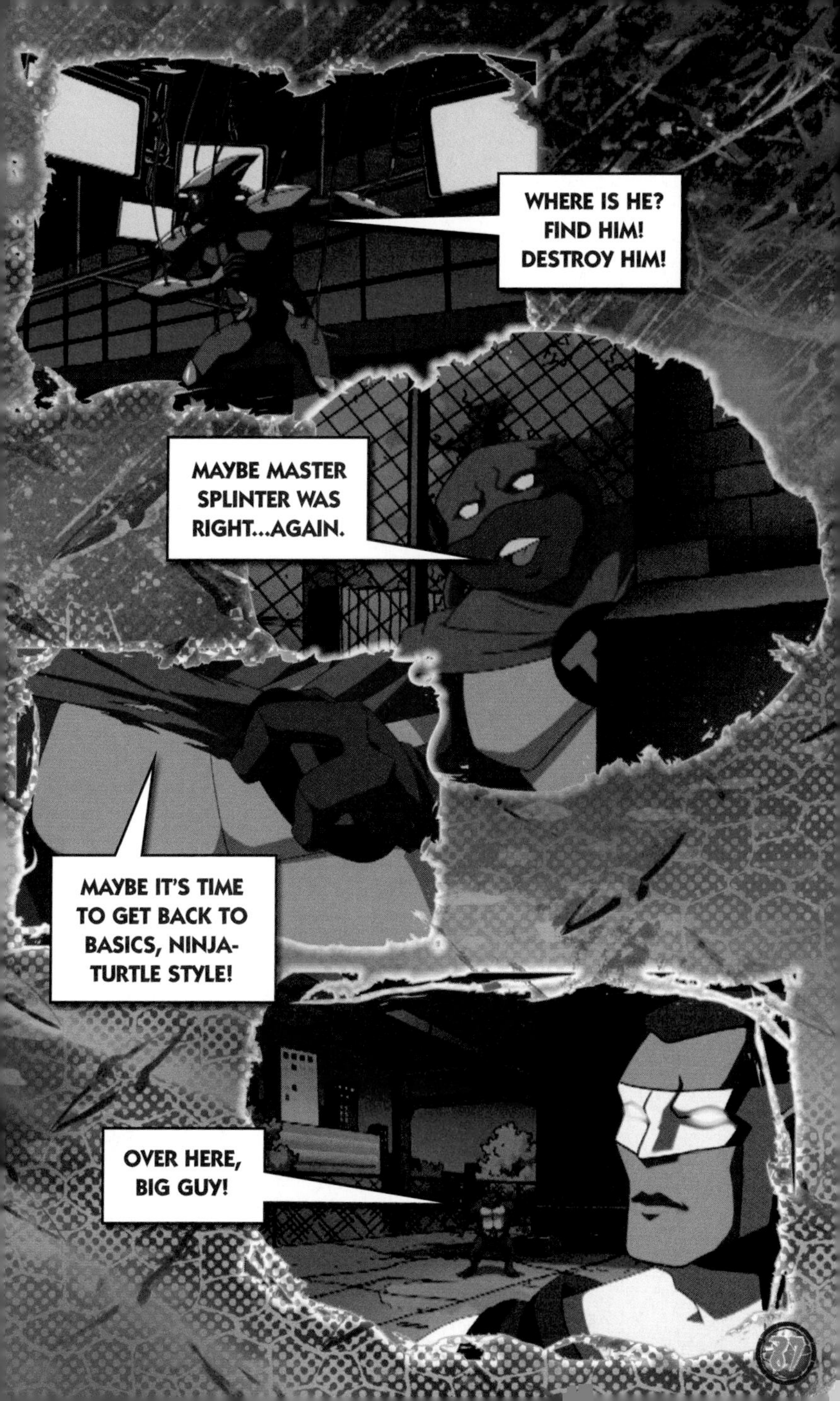
WHERE IS HE? FIND HIM! DESTROY HIM!
MAYBE MASTER SPLINTER WAS RIGHT...AGAIN.
MAYBE IT'S TIME TO GET BACK TO BASICS, NINJA-TURTLE STYLE!
OVER HERE, BIG GUY!

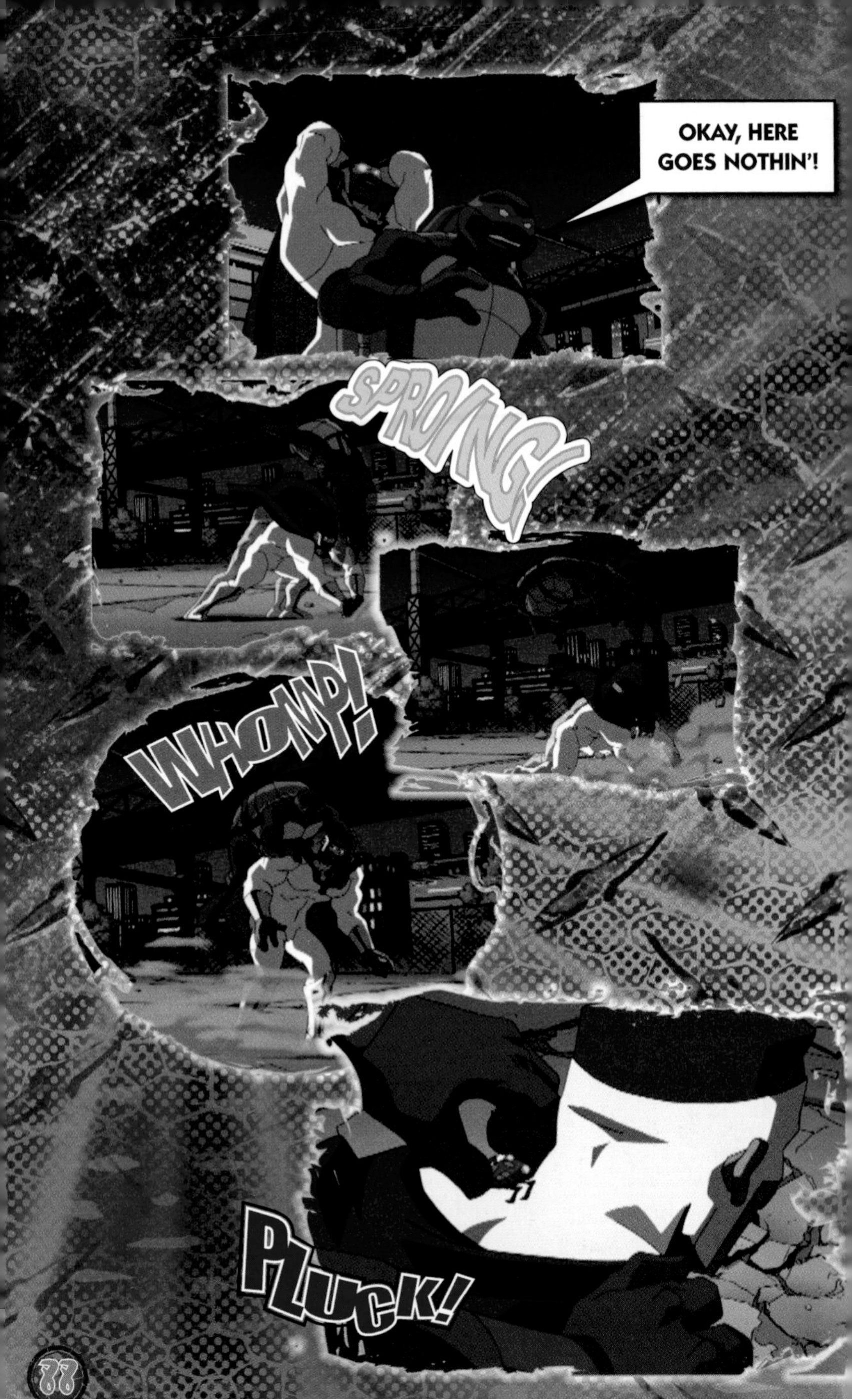

OKAY, HERE GOES NOTHIN'!
SPROING!
WHOMP!
PLUCK!

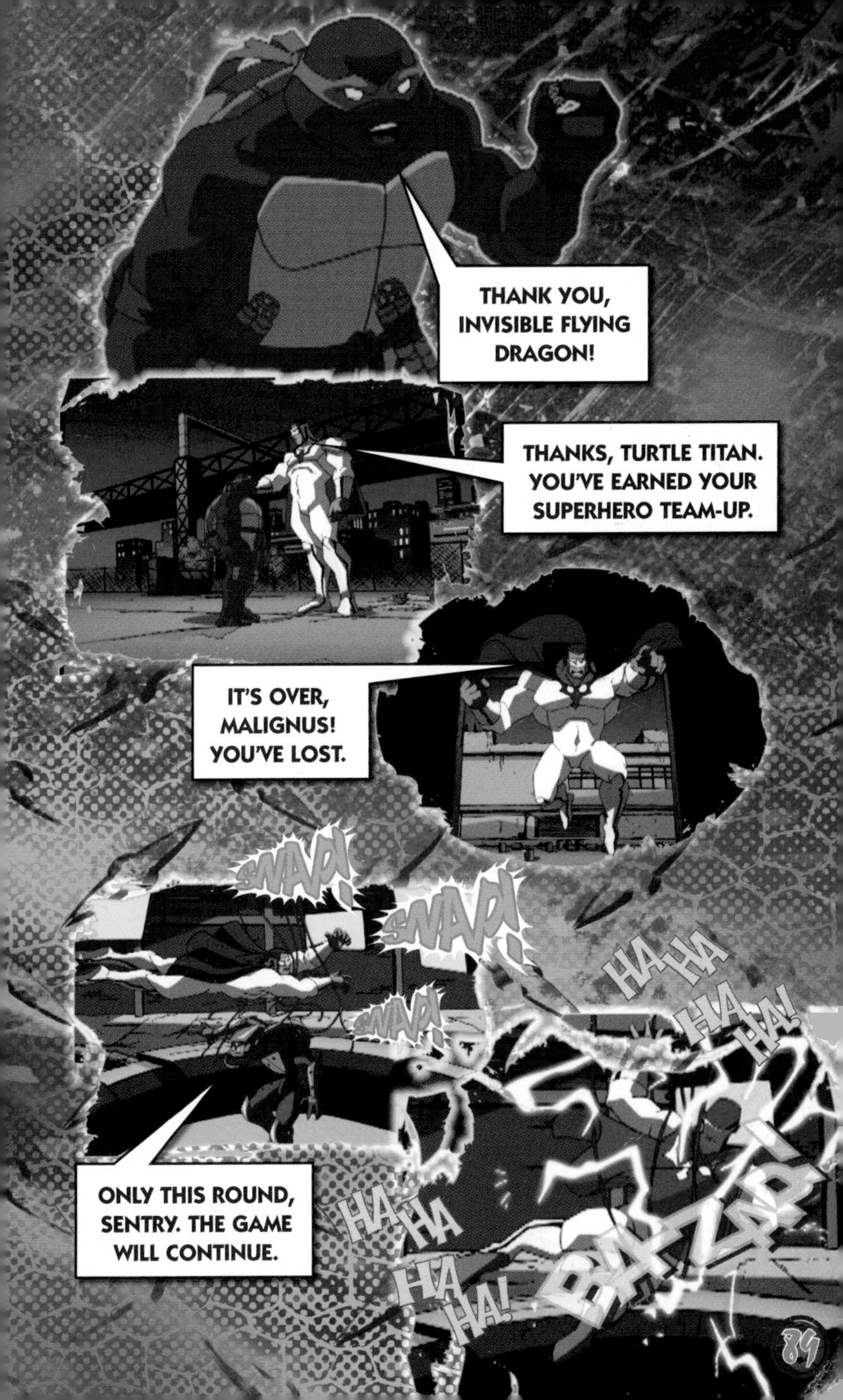
THANK YOU, INVISIBLE FLYING DRAGON!
THANKS, TURTLE TITAN. YOU'VE EARNED YOUR SUPERHERO TEAM-UP.
IT'S OVER, MALIGNUS! YOU'VE LOST.
SNAP!
SNAP!
SNAP!
ONLY THIS ROUND, SENTRY. THE GAME WILL CONTINUE.
HA HA HA HA!
HA HA HA HA!
BATZAP!

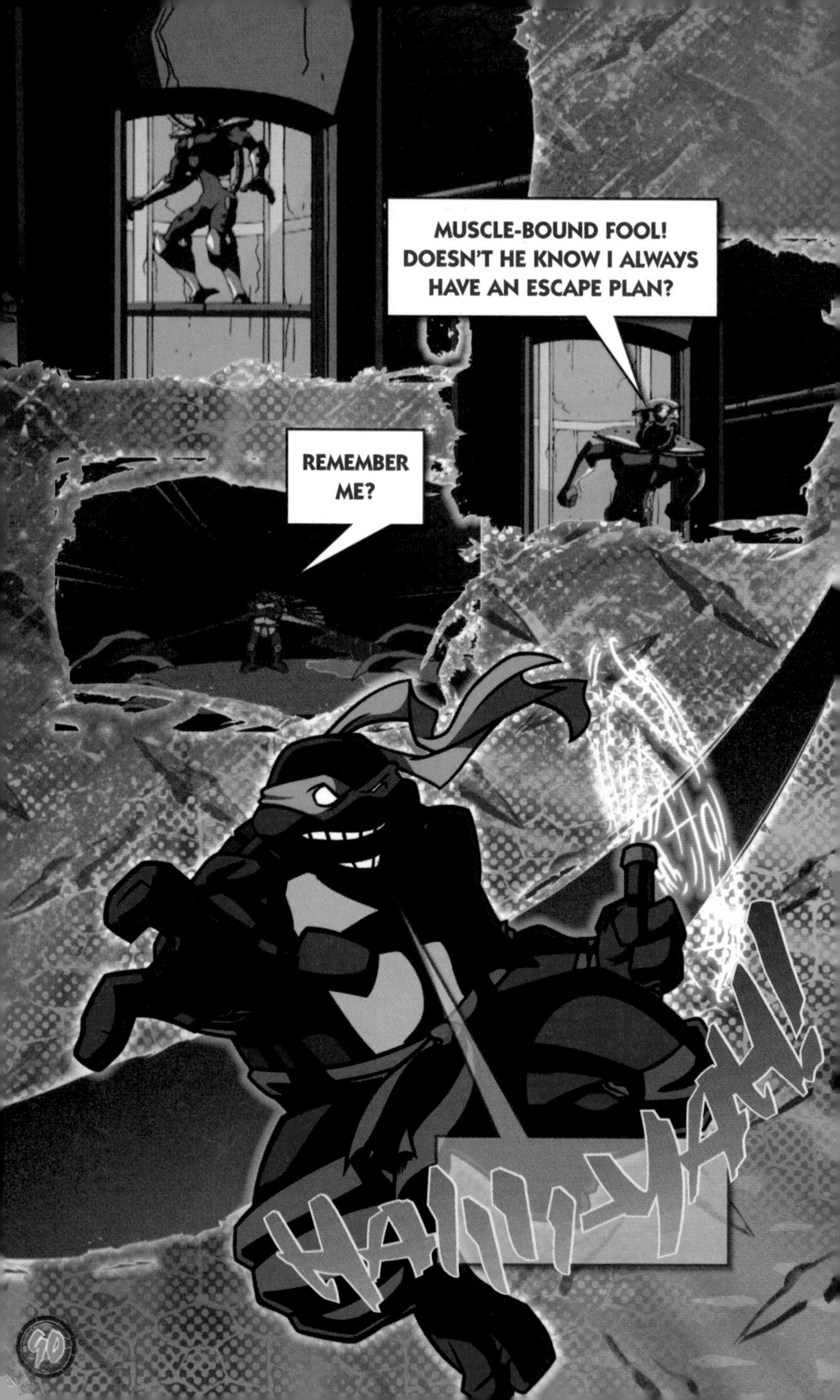
MUSCLE-BOUND FOOL! DOESN'T HE KNOW I ALWAYS HAVE AN ESCAPE PLAN?
REMEMBER ME?
HAIIIYAH!

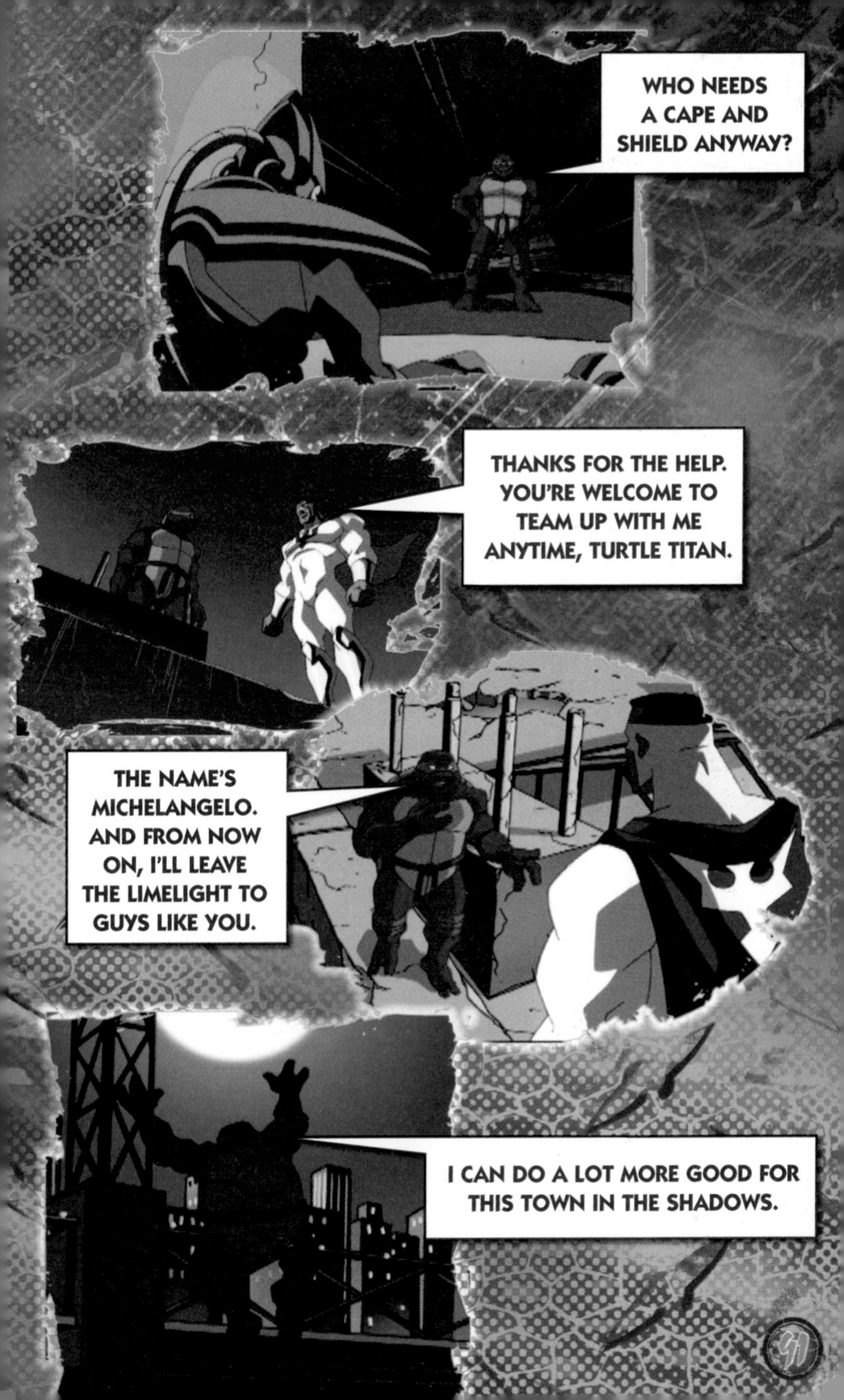
WHO NEEDS A CAPE AND SHIELD ANYWAY?
THANKS FOR THE HELP. YOU'RE WELCOME TO TEAM UP WITH ME ANYTIME, TURTLE TITAN.
THE NAME'S MICHELANGELO. AND FROM NOW ON, I'LL LEAVE THE LIMELIGHT TO GUYS LIKE YOU.
I CAN DO A LOT MORE GOOD FOR THIS TOWN IN THE SHADOWS.

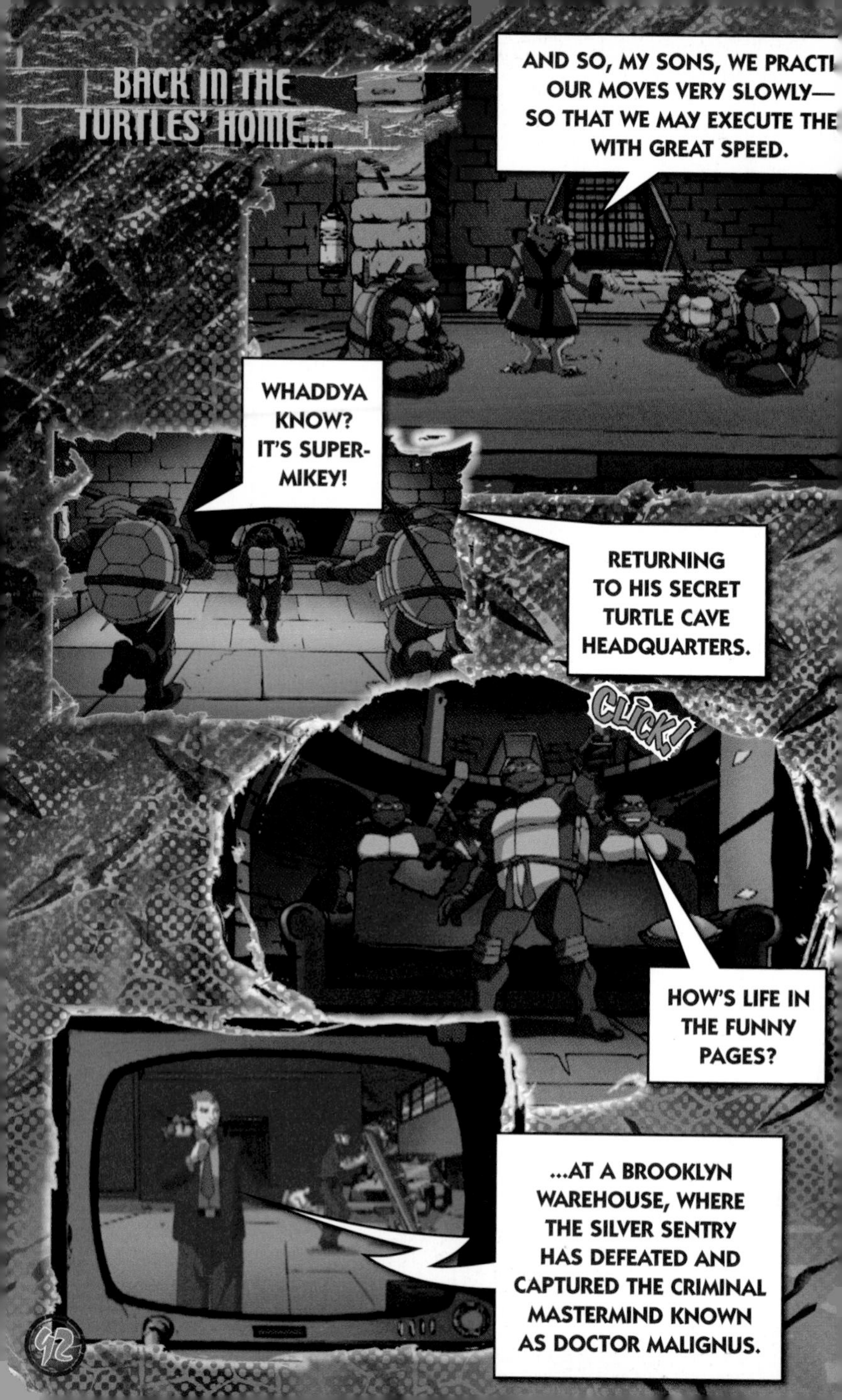
BACK IN THE TURTLES' HOME...
AND SO, MY SONS, WE PRACTI OUR MOVES VERY SLOWLY— SO THAT WE MAY EXECUTE THE WITH GREAT SPEED.
WHADDYA KNOW? IT'S SUPER-MIKEY!
RETURNING TO HIS SECRET TURTLE CAVE HEADQUARTERS.
CLICK!
HOW'S LIFE IN THE FUNNY PAGES?
...AT A BROOKLYN WAREHOUSE, WHERE THE SILVER SENTRY HAS DEFEATED AND CAPTURED THE CRIMINAL MASTERMIND KNOWN AS DOCTOR MALIGNUS.

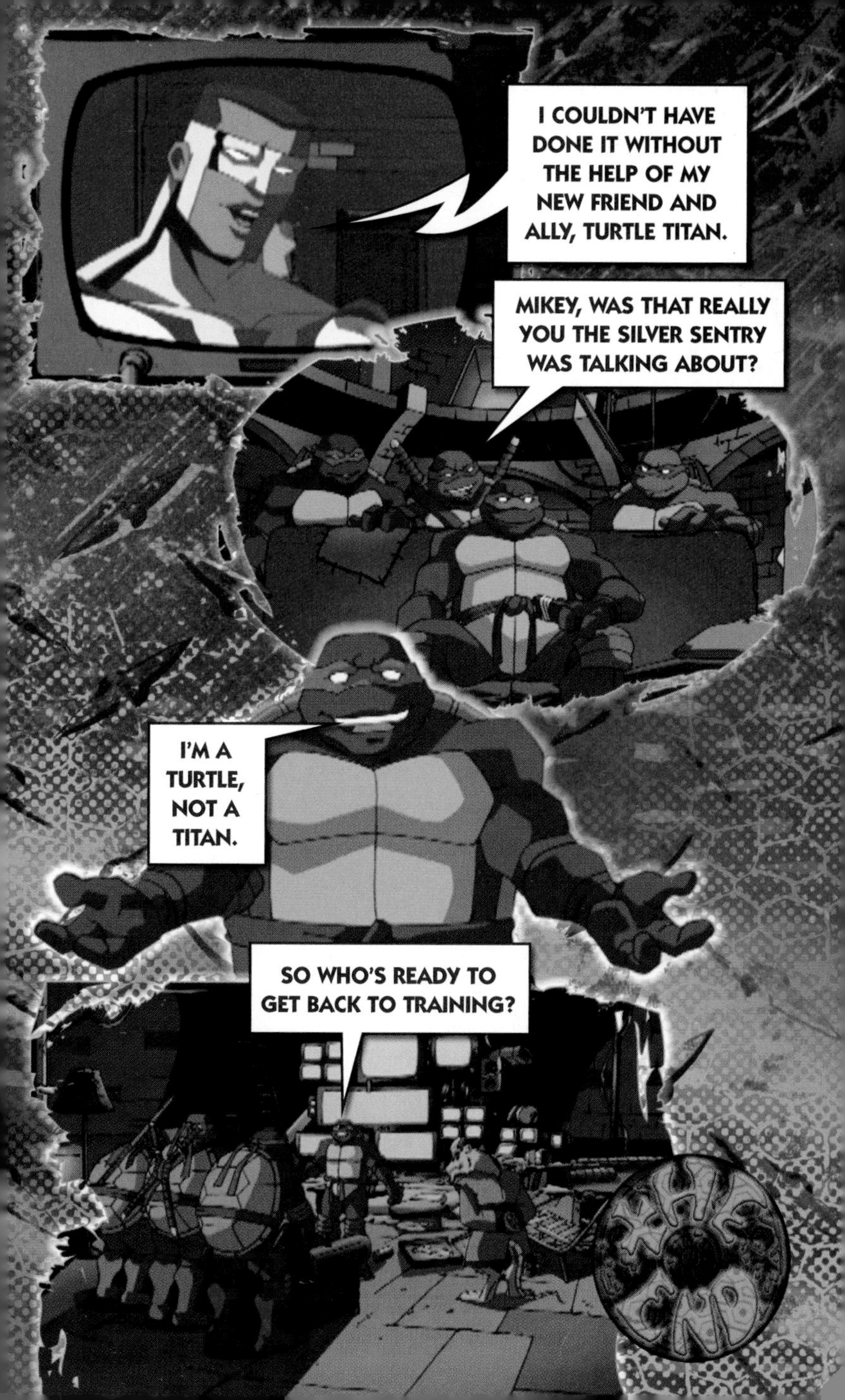
I COULDN'T HAVE DONE IT WITHOUT THE HELP OF MY NEW FRIEND AND ALLY, TURTLE TITAN.
MIKEY, WAS THAT REALLY YOU THE SILVER SENTRY WAS TALKING ABOUT?
I'M A TURTLE, NOT A TITAN.
SO WHO'S READY TO GET BACK TO TRAINING?

ALSO AVAILABLE FROM 🕐 TOKYOPOP

MANGA

ALSO AVAILABLE FROM TOKYOPOP®

You want it? We got it!
A full range of TOKYOPOP
products are available now at:
www.TOKYOPOP.com/shop

04.23.04Y

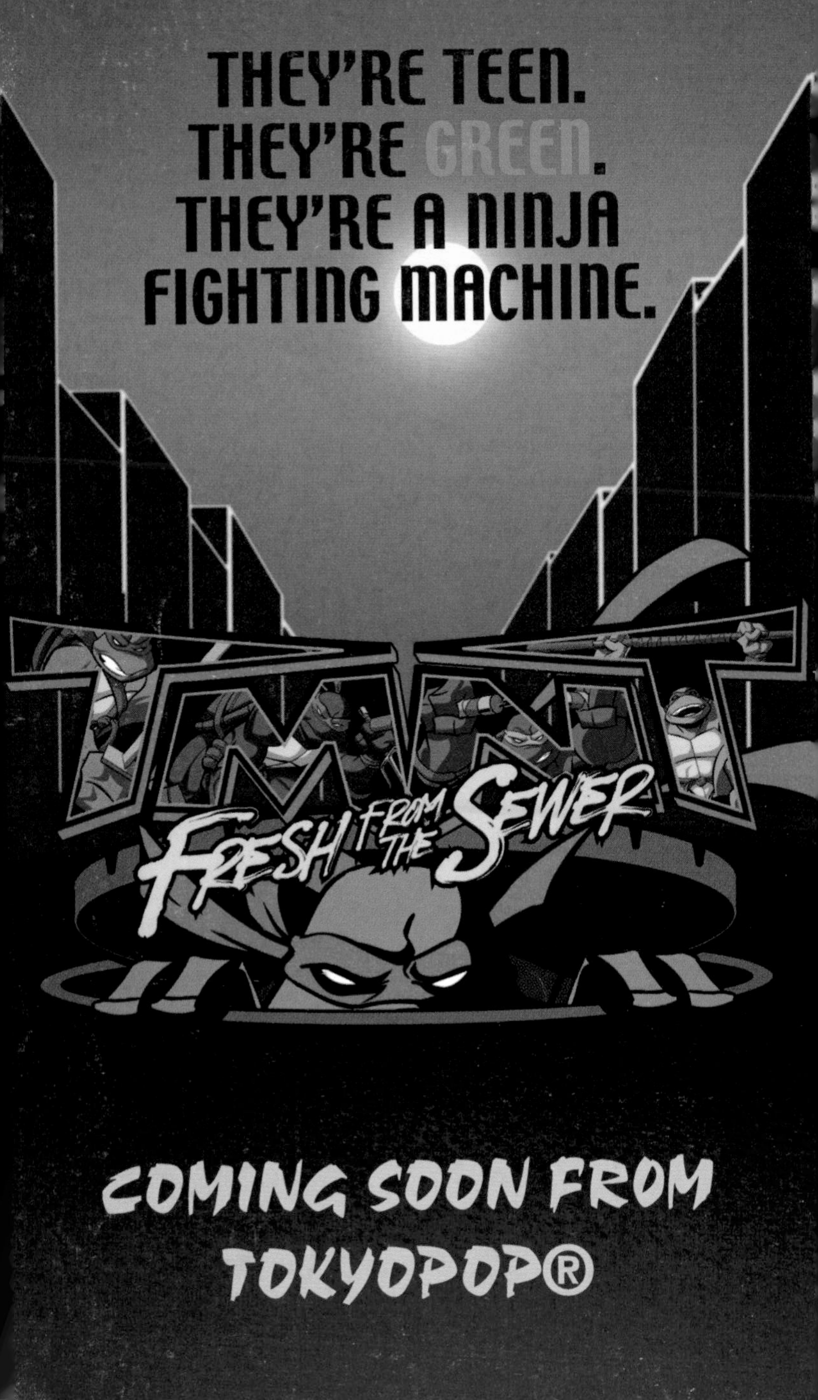
THEY'RE TEEN.
THEY'RE GREEN.
THEY'RE A NINJA
FIGHTING MACHINE.
TMNT
FRESH FROM THE SEWER
COMING SOON FROM
TOKYOPOP®